# Third Life: Taken

RJ Crayton

ISBN: 1496039343
ISBN-13: 978-1496039347

# DEDICATION

This book is dedicated to my siblings: Herman, Teresa, Jamaal and Nuri.
Life is always interesting with them around.

# ACKNOWLEDGMENTS

I want to thank my fans, for letting me know how much they enjoyed these books and that they wanted more. That always inspired me to get it done, even when other things crept up to cause delay. I want to thank my family for being supportive of my writing. I want to thank my wonderful beta readers in the Mitchelville Writers Group. The group as a collective offered advice on excerpt. Individually, I am so thankful to the following people who took the time to read the entire manuscript and offer priceless feed-back that improved the novel: Jim Brown, Lee Bruno, Stafford Battle and Shirley Hayden. I also want to thank my friend Joan Conway, who is such an inspiration to me with her cheery attitude and in her ability to write so much so well.

A special note to thank those who entered the Goodreads contest and won this Advanced Review Copy. I hope you enjoy it.

# MONDAY

# 1

## KELSEY

The doorbell startles me because we so rarely have visitors. More importantly, unexpected guests make my pulse quicken. It's been 17 months since the bounty for my capture was removed, and after narrowly escaping being shot to death because people wanted reward money, I never feel completely safe.

I am in the kitchen and have just poured Major Nelson, our 100-pound Black Russian Terrier, a bowl of dog food. "Come on," I say to him, and he turns his boxy, fur-covered head away from the food and looks at me curiously. I take him by the collar and lead him through the doors separating the kitchen and family room of our cozy one-floor home. Major Nelson is a well-trained dog, so he comes without much difficulty, despite leaving food behind. We head through the family room. In the corner, I see my 18-month-old daughter is stacking blocks in her play area, which is cordoned off by safety gates. We round the corner and head to the front door.

Major Nelson's panting presence by my side gives me a boost of confidence as we reach the door. I look through the peephole and laugh when I see who is standing on the other side. "One minute," I call through the door.

"Go on and eat," I tell Major Nelson as I release his collar. The kitchen is the best place for him while I have company. I point at an angle toward the kitchen door, which can't be seen from here. Major Nelson gives me a put out look and pads away. I take a few paces and watch him plod through the open kitchen door. Then, I practically skip back to the front door and open it.

Standing in front of me is a stocky man, 5 feet 10 inches tall, with black hair, brown eyes, and an uneven smile. "Greg," I say, taking a step toward him and wrapping my arms around him. "I am so glad to see you," I say as I release him and take a step back to get a better look at him. He looks generally the same: sturdy and committed. The perfect husband for my sister-in-law, who wanted to count on someone else after spending her childhood taking care of her younger siblings, following the death of their mother. But, he also seems tired. A hazard of traveling, I guess. But, that's unimportant, as I'm so happy to see a familiar face from back home.

I've forgotten myself. I step aside so Greg can enter the house. I am still grinning at the turn of events. As I shut the door, I instinctively give a quick look to see if Emmie, my husband's sister, is out there, even though I'm sure she's not. Luke would be ecstatic to see his sister. Emmie is 10 years older than Luke, and he adores her because she practically raised him. However, Emmie is eight-and-a-half months pregnant right now, so surely she wouldn't travel by plane, the quickest way, and probably not by vehicle, as I could think of nothing less appealing to a pregnant woman than a 12-hour car ride. I feel my smile begin to fade as I realize how odd it is for Greg to come all this way, to a foreign country, given how far along Emmie is. "This is such a surprise," I say to Greg. "What are you doing here?"

Greg smiles and looks around, but doesn't respond.

His unexpected appearance coupled with his silence makes me worry something has happened to Emmie or the baby. "Is everything alright?" I ask.

"Everything's fine," he says, widening his smile. Greg's skin is a little pale, and he has bags under his eyes. His hair is neatly combed, and despite the heat and humidity, his clothes are crisply pressed. But something about him is off. I can't quite put my finger on it.

"If everything's fine, why are you here?" I ask, then blush, as I realize just how rude that sounds. "I'm sorry," I say, and motion him to follow me further inside. We head toward the family room, where there's a sofa, a flatscreen, a couple of easy chairs and Penelope's play area. Unfortunately, the floor is littered with toys. We — I guess me, really, as Penelope isn't entirely helpful — generally tidy up a bit before Luke comes home. However, since that is a few hours away, it basically looks like a cyclone blew through. "Come in. Have a seat."

Greg follows me, stepping awkwardly to avoid tripping over a plastic block. I point to a chair, kneel to pick up a couple of toys that are clearly walking hazards. As I stand to carry the toys to the gated play area, I notice that Greg is still standing.

"I'm just going to put this away," I say, as I walk toward Penelope's play space. "Go ahead and sit, and you can tell me what brings you here."

"Why I'm here," he says, pausing and fumbling with his hands. "I apologize, but I don't have a good answer."

I set the toys I'm carrying next to Penelope, and then take a couple of steps toward him. I stare, waiting for him to say more, hoping I don't look as bewildered as I feel.

"It's something private that Emmie sent me to discuss with Luke," Greg says, shocking me. "Is he here?"

I shake my head, speechless. He's shown up out of the blue to discuss something with Luke. Without calling. Without even checking if Luke would be here. Something Emmie doesn't want me to know. I'm not related to Emmie by blood, but I still thought we were family. It hurts that Emmie doesn't trust me. Though maybe she resents me. I fled after refusing to participate in a government-mandated kidney donation. I'm a fugitive from the Federation of Surviving States (FoSS), the country that emerged after pandemics wiped out much of the United States population. Not every state joined FoSS. The former Florida along with a couple other parts of the gulf coast formed Peoria, the nation I live in. When I left FoSS, I took Luke, Emmie's favorite brother, with me. So maybe she has reason to cut me out.

I try to shake off the slight. Greg is staring at me, waiting for me to answer his question about whether my husband is home. "Luke's at work," I manage, trying not to look as wounded as I feel by Emmie's request to keep me out. I look up at the wall clock. It is almost two. "He won't be home until five."

"Mama," I hear. Penelope is apparently tired of being ignored. I look toward her play area in the corner. She's too old for a playpen, but we have gates that snap together and keep her from roaming the house unattended. "Have a seat," I say again, sweeping my arm in the direction of the sofa and armchair.

I walk over and pull Penelope from her play area, smiling while I do. She always does that to me: makes me forget everything else that is going on, because I am so happy to be with her. She has Luke's beautiful blue eyes but everything else about her is distinctly her own. She's slightly big for a year-and-a-half and brilliantly smart, I think. But that's probably just maternal bias.

I pat her diaper through her pants; it still feels dry. I just fed and changed her not five minutes ago, but I want to make sure she hasn't peed again. I wouldn't want her stewing in a wet diaper while Greg and I chat. I kiss her cheek and set her back down. I turn to join Greg, only he is standing right behind me. I step back, gasp and clutch my chest.

"Sorry," he says. "I didn't mean to startle you." He smiles and waves at Penelope. She looks at him curiously. "She's a lot cuter in person," he says, looking at my darling carrot-topped wonder.

"Thanks," I say appreciatively, as my heart rate winds back to normal following his abrupt appearance behind me. I turn to my daughter. "Penelope," I say, "this is your Uncle Greg."

She looks at him with renewed interest and giggles.

Grrr. I hear a low, throaty growl as I turn to see Major Nelson head through the open kitchen door and into the room. Greg takes a step back as Major Nelson pads over, growling hostilely the entire way. "He's not used to guests," I tell Greg, as I grab Major Nelson's collar. "I'll take him out back. Could you keep an eye on her for a second?"

He nods, then bends down, picks up a stuffed monkey and starts waving it cheerfully in front of Penelope. I pull Major Nelson back toward the kitchen, so I can take him out through the back door, but he isn't cooperating. Instead of going kindly with me, he pulls toward Penelope. I wish he'd stop. He's a very useful guard dog, in that he hates everyone new. But in situations like this, it's a pain. "Come on, Major Nelson," I say sweetly, trying to coax him. However, it's not working. Usually he's incredibly obedient, but he's trained to be hostile towards strangers and Greg is a stranger to him. I struggle with Major Nelson all the way through the kitchen, to the back yard. He even knocks over his half full water bowl and then barks furiously at me when I close the sliding glass door to the kitchen. The yard is fenced in, so I expect him to forget about Greg and roam free, perhaps tear into the new bone Luke brought him yesterday. Instead, he stands at the door, his paws banging against the glass. I grab a few paper towels and clean up the water he spilled as I was taking him out. When I'm done, I look up and see Major Nelson still standing there, watching. I give him a frown before turning and heading back.

"I'm sorry it took so long," I say, as I walk through the kitchen door and into the family room where I left Greg and Penelope. My stomach drops. The room is empty. Penelope is not in her play area and Greg is not here, either. My heartbeat quickens as I take a few frantic paces and see the front door wide open.

I am still trying to comprehend what is going on, what could be happening, when Penelope enters, pulling Greg along behind her. She looks confused by my panicked expression and says, "Fow-er."

Greg, who is not at all confused, gives me an apologetic glance and says, "She wanted to show me flowers."

Penelope toddles over to me in what a generous person might describe as a run. It's an awkward, speedy walk that Luke and I find adorable, and I'm incredibly happy when she reaches me. I pick her up and hold her close, feeling Penelope's warm body right next to mine. Having her near, feeling her grab a strand of my shoulder-length brown hair and twist it in her fingers, calms me just a bit. For some reason, I still feel panicked, even though it should have subsided now that she's back and fine. I slide her fingers from my hair and look at her and her sparkling blue eyes, the mirror image of her father's. Greg closes the front door with a thud and I look up at him.

"You know, Luke used to walk just like that," he says.

"What?" I ask, taking a step back, trying to parse out why I am feeling so ill at ease.

"When he was little," Greg clarifies. "When I was 12, I used to come over and help Emmie with her science homework and we'd get such a kick out of it whenever Luke ran through." He smiles at the memory, and it should give me comfort to think of my husband as a toddler. It should give me comfort to remember that Greg has known my husband for a quarter of a century, and that Greg has lived two doors down from my husband's family all his life. But it doesn't. Greg smiles again, but something about it feels sinister.

"You should go see Luke at the office," I say.

"You're right," he says, moving closer to me and reaching into his pocket. He pulls out something small and black and I stare at him trying to figure out what it is. He is holding a small mobile phone. "Before I go, I want to get a picture of the two of you."

Emmie has tons of pictures of us. Luke sends them all the time. He sent one last week, in fact. "I'm sure Emmie would rather see one of Luke with Penelope," I say, brushing off the suggestion.

"No, it'll just take a second," he says. "Smile."

Since Penelope is in my arms already, it seems easier to smile and look at the phone than to protest further. He takes a few shots, the electronic camera click the only sound in the room, and says, "These are great."

I nod. "Luke's office is in the Bradley building," I say, hoping it will nudge Greg out. "Room 481."

He is still looking down at the photos on the tiny screen. "Come take a look," he says.

"I'm sure they're fine," I say, not moving.

His expression is jovial, yet there is an undertone of strain in his voice. "No, you've gotta see. Here," he says this last bit and steps closer to me. Feeling the need to separate him from Penelope, I back away, making my way to the play area, where I set her down. He either doesn't notice or care about my apprehensiveness, as he keeps coming at me, his phone in hand.

"See," he says, standing right in front of me. Then he turns so he and I face the same direction. He stands beside me, shoving the tiny screen right in front of me so I can see Penelope and me in the still image. "Take it," he says. I grab it, unsure of how to refuse.

"Just hit the arrow on the side to see the other ones." I nod, despite not really wanting to. All I want is for him to leave. But what harm could tapping an arrow do?

"The Bradley building's part of the hospital?" Greg asks, shuffling through his pocket, probably for a pen and paper.

A wave of relief hits me now that he is on board with leaving. I tap to see another photo. "Yeah, just follow the signs from here. St. Francis Hospital."

I tap the arrow a few times looking at the pictures. Penelope always looks great. But me, not so much. I wish I'd done something to my hair this morning. It normally has a mild wave, but it looks frizzy, which can't be helped with all the humidity. My eyes look bright, brown and cheerful, but it's obvious the smile is fake. I still look chubbier than I'd like. Love Penelope, but I've still got 5 pounds of baby weight that I can't shed. Tired of dissecting this photo, I tap the arrow once more and see a photo of a woman on some type of hospital bed. Her hair is jet-black and matted, and her arms and legs are held in place by leather straps with buckles. I pull the screen closer to my face trying to make out where this was taken, who it is. The woman looks at once familiar but like a stranger. I feel like I should recognize her, but I don't. The face is turned in profile so I can just see half of it, and not that well. Then I see it: those features I know so well. They are family features — a face shape, a nose profile — they all have. I look more closely at the abdomen: a slight rounding, but definitely not eight months pregnant. I am so confused. "Is...," I stammer. "Is that Emmie?"

As I am turning to get my answer, I feel the cloth on my face and the weird odor emanating from it. Sharp, burning, unpleasant. I struggle for a moment, but Greg is behind me and has wrapped one arm tightly around me while he uses the other to hold this drug-soaked rag over my face. I know I am in danger. I know I have to get away. But I also know I am about to pass out.

# 2

## KELSEY

My mouth is dry and my head pounds. I wonder if I'm hungover. People who've experienced it say it's miserable, and I certainly feel miserable right now. Before, I'd had one glass of wine too many and a tough morning the next day, but nothing like this. This is 10 times worse than that.

"Luke, I feel awful," I mumble, my eyes still closed, as I try to place what led to this predicament.

I am going to ask Luke if we had champagne last night, but I become preoccupied with the fact that my wrists hurt. Something is cutting into them. It almost feels as if my hands are bound with ropes.

My eyelids pop open. Bright sunshine streams in, nearly blinding me, so I close them again.

In that second, I know. Everything comes back to me. Greg. The rag over my face. Penelope. I open my eyes again, this time blinking to adjust to the sunshine. Taking in my surroundings, I see I am in the backseat of a sedan, tilted to the left side leaning against the window, but strapped in a seatbelt.

Thin brown ropes bind my wrists, which sit in my lap. I look to my right and see Penelope strapped into her car seat sound asleep. I gasp.

"You're awake," Greg says, perturbed. "I was hoping you'd sleep until we got into FoSS."

His voice is cold and so unlike the gentle Greg I remember. "I don't understand Greg," I say, my voice hoarse, probably from the chemical he used to knock me out. "Why are you doing this?"

He chuckles. "Because you deserve it. You saw that picture of Emmie. That should be you, not her."

The image, one of a woman I barely recognized, a woman who looked vacant, who looked dead. That was Emmie. And the baby. She didn't look pregnant. Part of me doesn't want an answer to my question, but I know the answer is crucial to why I'm here, so I ask it. "What happened to Emmie?"

He doesn't respond. We drive in silence. I look at Penelope, her lips making sucking motions, probably dreaming of a bottle. I now notice that next to me on the area between us, Penelope's stuffed monkey, Mr. Giggles, lies in a heap. She takes Mr. Giggles everywhere. She must have had him when Greg brought her to the car. It likely fell from her arms after she'd fallen asleep. I've got to get us out of here.

"Please," I say softly, looking back at Greg. "I'm worried about Emmie, about the baby. What happened? "

"The baby's dead. Stillborn. She stopped feeling movement, so we went in; they had to deliver immediately. Only it was too late." His voice is devoid of feeling, as empty as Emmie looked in that photo. "Emmie couldn't cope. They put her in a mental institution. They want me to bring you to them, and then I can get my wife back."

# 3

## KELSEY

I can see Greg's face reflected in the rearview mirror. His eyes are wild and desperate. I know I need to escape. Only I don't know how. I need time to think. For the moment, I decide I should keep him talking, distracted.

"Greg, you don't have to do this," I plead, wiggling my wrists, hoping to loosen the ropes encircling them. "If we get Luke, he can help you figure out a way to get Emmie back."

Greg glances at me using the rearview mirror. His eyes are cold and hard. "This is the best way, Kelsey."

I try to be inconspicuous as I work furiously at loosening these ropes binding my hands. "There has to be another way. One that doesn't end up with Penelope's mother dead. You don't want her to lose her mother."

"You're kidding, right?" he asks, full of disdain. "You don't have to die, Kelsey. This is the thing I've always hated about you. You're selfish and self-involved. If it's not your way, then it's just wrong and dire, and the world is coming to an end."

He breathes out and changes lanes on the road. "Tell them you renounce this stupid anti-Life First sentiment, and raise your daughter in peace in FoSS. It's really simple."

Gee, I had no idea my brother-in-law hated me and thought I was selfish until this very moment. Yes, I guess I should have clued in when he kidnapped me. But, I thought that was more about saving Emmie's life. Now, it sounds like kidnapping me and turning me over to FoSS is something he'd be happy to do without Emmie being institutionalized.

I am not sure where to take the conversation now. Arguing with him seems like a bad idea. FOSS wants me dead. When I was selected, or marked, to donate a kidney, it was because of the Life First policy, which dictates we endeavor first and foremost to preserve human life, even if it means sacrificing our organs. Unfortunately, I don't think FoSS cares whether I renounce my beliefs or not. They think I've started a movement and I think they just want me dead more than anything. But, I won't be able to convince Greg of that. Given his disdain, I don't think I can appeal to his sympathy for me. I try pulling my wrists apart some more, but it seems like the ropes are getting tighter, not looser.

I look out the window and see a road sign indicating we are getting closer to the border. I have to think of something right now. Once we are in FoSS, I am dead, and I have no way to make sure Penelope is safe and returned to Luke.

"OK, I'm selfish," I tell him. "I admit that. I'm sorry."

I can hear the panic in my voice. This is not going to go over well. I have to compose myself. I look at Penelope, innocent in her car seat. I have to figure this out for her.

"But, just because I'm selfish doesn't mean you should trust FoSS," I say, trying to steer this conversation away from me and my misdeeds. "Just because you deliver me doesn't mean they'll give her back to you."

His eyes find mine in the mirror again, and part of me hopes he'll crash the car — not a real smash-bang-everyone's-dead-crash — but a fender bender that would bring help my way. His eyes express uncertainty.

"You can't game me, Kelsey," he says, without much force.

"I'm not trying to game you," I tell him. "It's just that you could ruin my life and Penelope's life and Luke's life and still not get Emmie back."

He shakes his head, the helmet of black hair bobbing rhythmically in front of the headrest. "We've signed an agreement. I bring you in, and they give me Emmie. Simple as that."

"What if they rip up the agreement when you hand me over?"

He is silent; I am too. My skin is bleeding now. The ropes are cutting into me way too badly.

Penelope is still asleep, her red curls falling into her eyes. Please dear God, let her stay asleep. If she sees me like this, tied up, bleeding wrists, she's going to panic and cry. Who knows what Greg will do? If anyone had asked me yesterday if my brother-in-law would hurt anyone, I would've said no. But now I can't trust him at all. I can't trust that he won't hurt my daughter if I do something he doesn't like.

"Kelsey," Greg says, softer. "I know you don't want to go back to FoSS, and the truth is, I don't really care to take you back. But this is the position we are in now. So, buck up and deal with the situation. Stop trying to use Psych 101 to get me to let you go. It's not gonna happen."

I grit my teeth. This is so frustrating. Mainly because I know he is right. There is nothing I can say to him that is going to change his mind. I am a selfish person, his wife isn't, and he is going to sacrifice me for her.

If given the choice, I wonder if Luke would do the same: sacrifice someone else — someone who had never hurt him — to save my life.

No, no he wouldn't. He'd find another option. Something that didn't involve hurting people to get what he wanted.

"How is she?" I ask him.

"Who?"

"Emmie."

A long breath sails out of him, almost as if he is being deflated, having all that is in him sucked out. "She's not well, Kelsey," he says. "She could get well with medicine, but they want you back before they give her that help."

I want to reach out and slap him. I would if I weren't tied up and bleeding. "Now it's my turn to ask: are you kidding?"

"What the Hell's that supposed 'ta mean?" he asks, indignant.

"You may think I'm a selfish bitch, but I'm not withholding psychiatric medication from someone who needs it," I spit. "And you really think they're going to let her come back to you when they won't even help her get well."

He reaches his hand up and pulls it through his hair. "The reason they won't help her is you," he shoots back with venom. "Anyone else they would have helped a long time ago. But, because she's Luke's sister and he's with you, they won't help her. So, if you hadn't up and walked out on FoSS without doing your civic duty, my wife would be fine."

"Her break down is not my fault. And it's FoSS that won't treat her, not me."

He glances at me in the mirror once more, his eyes full of anger and pain. "It is your fault Kelsey. Don't you get that? You never do get anything unless it revolves around you, do you?"

I soften my tone. "I'm sorry, Greg, I don't understand how it's my fault. I thought you said it was the stillborn."

"It was," he says. "That was the trigger."

"So I don't see how that can be my fault." I manage to sound gentle, even though I am frightened by the situation. Despite my earlier desire to soften him up and escape, it seems I am only making him angrier. At me, no less.

"Let me ask you a question, Kelsey: Were you surprised to learn Emmie was pregnant?"

Whoa. I'm not sure where he's going with this. I think back to Luke telling me. And the truth is that I was surprised. "A little," I say, tentatively, not wanting to anger him with the wrong answer.

"Why?" he asks, as if my answer was correct.

I want to answer correctly again, so I try to think this through. It's a tough one, because the why is hard to pinpoint. It just seemed that Emmie never really wanted to mother more people. With her own mother mentally ill and a father who worked all the time, she'd lost her childhood mothering Luke and Chase. It was as if she'd given all her love to her younger brothers, done all the mothering with them, and she simply wasn't interested in it. I mean, she is 10 years older than Luke and she doesn't have any kids.

She'd been pregnant once before, and that had been at Greg's insistence. When the baby didn't make it, they seemed resigned to being childless. "I don't know exactly," I say softly. "She just seemed happy to have raised Luke and that's it."

We are at a stoplight. He turns and flashes a smug grin. "See, you can actually think beyond yourself if you pay attention, Kelsey."

He turns back to the road. "Somewhere deep, I think she did want another baby, but on the surface, she was done. Luke was her baby. She loved him like a son, and she was proud of him and content with him and that was enough. She was also scared about mental illness and pregnancy and being like her mother. It was the stillborn baby that had cemented her mother's descent into madness," he says with a sigh. "I guess she was right to be worried, in the end. It's what caused Emmie to go mad, too. But, she was pregnant, and she wanted a baby because she missed her baby. She missed Luke. She missed Luke because you took him away from her. So, this started with you, and it's going to end with you."

I want to kick the seat. I know I can't, but I really want to. This is surreal. At least I can see why it is so easy for him to kidnap me. He's put all the blame for this situation on me. And maybe he is even right. Maybe, Emmie would be fine if I had just done my duty and not taken Luke from her. I don't know. What I do know is, Penelope and I need to get out of this car and away from Greg. "I'm bleeding," I say.

His eyes glance back in the rearview again. I hold up my bloody wrists. He rolls his eyes. "Trying to escape, huh?"

"No," I insist. "I just want the ropes to loosen. They're too tight."

"It's a constrictor knot," he informs me, dispassionately. "The more you try to loosen it, the tighter it gets."

I nod, although I'm not sure he notices. What he said makes sense. I wish he'd told me that from the get-go. I probably still would have tried to loosen them, but not for as long as I did.

"I'm a bad person and I've caused problems for Emmie. I realize that," I say, trying to sound forthright, "But, Penelope doesn't deserve to see me like this — my wrists covered in blood. It's going to scare her. Can you please just stop, loosen the ropes, and maybe wipe up some of the blood?"

He sighs. "It's just 15 more miles till we get into FoSS. I'll do it then," he says.

"The ropes have already cut my skin. What if they slice into a vein or something? Can you just stop and make it more comfortable for me? I promise you, I won't try anything. I just want a little relief. And it will really help Penelope if I'm not covered in blood when she wakes up. You know Emmie wouldn't want to upset Penelope."

He doesn't look back at me, but I can see him in the mirror. He is contemplating what I said. He keeps driving, and after a minute more passes, I am feeling desperate enough to say something that could sway him, but also runs the risk of further enraging him. "Penelope is Emmie's niece. Think of what Emmie would say if she found out you let her wake up to find her mother bound and bleeding in the back seat."

He still doesn't speak to me, and I'm not sure what to make of it. He could be hostile to me for trying to use Emmie to play on his sympathies. Unfortunately, that's the only option I have left at the moment. I feel the car slow and in a few moments we are easing to the side of the road.

We pull to a stop and he gets out, leaving the car parked and idling. Instead of opening my door to check on me, he goes to the trunk. I look out the rear window, but all I can see is the top of the raised trunk door. When he closes it, he has something gray tucked under his arm. Finally, he swings around to my door. He is about to open it, so I get ready. I know this is the only chance Penelope and I will have to escape.

# 4

## KELSEY

Greg opens the door to the car and leans in. He looks over at Penelope and finally at my bleeding wrists. "Kelsey, I am sorry about this," he says, and he seems to mean it. "But, I can't loosen the ropes. I brought you this blanket. It will cover your hands, so when Penelope wakes up, she won't see any blood."

I want to roll my eyes, to spit in his face, but I can't. "Can you maybe unbuckle the seatbelt, so I can get repositioned and just get a little more comfortable?"

He gives me a scrutinizing look and I try to appear sincere. He clicks his tongue against his teeth, sighs and then unbuckles my belt. Afterwards, he begins to unfold the gray fleece blanket and place it over my hands. When his head is close enough to mine, I say his name softly. He looks me directly in the eye, expectant. Our faces are level, so, with all my might, I tip my head forward and headbutt him. I read somewhere that headbutting hurts the person who isn't expecting it more, but after doing it right now, I'm not so sure.

My head is aching, but I can't focus on that. Greg yelps and I fall on my back, pull my knees to my chest then thrust my feet forward, kicking Greg to the ground. My hands are still tied in front of me and hurt like hell. I wish he'd untied me, but he is not an idiot. At this point, I've got to get away, but my hands are a problem. I sit up in the seat, and through bound hands, try to grip the door well enough to pull it closed. If I can just lock him out of the vehicle, I'll have more time. The key is still in the ignition. I just have to keep him out. I've got hold of the inside door handle and am pulling, but suddenly Greg sticks a foot in the door, and while I'm pulling with all my strength, it's not going to close as long as his foot is there.

He prises the door open with his fingers and his face is contorted with rage. He looks like he's going to hurt me. But I know he wants to turn me over alive to FoSS, so I throw myself at him, knocking us both out of the car and onto the ground. I'm lying on top of him, but he doesn't immediately grab for me. I'm not sure if it's because he's so startled or because I've knocked the wind out of him. I roll off and steady myself to stand up. We're on the side of the road. Maybe I can flag down help.

I'm on my feet when I feel him grab my leg. "Get back here, bitch."

I shake my leg, trying to loosen his grip, but he hangs on and pulls. I lose my balance and fall to the ground, just barely getting my arms out in front of me, so I don't smack down face first. He rolls me over and climbs on top of me. "Looks like you need to be out for the rest of this ride," he says. I struggle beneath him, but he's too heavy for me to budge. He pulls a bottle from his jacket pocket and the rag again. Not more of this. Dear God. As he puts the rag over my face, I bite his hand. He wrenches his hand back, screams in pain, looks at me with pure venom and slaps me hard. My face explodes in pain. I hear tires squeal and try to turn my head to see where the car is that's making the noise. But then the rag covers my face again.

# 5

## KELSEY

When I come to, my head is pounding again. I am lying on a bed of some type, and my eyes feel leaden. There are strange noises. Beeps and whirs. My wrists hurt. A dull throbbing intensifies the more alert I become.

"Penelope," I whisper, but I don't open my eyes. "Penelope."

"Kelsey" says a familiar voice. It is kind, yet authoritative. "Kelsey, I've called Luke and he is on his way. I need you to open your eyes if you can."

My lids flutter a moment, before letting in slits of light. Slits of vision through which I see a tall, lean blonde man with turquoise eyes and an easy smile. Shit, I think. I wonder for a moment why that came to mind, but then I recall that "Shit" is the first thing Jasper Christensen ever said to me. "Jasper?" I squeak out, my throat dry and raspy.

"Yes, Kelsey, it's me," he says, standing at my bedside looking down at me with a serious expression. "We need to know what happened. Where is Penelope?"

The fog in my mind clears and terror replaces it. I try to sit up, to a swooning effect and lie back down. "She's not here?" I screech.

"No, Kelsey," he says, shaking his head adamantly. "The man who found you said someone was attacking you on the side of the road, when he drove up. His arrival scared off your attacker and then the man called an ambulance that brought you to the emergency room. I happened to be here for an emergency consultation and saw you. I identified you and called Luke. But he had no idea what had happened and he says Penelope's not at your house."

My breath catches in my throat. I think I'm going to be sick. "They took her, Jasper," I say, the guilt of abandoning my daughter and getting out of the stupid car, weighing on me like an anvil. “FoSS took her.”

# 6

## SUSAN

I'm almost done. I sigh and plop down on the sofa in my living room. My one bedroom apartment is almost completely packed. A neat pile of 25 boxes occupy the other half of the room, and the movers are coming for them tomorrow. Given how much time I spent at my fiancé's place, I'm shocked at how much stuff I've managed to accumulate here in a year.

My phone rings, so I pull it from my pocket, look to see who it is and then answer. "Hello, Dr. Donnelly," I say.

"Hello, Mrs. Donnelly, almost."

"Five days, 15 hours, and counting," I gush. I'm giddy with excitement over this, which is not what I expected. It's not me to be a simpering, gushing fool, but this wedding has done it to me. I look at my watch. "Are you in the car?"

Nothing. I wonder for a second if I've lost my signal. "Erica said she needs five minutes of my time," he says.

Good grief. His boss is a total chatterbox. "So, you're saying you're going to be delayed by an hour?"

"Between the wedding, the honeymoon and moving into the house, we're gone for a month," he reminds me.

Maybe he's right, but I'm not sure I actually understand why he even needs to be there. "You submitted everything a while ago, and I thought it was going to be at least another month before you got approval for a human trial."

"It's supposed to take a month, but Erica got word they're fast-tracking us," he says. "It will probably take two more weeks for them to approve it, which means I'll be out of the office. That's fine, because we have to solicit patients and approve them. I made one last change to the solicitation, and I think she just wants to make sure we're on the same page."

I sigh, realizing he's right. This is important work. Finding a method to reverse paralysis that doesn't use illegal stem cells is important to him, and if his research is right, he's found one. One that works on primates, but he needs government approval before the human trials start. Only, I wish he could wait patiently at home, rather than finding excuses to go into the office. "Fine," I say, more pouty than I actually feel. "Have your meeting. Since you're going to be awhile, I'm going to hop in the shower. I'm hot and sweaty."

"That's my favorite way to find you."

"You sure? Because, if you can actually keep Erica to five minutes, I'll be all wet and slippery when you get here."

He pants into the phone. "I stand corrected," he says. "I'm going to go talk to Erica for exactly five minutes, because I definitely think I'll like wet and slippery much better than hot and sweaty."

* * *

I've showered, and am wearing my robe and nothing else. I figure Rob will like that. I even took a minute to put on the lipstick he likes: hot red cherry. The color is exactly what one would imagine based on the name, bright, bold and sexy as hell.

I check my phone, which I'd set on the table next to the sofa. Two texts. One from Jane — my soon to be sister-in-law — telling me I'm going to love my bachelorette party. The next text is from Rob from ten minutes ago. "Did it! Five-minute meeting. Forgot my key to your place, but will be there soon. I expect a reward for my promptness; something that takes longer than five minutes. :)"

I smile. Perfect. There is a knock at the door. Ha, that was quick. He must have high-tailed it over here. I head to the door and start speaking as I open it. "So what would you like for your re —"

I stop short, stunned by what I see. My first impulse is to slam the door shut. That would stop my racing heart and perhaps end the panic setting in, but that is not the move of someone who is alright. Not something someone who has moved on would do. Instead, I swallow hard, my hand clutching the doorknob tightly for support, and say, "Kevin."

My former fiancé hasn't changed much since we last saw each other. Same inky black hair, brown eyes, chiseled jaw, slender nose. And that same smile — two rows of perfect white teeth, from birth, not braces — that makes you feel like you are the only one in the room.

In this case, I am the only one in the room. I want to look away, before I'm caught up in memories of all those good times, before everything went south, but I fear he'll know what I'm doing. That I'm avoiding his gaze, so instead I maintain eye contact, like someone who is fine. Like someone who he didn't hurt immeasurably.

His eyes linger on me. His gaze is so intense, it feels like he wants to suck me into his vortex. "May I come in?" he asks.

No, I want to say. I should say. I don't say. "Sure," I tell him, cinching my robe tighter, sliding the door wider and taking a step back so he can enter. Once he steps inside, his black dress shoes padding softly on the floor, I close the door and stand next to it. I should offer to let him sit, but I don't have it in me. I need him to say his piece and leave.

"May I sit down?"

I shake my head. "Kevin, I'm not really dressed for company," I say, as I start feeling conscious of my robe. "Now isn't a good time."

For the first time, he doesn't look like the confident Kevin of most of my memories. He looks unsure, unsteady, the way he did in our last conversation. "Sue," he says. He always called me Sue. I liked it. It was special, something he alone called me. But, now it has the effect of nails scratching a chalkboard. It grates on me. "I'm sorry to come right now, but I found out some disturbing information you ought to know. It's about your marking surgery."

# 7

## SUSAN

I usher Kevin into the kitchen, then run to my room and make a quick change into jeans and a t-shirt. When I return to the kitchen, I find Kevin waiting patiently. He is wearing black slacks, a white shirt, a tie and a blue blazer; overdressed for sitting in a wooden folding chair at my circular table.

I sit across from Kevin, ensuring there is the appropriate distance between us. I would have had him sit in the living room, but only the sofa remains and I don't wish to sit so close to him. I'm nervous about what he has to say. My experience being marked and its aftermath was a dark time in my life.

He pulls a sheet of paper from his breast pocket and hands it to me. Taking it, I scan the first few lines. Once I realize what it is, I set it down. My eyes squint at him in confusion. "This is the recommendation Sen. Reed wrote me for the FoSS National Honors Architecture Masters Degree program," I say. "How did you get this? It's a sealed recommendation. I've never even seen it."

He takes a quick breath, picks up the letter and pushes it back in my direction. "Look at the highlighted section."

I'm hesitant, still not sure what this letter means or why he has it. I look down at the paper, limp in his hand and take it. I skim to the bottom, where a yellow highlighter has illuminated two lines: "I've known Susan since she was five-years-old; she's my daughter's best friend and like a daughter to me. I think she would make a wonderful addition to the Honors Architecture program."

The words warm me. Sen. Reed said as much to me last year, but I hadn't realized he'd told anyone else. "Why do you have this?" I ask him again, letting the letter fall to the table.

"I've been working part time for Dr. Rounds," he says, as if this name should have meaning to me.

"Who is Dr. Rounds?"

He doesn't answer immediately. Instead he lifts the letter, folds it and puts it back in his pocket. Softly, he says, "He's in charge of the Universal Program to Preserve Life through Citizen Donation."

Only Kevin would feel compelled to call the program by its full name. I frame my question the way any normal person would. "The marking program? You're working for the man who runs it?"

Kevin slowly nods his head, his expression inscrutable. I try not to grimace. The Citizen Donation program, which most people just call the marking program because once you've been selected or marked, you're required to help needy patients through live donation. Selections are made based on DNA. Everyone's DNA gets uploaded into a database at birth and when a person gets gravely ill and needs life-saving procedures, the marking program finds the best match and marks that person. I was obligated to donate bone marrow to a needy patient, and an infection after that surgery left me paralyzed from the waist down. My friend Kelsey fled the country to avoid a forced kidney operation after she was marked. I'd still be in a wheelchair if it weren't for a miracle medical procedure performed a little more than a year ago. Even though I can walk again, mention of the marking program sends shivers up my spine. I give Kevin a bewildered look. "I don't understand. What does this letter have to do with Dr. Rounds? With the marking program?"

Kevin looks around the room, as if it might be bugged, then slides his chair around so it's right next to mine. He's violated every tenet of personal space and is close enough that his leg brushes against mine. "This was in Dr. Rounds' personal file cabinet."

I put my hand up to get him to pause. "Why would he have this?" I ask, baffled.

"That's what I wanted to know," Kevin whispers. "So, I went ahead and looked at the records for your marking surgery."

I slide my chair away, stand up and take two paces from him. The blast of anger that has erupted in me spills out when I speak. "You did what?" The idea that he would go through my medical records — through those medical records — infuriates me. He hadn't wanted to know at the time. He hadn't stuck around to help or ask questions when I needed him most. He abandoned me, but now when we're through, he violates my privacy and gets those records. I point a finger at him and snarl, "You had no right, Kevin."

He stands and walks over to me, contrite, and stops right in front of me. "I'm sorry," he says. "You're right about that. I just was concerned about why he had the note."

I take a step back. "Did you ask him?"

"Of course not," he tells me. "I wasn't supposed to have found it. I wasn't supposed to have been in his office, in that drawer, OK? But, once I found the note, I copied it, and I went looking in your medical records." He reaches out his hand and puts it on my shoulder. "I think you should sit back down."

I want to say, no. But something in his tone tells me I shouldn't. I sidestep the arm on my shoulder, walk back to the table, slide his chair further from mine and sit. He follows and sits. "I've seen my medical records. I know the surgery went wrong. I lived with the consequences of those mistakes for more than a year. I'm not sure how anything in my file changes that."

He purses his lower lip. "It's not the file that relates to what happened after you were marked, Sue. It's the marking file, the one that shows the match results. The one that shows which people would be the best genetic match for donation."

I tilt my head toward him.

"Sue, you weren't the best match for that man. There were 92 people better suited to be his donor," he says, his voice soft, yet full of gravitas. "Someone moved you to the top of the list, and I think your connection to Sen. Reed is the reason why."

# 8

## SUSAN

What he is saying can't be true. My darkest moments. A surgery that left me paralyzed; a paralysis that resulted in my fiancé abandoning me; a paralysis that made me restructure my life — it didn't have to happen?

His brown eyes are deep, unanswering pools when I look into them. "You must have made a mistake, Kevin," I tell him. "They wouldn't move me up just because of my relationship with Senator Reed."

"I looked up Kelsey's record," he says.

My stomach feels like it just dropped a thousand feet. I don't want to hear what he says next, but I can't help looking at him expectantly.

"Seventy four people were a better match."

I put my head in my hands and close my eyes. This is too much. I can't believe this. Our lives ruined for no reason. Kelsey's life. My life. I raise my head and look at him, hoping he has the answers. "I don't understand. Why would someone do this? Why wouldn't they just hurt the senator? Why would they hurt me and Kelsey?"

His voice is thoughtful when he answers. "I think you have to ask yourself what they would gain by moving you and Kelsey to the top of the list?"

I drum my fingers on the table, unwilling to speak yet. I need time to think, to process this. My thoughts are running through my head too quickly, all jumbled and uncertain. I find myself staring at Kevin's breast pocket, where I saw him tuck the note. Only the note is not visible at all — not even a slight bulge or sagging of the fabric to indicate his jacket holds anything. Even now, the note remains a phantom.

Kevin, I notice is grinning at me dreamily. "What?" I ask. There seems nothing about this situation to inspire that look upon his face.

"It's just that you haven't changed," he says, shaking off the whimsical look. "You still like that apple-cinnamon scented shampoo. Your hair is a little shorter, but it's still that brilliant red that is as determined and strong as your personality. You have the same habits: you still drum your fingers and get this intense look in your eyes when you're deep in thought."

His eyes are soft and warm and they remind me of how he looked the first time he kissed me: yearning, hopeful. I slide my chair away from him a little. We need distance. I'd ask him to leave, but I need answers. I harden my expression, hoping he'll stop looking at me like that. "What is it that you think someone had to gain?"

Kevin's face dims a little, his eyes turning down at the corners, his mouth tightening. "Political favors. Maybe a political favor in exchange for removing your mark."

That doesn't make any sense. I am shaking my head. "He never asked to get us off the list; he never asked them to unmark me."

He raises an eyebrow, reaches out and touches my hand. "Are you sure?"

The spot where he's touching me feels warm, like it's near a flame, one that's going to burn me if I don't move. Kevin is close enough that I can smell his aftershave; the same one he used to wear when we were together. I want him to go. "Thank you for telling me this." I stand and he looks startled by the suddenness of it. "Come on," I say, forcing a smile, trying to lead him out of the kitchen. He doesn't immediately follow, but after a moment, his chair sweeps across the tile and he is walking right behind me, back through the living room, toward the front door.

I stop at the entryway, or more importantly, Kevin's exit route. "You should tell Sen. Reed this," I say, wanting more than anything for him to leave. "He can help you figure this out."

He searches my face for a moment. He knows I'm trying to get rid of him, and he'd like to figure out why. I guess, the two of us really haven't changed that much if we can still read each other so well. I reach for the knob to open the door, but he grabs my hand. "I know what you're doing, Sue."

I give a light chuckle. "Opening the door," I say dryly. "You really are going to be a brilliant doctor if you figured that one out all by yourself."

He smiles back, and takes a step closer to me, again violating the boundaries of personal space. "As awful as I was to you, I didn't kill what we had, Sue. I can still feel it. You can, too."

The air between us is buzzing with a quiet electricity, and I want it to stop. I slide my hand out of his and take a step back, knowing fundamentally he's wrong, but wondering why his presence so close, so near, still makes my pulse rise. "I'm getting married at the end of the week."

He shakes his head. "You don't have to."

"I want to," I tell him. And in my mind I see Rob's face, his hazel eyes, his dirty blonde locks curling slightly on his head, his adorable nose. The way he looked at me the first time we met, the way he looks at me now, like I am the only woman for him. I want to marry Rob. I want Kevin gone. "Look, I appreciate you coming here, you telling me this, but I don't feel comfortable discussing this with you."

"I'm sorry, Sue," he says, his eyes pleading forgiveness. "I'm sorry for leaving you the way I did. I was wrong. I was a fool."

My entire body stiffens and I feel like shutting down. I can't deal with this. Everything surrounding my paralysis — from the procedure itself to Kevin breaking our engagement — was traumatic and him dredging it up makes me want to shed my skin and slither into a hole. "I don't care," I say, looking him directly in the eye. "It doesn't matter. It's over. We're over. That time is over."

He grabs me, placing one hand behind my back and pulls me into him, his lips pressing against mine. His grip is vice-like, his upper body pressed against mine, trying to will me to reciprocate. I keep my lips shut. I feel his tongue attempt to find mine, but meet the wall of my closed mouth. I try to pull away, but he's holding me tightly. I have to breathe; I open my mouth; his tongue takes advantage, sliding in and mingling with mine. I tug away again, considering a knee to the groin, but as I'm thinking about it, he relents and lets me go. I stagger back two steps and gape at him.

Why would he do that? Now that I'm healthy again, he wants me back. It hurts. I take a step toward him. The corners of his mouth glide upward, as if he believes he's going to be vindicated, so I relish even more the pain that appears when I slap him.

He grimaces and rubs his cheek consolingly.

"I'm getting married," I tell him, ignoring the stinging in my hand. "I love my fiancé."

"I was your fiancé once," he says, nostalgia playing across his face.

"And you abandoned me when I needed you most," I say. "You told me I was too paralyzed for you to be with." I let the words sit there a moment. Saying it to his face is cathartic. Seeing the red mark my palm left on his cheek is also cathartic.

"I'm sorry," he pleads, reaching out and touching my arm gently. "When they moved you up on that list, when they did that to you, they ruined your life and mine too. We could've been happy," he says, grazing his fingers along my upper arm. "We would have been happy, you and I, if not for that surgery."

We were happy, and we could've still been happy if he had just stayed. I clutch my hands tight to my sides and will myself not to move, not to flinch and to keep Kevin in my sights. "Is that letter real, or did you make this whole thing up to come over here, dive into our past and assault me?"

His face falls and he staggers back a step as if I've literally wounded him. "Sue, I would never do that," he says. "I wouldn't make it up. And the kiss... I just wanted to remind you what we had. I didn't mean for you to look at it that way."

I close my eyes and breathe out. "This is why you have to go, Kevin. You can't do that to me. OK?"

Nodding, he reaches out and takes my hand. "Sue, I'm sorry."

"May I have the letter? The one from Sen. Reed. I want to keep it."

He hesitates and then reaches into his breast pocket to retrieve it. "It's just a copy, you know."

"I know," I tell him as I take it. I need to show this to Rob, so we can figure this out. "You should go, Kevin. I need time to think."

He nods. "Why don't you look that over, digest it some more, and then maybe I could come back later; we could talk. I could show you the marking results; the originals and the doctored ones."

"Sure," I say, though I'm not sure I mean it. I'd like to see the paper trail, but I don't want to see Kevin. He and I had a good relationship until the end, but the last time we saw each other was one of the worst days of my life. I don't like having those feelings resurrected.

"And, with you finding this out, maybe now is not the best time to leave town. Maybe you shouldn't have this wedding until you can figure this out."

I'm flabbergasted at this suggestion, but I hide my shock, instead swallowing and reaching for the doorknob. I pull open the door to let him out and there is Rob, hand poised to knock.

Rob looks from me to Kevin, but says nothing. I feel my cheeks heat and notice that my lipstick is smeared on Kevin's mouth.

"I'm Kevin," my former fiancé says, introducing himself to my current fiancé.

"Rob," my current fiancé says, reaching out to shake his hand.

"Good to meet you," Kevin says, then runs his tongue across his upper lip. He smiles as if the taste of my lipstick gives him immense pleasure. He turns to me and says. "Sue, think about what I said." Then he heads out the door, disappearing down the hallway.

Rob comes in silently and stands just inside the entryway. His lips are pressed firmly together and he's crossed his arms. "Care to explain that," he says coolly, then adds, "Sue."

"I will," I tell him, turning and walking toward the sofa. "But you're not going to like it."

# 9

## SUSAN

We are sitting next to each other on the sofa, and I have told Rob everything that transpired between Kevin and myself. Now, he sits rigid next to me. Throughout my story, he didn't say much, except to ask if Kevin hurt me when he kissed me. My pride, yes, but my body, no.

He blows out a short breath that should be stress relieving, but he doesn't seem any less tightly coiled afterward. "You told him he could come back?"

The air in here seems too still. The only noises are the gentle hum of the ancient refrigerator in the next room, and Rob's and my breathing. His face loosens a bit, his eyes watching me, trying to figure me out. "I just wanted him to go. I thought he'd leave more quickly if I said we could talk again. I don't want to talk to him again."

He pauses a moment, as if deciding exactly what to say. "I know things ended badly and quickly without a lot of resolution," he says in a low, deliberate tone. "I just want you to know, if his visit stirred up, uh, unresolved feelings, I understand. You can tell me."

For Rob to ask, he must be bothered by it. He's right: Kevin's visit stirred up unresolved feelings. But, they're not going to impact my relationship with Rob. "I would be lying if I said I wasn't surprised to see Kevin. Everything about his visit was a bit stunning. If I seem different, I'm just a little stunned, still. I don't have feelings for Kevin. I love you, and I am looking incredibly forward to becoming Mrs. Samuel Robert Donnelly."

Rob leans in and kisses me, a soft, delicate kiss, which is what I need at this moment.

When he pulls away, he seems a little more reassured. He takes my hand and says, "If what he said is true, we should find out what happened with your marking. We don't have a lot of time before the wedding, but tomorrow's pretty free. Do you want to try to figure some of this out now, or wait until after the wedding?"

I press my back into the sofa, trying to get some support. A good question. I want to know right now. But, he's right. We're supposed to leave for Georgia on Wednesday, and that's cutting it short, as it is. "Obviously, the wedding comes first, but I'd like to spend a little energy figuring out what we can before we leave. I'll call Sen. Reed, and maybe you can use your tech skills to try to figure out who moved me to the top of the list, and why."

"If anyone actually did move you," Rob says, skeptically.

"You think he's lying?"

"I think that his objective in coming over here was to see you again," Rob says harshly. "Maybe it is true, but if his goal was to help you by sharing this information, he would have brought the marking results, not told you he needed to come back later."

I drum my fingers on my thigh. I'd suggested Kevin was lying but I hadn't really thought it was true. I'd just wanted to throw him off balance, to get him to stop looking at me like I was the woman he adored. Rob is right. We can't take what Kevin says as gospel. I turn back to Rob. "I'll ask Kevin to come back with the results. Only I want you to be here this time."

"Of course," he says, almost before I've finished speaking. "I'm not leaving you alone with him again."

Part of me wants to challenge him on this, to say I can be alone with anyone I damn well please. But, Rob isn't trying to push me around. He's concerned about my safety, and I can't blame him after Kevin kissed me like that. Still, I'm not some helpless victim who Rob has to look after. "About Kevin," I say. Rob bristles at the mention of Kevin's name. "I want you to be around, but I can take care of myself. I can handle him."

"Like you did today, when he kissed you, against your will?"

I glower and straighten my back. "I slapped him across his face."

"Maybe he enjoyed it."

Uggh. Really? I gape a moment. Before I can respond, I hear a familiar jingle from atop the end table next to us. It's my phone, so I turn away to answer it, glad for the interruption.

"Hello," I say.

"Susan, this is Lewis," says the raw voice on the other end of the line.

I mouth 'Senator Reed' to Rob, and give a confused shrug. Part of me wonders if Kevin has spoken to him already, but it seems too soon, and the senator sounds a bit too distraught for it to be about the markings, which happened almost three years ago. "Is something wrong?"

"Yes. They've kidnapped Penelope and I need your help."

# 10

## KELSEY

Jasper said they'll release me in an hour. It seems the drug Greg used to knock me out shouldn't have any long-term side effects. Luke and I are alone now. He's sitting in the chair at my bedside; he hasn't said much since I told him exactly what happened. His head is down and I can't see his reassuring blue eyes; only the top of the fuzzy brown buzz cut he now sports.

I feel horrible. It's my fault Greg has Penelope. I should've trusted my gut inside the house, or at least Major Nelson's. He knew. Instead of listening, I locked him outside the kitchen, his paws banging for me to understand.

Then, once Greg had us, it was stupid of me to get out of the car. I play the scene over and over in my head. If I'd just been willing to take some more abuse, if I just hadn't panicked, if I had somehow kept us on that roadside a little bit longer without getting out of the car. I wanted Greg away from Penelope, but I shouldn't have gotten out of the car. That was stupid. Now, who knows where she is.

I am holding Mr. Giggles. He apparently fell out of the car during the struggle. The paramedics brought it to the hospital with me. The toy monkey is nestled in my arms, the same way Penelope used to carry it. I feel the need to hold it, as it reminds me of her, but it's also a reminder of how I failed as a mother. I did everything wrong, and FoSS has her, because of me.

"I'm sorry," I whisper to Luke, whose head is down in thought.

He looks up at me, confused. "What?"

My eyes are starting to tear and my voice breaks. "I'm sorry I let him take Penelope."

Luke takes my hand in his, his skin feeling so much warmer in this cool hospital room than mine. "Kelsey, it's not your fault," he insists, his voice low and soothing. "This is Greg's fault. I can't believe he would try to take you back; that he would leave my sister in an institution and think kidnapping my wife and baby was the way to fix it."

His voice is brimming with anger, his eyes are distant and, for the first time ever I've seen, cruel.

"Luke," I say, pulling my hand free from his to wipe away tears. "How are we going to get her back? What are we going to do?"

Luke rubs my shoulder, his cruel mask fading away as he tries to look strong for me. "I have to go back to FoSS. She's my daughter, and there aren't any charges against me. I have to go and fight for her."

I grab a few strands of my hair and twist them around my finger. I've had so little hair and so little cause to worry recently, I've not relied on this nervous habit in a long time. Now I've got plenty to worry about, including Luke's plan. "Go back to FoSS," I say, unable to keep my anxiety from creeping in. "That's crazy. What if they decide to charge you with helping me?"

"It's been two years. I don't think they will," he says, as if he's thought about this for a while.

But it doesn't make any sense that they'd give her back and let Luke bring her home to me. She's their only bargaining chip at this point. "Luke, I don't think it will be so easy. Have you talked to my father?"

He looks away briefly, then back to me. "Yes, I told him they have Penelope. He's trying to find out who, and see if he can negotiate her release."

My father is a brilliant negotiator. If anyone has a chance of getting her back, it's him. Suddenly, it hits me; he's got something to work with. "This violates our bargain," I say, thinking back to the agreement we made with Gen. Xavier Tisdale. He's a military leader who secretly kidnapped — and almost killed — Susan almost two years ago. The deal was we'd all be safe — Luke, me, Penelope, Susan and Rob — as long as we kept secret what the government had done.

Luke grimaces and then he says without preamble, "Tisdale died yesterday. Cancer. He's been sick for a while, and finally passed away. Your father thinks our deal is void. At this point the government could say Tisdale acted alone, a rogue official. It's still not good if we were to produce the recording, but there's a lot less damage for

FoSS."

I close my eyes, relishing the darkness it brings. This is not the answer we need. Not when our daughter's life depends on it. Deep breaths. I try to pull in deep breaths so I can calm down, so my head can clear, so I can think. I squeeze the little toy tighter. I need to get my daughter back, and the bargaining chip we have is not very good anymore. There is an obvious solution to getting her back. I should turn myself in. I mean, even if we get Penelope back, we'll spend the rest of our lives looking over our shoulders, wondering if someone is coming to get me. Wondering if they'll try again to take Penelope as a bargaining chip. I can't do that.

"I think you're right," I say to Luke.

"About the deal being void?"

"Yes," I tell him, giving a sober look. "And about getting her back. I think it's best if you go back to FoSS to bargain for her."

He gives a resigned head bob.

"But I should go, too," I tell him. "We both need to get our daughter."

# 11

## KELSEY

"Kelsey, you can't go back," Luke says, his voice pleading. "They'll kill you. You have to stay here where it's safe. I already checked with Gen. Maylee. He said you can go back to the compound."

I stare at my husband, disbelieving. "You already talked to him?"

My husband smoothes out my blanket, finds my left hand and lifts it into his, running his pointer finger along my wedding band. "I don't know where my daughter is or if she's alright," he says, his voice soft and desperate. "I need to know that my wife is safe. Kelsey, please give me that peace of mind."

This is eating at his insides, slowly gnawing away at who he is. Luke has always been a protector, first mine and now Penelope's as well. He relishes that role. With this kidnapping, he feels he's failed Penelope but still needs to protect me. I want to give him peace; I want him to rescue our daughter from wherever she was taken. The problem is, I'm afraid he can't. I'm afraid that I am the only thing we have to bargain with to bring her home.

"Luke," I whisper, putting my right hand on top of his. The hairs on the back of his hand brush against my palm. "I want you to have peace, but I need to go with you."

Staring down at our meshed hands, he shakes his head, refusing to look at me. "Kelsey, I can't lose you both," he says. "You need to stay here."

I can't tell him yes, so I sit there with him, breathing in and out, listening to the machines in my room. They whir quietly. There is a glass window with horizontal blinds, which are half open. I can see silhouettes pass by, in what is presumably a busy hospital. A place busy with the business of saving lives. I need to save my daughter's life. I need to go.

"Luke, I promise you, I will be safe if I come with you," I say, my voice resolute. "I will do everything you ask me to do in regards to safety. I need to go with you to find our daughter. The little girl I almost died giving birth to. The little girl I've held and cradled every day since we brought her home from the hospital. I need to go with you, Luke, just as much as you need to know I'm safe."

There is silence as I wait for Luke to speak. I can feel the pulse beat beneath his thumb, as his hand gently presses into mine, clinging to it like a lifeline. Only, he's my lifeline, too. Can we really tether each other when we're both adrift?

Luke takes his gaze from our hands and looks me in the eye. His expression is weary, and he says. "If we can figure out a way to get you in safely and you promise to do everything I ask, we'll go get our daughter together."

# 12

## SUSAN

The senator, Rob and I are huddled around my tiny kitchen table strategizing. The senator thought it was easier to stop by here than have Rob and I come over.

He received a note at his house with four sentences. "P is fine. Keep her that way. Tell no one. Further instructions will come." It wasn't much, but enough for us to know that Penelope is in danger and needs our help. So, this little session hopes to address two problems: (1) how to find Penelope and (2) how to find Emmie. Then we have to rescue them.

"I'm still friends with some of Molly's colleagues," Rob says. "One of them is hooked in enough that I think I can find out where Emmie is, if it's an actual mental institution."

I pat Rob's hand. "Thank you." Molly is Rob's deceased wife. She was a psychiatrist whose research made her a rising star in the field. Her untimely murder by a patient five years ago left Rob a widower at 26.

"Lewis," I say, conscious of the fact that I am using his first name. It is at his insistence but I still feel awkward, having called him Senator Reed most of my life. "Have you been able to find out anything about who's holding Penelope?"

His eyes are downcast and his cheeks sag as he shakes his head. "I'm still trying, but so far everyone I talked to is denying having any knowledge of Greg returning to FoSS with a child. I plan to corner someone at the funeral tomorrow. Everyone who could have answers will be there."

I reach my hand up to my neck, feeling the soft skin there, a chill running through me. Gen. Tisdale being dead changes everything. Rob told me about it shortly after Kevin left. He'd finished with his boss in five minutes, as promised, but he'd gotten delayed when his mother called with the news of Tisdale's death. The general had ordered me held captive two years ago, while he mounted a propaganda campaign against Kelsey using videos I was forced to make. Tisdale eventually ordered me murdered, but I managed to escape and the senator brokered a bargain for our safety. With the general gone, we all feel a bit precarious. Our safety, our bargain was all tied to this man, and now he is dead.

The senator gives me a sympathetic look. "You don't have to go, Susan," he says. "Rob is the only one who actually knew him, and given that you two are getting ready for your wedding in a few days, no one would expect you to be there."

Part of me would like to ditch the funeral of the man who ordered me poisoned, and almost killed Rob's brother in the process; the rest of me wants to go. To see the monster dropped in the ground and covered with cold, black dirt, to know he will never rise again. To spit on his grave. Well, even though I'm going, I can't do that. That would defy proper decorum and go against our purposes, which is to find out who's got Penelope and how to get her back.

"I'd prefer to go," I tell the senator. "I'd feel like I was doing something."

"Speaking of doing something," says Rob, his voice cold. "What about Kevin's information? Do you think he's onto something or is it bogus?"

The senator looks down at his hands in his lap. He doesn't meet my eyes when he speaks. "You should see whatever information he has to give you and assume it's true, that Kelsey and Susan were targeted because of their connection to me."

He still hasn't looked up, and I feel dread creeping up my spine. "You seem to have given this some thought," I say, softening my voice to avoid sounding accusatory.

The senator smoothes a hair behind his ear. It's something he does in a debate if he wants a moment to think. I've spent too much time with his family, with Kelsey and political strategists. I wish I didn't see small things like this. He is raising his eyebrows slightly and loosening his face, an attempt to appear open. "It never occurred to me that you or Kelsey were being targeted. But, in retrospect, there were clear overtures from a person on my staff trying to get me to pull strings to get your name removed from the list."

My heart stops for just a second, and I feel my entire body harden, as his words sink in. Someone asked him to get me out of it, and he said... what? "They tried?"

He reaches out his hand and touches mine. "I didn't think you didn't want to do it. You seemed fine with doing your civic duty. It didn't seem fair for me to pull strings when everyone else had to deal with the consequences when they proved to be a match."

I slide my hand out from under his, his touch suddenly feeling deadly cold. I steady my breathing and try to think about this rationally. I wasn't bothered by the marking. I did want to do my civic duty. But, the me who knows the end result, the me who knows how everything went wrong, is brimming with anger that he had an opportunity to stop it all from happening, but chose not to. "And Kelsey? Could you have stopped Kelsey's marking."

"Yes," he says, barely audible.

I look at him, daggers in my eyes. "You knew she was upset. You knew she wasn't coping well."

His lips tighten and cheeks sink in. "At first, I thought it was normal concern," he says, his voice pleading for the kind of understanding I don't think I have in me right now. "Then, when I realized how truly panicked she was about it, it was too late. The news of her marking had been made public. Even though I wanted to pull strings, I couldn't do it without people finding out. So, I did what I could. I tried to convince her she'd be alright, and I asked they bring in the best transplant surgeon: Dr. Ekkels, from Baltimore. Even that wasn't really fair, me pulling strings to switch doctors. She'd been marked. It was her duty, so I told myself that in the end, it was the right thing. I mean, if she truly had been the best match, it would have been right for her to donate."

He chose his political career over his daughter. He'd wanted to help her, but he was afraid the public would find out. And worse still, he never even considered helping me. I gently squeeze a fold of neck skin between two fingers, hoping to alleviate some of the anger I'm feeling, without saying something regrettable right now.

"I would have tried to get you out of it, Susan, if I had known for a second it would go wrong, if I'd thought you didn't want to." My face must be completely transparent today, broadcasting all of my thoughts, if he is responding without me speaking. My eyes must accuse him, where my voice fails.

"Susan knows that, Lewis," Rob says, placing a hand on my shoulder. "I think she's just a bit surprised to realize that Kevin was telling the truth. He seemed more intent on rekindling their relationship than relaying pertinent information."

I turn and give my fiancé a hostile glare. He is trying to be a peacemaker, to improve a situation that will deteriorate if I speak my mind. Only, that's not what I want right now. I want to be angry and I want the senator to know it. I am hurt to know that he could have helped me and chose not to.

Senator Reed offers Rob a sheepish look. "I'm sorry," he says. "I think Kevin's renewed interest in Susan is my fault."

I steal a glance at Rob, whose nostrils have flared with that little tidbit. Well, at least he'll stop trying to smooth things over. "What do you mean?" I ask. Perhaps moving off the subject of my marking will help my anger to subside.

"Ever since Kelsey torpedoed Kevin's career using my contacts, I've felt responsible for helping him recover," Senator Reed says. Kevin had been awarded the prestigious Lazenby Scholar award, but somehow Kelsey managed to get the offer rescinded after he broke up with me. I can see why the senator might want to lend a hand. He looks at Rob briefly, perhaps trying to gauge his reaction, then back to me, and continues. "We talk from time to time and recently I told him I was proud of his changes. That I thought he was a very different young man than the one who'd treated his fiancée so poorly. I even told him that you would like the man he'd become."

I keep my mouth clamped shut, though this is jaw-dropping news. I have no idea why he'd say such a thing to Kevin. The senator studies my face for a moment and then turns to Rob.

"I just thought he wanted confirmation that he's changed, that he's become a better man. I never imagined he'd want to pursue Susan again," he says to my fiancé. "I told him that Susan is very happy, that she's getting married."

The words are right, and maybe they even had the right sentiment when he expressed them to Kevin, but I'm sure Kevin didn't hear that. I'm sure he looked at the situation the way Sen. Reed did last year. Lewis told me he thought Kevin and Rob were similar, with Rob being more mature. Kevin sees my involvement with Rob as me seeking a new and improved version of him. He thinks he can win me back by showing me that he's the version I want.

"If what Kevin said is true, can you use it as a bargaining chip to help get Penelope back?" I ask.

The senator doesn't hesitate. "Yes," he says. "If Kelsey wasn't really marked, she shouldn't be a fugitive. Having proof of that would change everything."

"Then, we need the evidence Kevin has. I'll call and ask him to come back."

# 13

## KELSEY

Luke ran home, packed us a bag and convinced our neighbors to look after Major Nelson for the next few days. Now the two of us have left the hospital with Jasper, who's bringing us back to his place. While Jasper was working for Dr. Grant when I met him, the two have parted ways and Jasper now has his own small practice in Peoria. It's not as large as Dr. Grant's, but is still something. Like his mentor, he's been doing some fascinating research into curing the diseases of pregnancy, both here in Peoria and back in FoSS. When I ask why he and Dr. Grant parted ways, he simply says it was just time for him to move on. I don't pry because he clearly doesn't want to discuss it. But, I do wonder if my dumping Dr. Grant's care for Jasper's impacted their working relationship. Or if Jasper just saw how crooked Dr. Grant was.

When we arrive at the small office complex, Jasper ushers us in. The clinic is closed for the evening, so there are no staff or patients to worry about seeing me. It's dark, so Jasper turns on the lights and herds us toward a back room.

Once inside I realize it's his office. Jasper's office is not as nice as Dr. Grant's was. It's a windowless room, with a desk, two chairs across from it, some shelves lining the wall and a few framed degrees or certificates. The tile on the floor is standard speckled white, which has a tendency to look dirty, whether it's been cleaned or not. It makes me wonder again why Jasper split from Dr. Grant. Despite Stephen Grant's self-absorption, he is known to be a brilliant doctor and very well connected. I'm not sure I'd leave all that power and sunny, swanky offices for this. Luke sets our overnight bag in the corner, while Jasper pulls his chair out from behind his desk. Jasper positions the chair near the other two, and the three of us sit in a circle. "So, you want to get both of you back into FoSS?" Jasper asks.

I suppose Luke told him this sometime between when we discussed it and I was released. Trusting Jasper appears to be something Luke has decided is OK. While I don't distrust Jasper, per se, this is a dangerous operation we're planning and telling the wrong person could land us in hot water, once we get back into FoSS. Luke has given a soft "yep," Jasper leans forward and speaks quietly.

"I have a van," he says. "It has a hidden compartment that will fit a woman. I've used it twice to help Zuri bring women across." He shakes his head, the memory nerve-racking enough to make him jittery in the present. "Getting across the border is tough on both sides, as no one wants defectors. But there usually aren't women trying to get smuggled across from here to FoSS, so I think we'll be fine. If you want to do it, I can drive you over the border tomorrow morning."

While this should be good, it feels almost deflating. Too easy. Just like that, we have a solution. Luke nods. I put a hand on his leg and give him a wait-a-minute look. He gives a barely perceptible head shake, as if I'm to drop it. But I won't.

"Jasper, why would you do that for us? You could lose your license to practice medicine if you're caught. You could go to a holding facility."

He straightens himself in his chair, his turquoise eyes glinting in the low light of the office. "I don't expect to be caught," he says, rather cockily. "And if we are, I'll deny knowing anything about my cargo."

But that still doesn't explain why. Luke takes my hand, pulls it into his own. I turn to look at him, and he shoots me a 'drop it' look. It's nice that he is so trusting, but I'm not. I turn back to question Jasper further, but he is standing now and sliding his chair back to the position it held behind his desk. "My apartment is upstairs," Jasper says, tossing Luke a set of keys. "You guys can stay there. It's two bedrooms. Use the first one, on the left. Clean sheets are in the closet. I'll be back in the morning. Clinic is closed Tuesdays, so we'll head back into FoSS tomorrow."

Luke gives a curt, OK. I'm still thrown off by his trusting Jasper so completely. "Jasper," Luke says. "It's imperative that you don't tell anyone but Sen. Reed that Kelsey is coming with me. I mean anyone." He says the last part with an eyebrow wiggle for emphasis.

"I understand," Jasper says, walking by us and out the door. "I'll see you two in the morning."

* * *

Jasper's apartment is small but quaint. We enter into a room that's split between the living area and kitchen. It's a bit cluttered, various exercise items like weights, springs and resistance bands, but it's clean enough. To the right is a hallway. We head down it and the first door, on our left is a bedroom with nothing but a mattress on the floor. There is nothing on it, not even a sheet.

"This must be it," says Luke, as we walk into the room. On the top shelf of the closet, set off by brown louver doors, are clean sheets, a pillow and a blanket.

Luke hands me the fitted sheet, and we head over to make the bed. I enjoy the peace and tranquility of doing something simple and mindless. When we've put the blanket on top, Luke puts the pillow on my side of the bed. "You should try to get some sleep, Sweetheart."

I reach in the overnight bag and pull out Mr. Giggles. I set him on the edge of the mattress, then sit next to him. Bringing my knees up to my face, I wrap my arms around them. "I can't sleep," I whisper. "Not with her gone, with Greg doing God knows what to her."

Luke walks round and sits next to me, folds me into his arms and holds me. It feels good for a minute. I can feel safe and warm and happy to be here with him, for a few fleeting seconds, but then the world rushes back, slamming into me like a brick wall. My daughter is gone. I haven't a clue where she is, except that she has returned to the one country that wants me dead. And I'm holed up in the apartment of a man I barely know.

I pull free from his arms. "Why are we here, Luke?"

"Kelsey," he says kindly. "I told you; we just don't want anyone to know where you went after the hospital. It's not a good idea to go back to the house right now."

I shake my head. "No, I know. That makes sense. But, why here? Why do you trust Jasper?"

"Because he's the kind of doctor Dr. Grant should be," Luke says. "He genuinely cares about people and genuinely wants to help. I've seen him at hospital events; we talk from time to time. And I know why he split from Dr. Grant. He's not going to turn us in. We can trust Jasper."

His eyes are reassuring and he seems completely confident in his assertion, but I don't know why. "How do you know this?"

Taking in a short breath, he stares at me head on, and says, "His split with Dr. Grant wasn't good. Jasper felt Dr. Grant wasn't being as forthcoming with some of his patients here, and called him on it. Dr. Grant didn't appreciate that, and he had Jasper brought before the medical board for falsifying work records."

My eyes widen and my mouth pops open. "What happened? Is Jasper in trouble?"

Luke shakes his head, reaches a hand out and places it gently on my back. "No," Luke says. "It was an issue of whether or not Jasper was working more hours than he's supposed to. A lot of doctors do it, especially when they don't have families. They put in extra hours off the books to help out in needier areas, but it's not legal. The board gave Jasper a slap on the wrist. After that, they parted ways."

I bite my lower lip and try to digest what Luke has just told me. While Jasper's reticence over discussing it hinted the split was not amicable, it seems odd that Dr. Grant attacked Jasper so openly. Dr. Grant doesn't seem the type to openly seek revenge. He's the type to bide his time and wait. Yet, he got into a smackdown with Jasper and forced him out. It's especially odd, because Jasper is a good doctor, a really good doctor.

"Why is Jasper still here, running this dingy clinic? Why doesn't he go back to FoSS?"

Luke shrugs. "He has a girlfriend here, and he likes being able to help. Feels he's needed here more than he is in FoSS."

That makes sense. I like Peoria, but it's not the same as FoSS. The people who rejected the sentiments of FoSS and the principles of Life First have created a vibrant nation. They live life as a whole, enjoying so many things, taking so many risks. In FoSS, so much of our lives are about limiting risk, preserving health and well-being. People here aren't cavalier, but they seem to recognize that while life is precious and should be saved, it's only lived once. I turn to my husband who is rubbing my back in gentle circular motions. "So, how do you know all this?"

"People talk," he says. "Hospitals are a small community." Ah. I see. Trading on his experience with Dr. Grant, after we moved to Peoria, Luke got a job as a hospital administrator. He was initially an assistant, but his boss went to another hospital last year, and Luke got a surprising promotion. It makes sense that he'd know about Jasper's trouble.

"You never mentioned it," I say, trying to sound nonchalant, though I find myself irritated that he wouldn't. It seems the kind of thing you'd mention to your wife.

"I told you Jasper left Dr. Grant," he says. "And you didn't seem that interested in hearing about anything to do with Dr. Grant, so I didn't go into all the details."

He's right. Ever since I realized Dr. Grant was not my friend, that he would betray me if someone offered him the right deal, I'd changed the subject anytime Luke mentioned him. If Luke was trying to tell me about Jasper and mentioned Dr. Grant, I probably did shut him down. I stand up and start pulling down the drawstring pants I'm wearing. I'm so tired. I need to rest.

"You ready for bed?" Luke asks.

"Yeah," I tell him, picking up Mr. Giggles. I pull the stuffed animal to my face and inhale. It smells just like Penelope. I wrap Mr. Giggles in my arms and lie down. "I need to at least try to sleep. I need to be rested if we're going to get our daughter back."

# TUESDAY

# 14

## KELSEY

I slept fitfully in Jasper's extra room, tossing and turning so much that at 4 am, Luke left. He told me he'd feel better going for a jog because it helps him to think and clear his head. I wish running helped me in that way; instead it makes me sore and irritable. But, probably today, running would have been better than lying here worrying about Penelope.

I'm in the bed still, the blanket pulled up to my neck, my eyes closed and trying to lie still. When I was young, my mother used to tell me it was less important to sleep than it was to let my body rest. "If you lie still and are very quiet, even if you don't fall asleep, your body will get the rest it needs," she would tell me. I realize now she just said that to get me to stop overthinking the issue. The second I lay there, not worrying about falling asleep, my mind would clear and I'd be asleep in moments.

But knowing that it's not true, even lying still and breathing steadily doesn't help. All I can think about is Penelope. She's never been without me. Well, she was premature and spent two weeks at the hospital, but I don't feel like that counts. Penelope was so little, she can't remember that. But now she knows me, she expects me and she expects Luke; but instead she's woken up in a car with a stranger. No, she woke up in a car with an uncle she'd just met, an uncle who'd intended to hand her mother over to be murdered. Instead, he's handed her over.

And she's all alone. I don't even know if they're taking good care of her; there's no reason to hurt a baby, but there was also no reason for Greg to take her, to involve her. I'm still in shock that he would take my baby to save Emmie.

There is a light tapping on the door. I open my eyes in time to see Luke poke his head in. "Kelsey," Luke whispers. "You awake?"

I sit up, letting the cover slide off me, and Luke frowns as he enters. "You don't look like you slept any better after I left. I thought maybe I was keeping you awake. I hoped if I got out of here, you'd at least get a little sleep."

I shake my head, noticing Mr. Giggles has fallen on the floor. I pick him up, my wrists still tender from being constricted yesterday. They bandaged them at the hospital and I should be able to remove it in a couple of days. I look from the bandage to Mr. Giggles and tuck the monkey under the covers, feeling somewhat better at the prospect that he is safe and sound. "No, you weren't keeping me awake. It's Penelope. We've got to find her. I feel like we should be doing something more than waiting around to sneak back into FoSS."

Luke shakes his head. "Your father got that note pretty soon after and it was clear what they were talking about. Greg's story checks out: Emmie had a stillborn and now she seems to have completely disappeared. He took Penelope for FoSS. That means they'll have demands. It's important to find out what they are, not spook them. We don't want them to do something…" he pauses, his face clenching as he tries to wrench the words out, "something they can't take back."

I shudder, trying to force the image of a tiny white casket being lowered into the ground out of my head. "When is Jasper coming?" I ask, trying to distract myself.

"He's here," Luke says. "Whenever you're ready, we can discuss the plan."

I climb off the mattress and walk over to the chair, where I've draped the drawstring blue scrubs that Jasper finagled me at the hospital. The pants I'd been wearing when I was kidnapped were covered in dirt, scrapes and blood (from my wrists). Since I was unconscious when they picked me up and my pants were bloody, they'd cut them off to check for injuries.

I'm not sure how long we'll be gone, so I'll wear these scrubs today, before digging into whatever Luke packed for me. I pull on the loose pants, tighten the drawstring and head out to the main room where Jasper is sitting on a beat up, but cozy looking chair drinking something hot and steaming. The scent of coffee is in the air, so I hope he's brewed an entire pot. I could certainly use a pick me up.

Luke grabs two wooden stools from the corner and sets them not too far from Jasper. "Help yourself to some coffee," Jasper says, pointing across the room to a countertop that divides the kitchen from this living area. I walk over and find a glass coffee pot, blazing hot when I graze a fingertip along the side. I grab a ceramic mug from a glass-doored cabinet above the coffeemaker. "You have milk?" I call over, and Jasper says it's in the fridge.

As I open the door to the refrigerator, I must admit that I like having free rein of his kitchen. At home, I like to get everything and I hate people meandering through the cabinets and leaving things out of order. I find the milk, add a dash, then walk over and stand near Luke and Jasper, who are already deep in conversation.

Jasper has just handed Luke something. I lean in and look at it — a small brown cover with gold lettering. "A passport?" I ask

Luke nods.

"Your father says Luke should just come back. He's a FoSS citizen and he'll use his passport to return. He'll say he's going to a friend's wedding."

I guess that's as good an excuse as any. If I weren't a fugitive, Luke and I would have been going to Susan and Rob's wedding. I sigh and watch as Luke opens his passport. Inside is a picture of him taken recently, his dimples showing, but his hair shorn to almost nothing, the way it is now. I miss the mop of hair he used to have, but perhaps that was a boyish look and this is more the man he is becoming: handsome, charming, but more serious.

"And me?"

Jasper purses his lips and gives me a delicate look. "How limber are you?"

I sit down on the stool and look to my husband, hoping he knows why Jasper has just asked me this really bizarre question. Luke laughs at my expression and says, "You get the secret compartment in the van. It has a false seat back and you kind of have to scrunch in there."

"And if I'm not particularly limber?" I ask, taking a sip of my coffee. It's hot and just a tad bitter, the way I like it.

Jasper half smiles and tips his head, his blond locks jiggling slightly as he does. "Then you're going to be even more uncomfortable than most people. The secret compartment is smaller than I'd like it to be, and it's fine for a short trip, but to be on the safe side, we're probably going to have to drive you all the way to Ashburn in it. That's close to two hundred miles of you crammed in there. Normally, I wouldn't ask a person to suffer through more than 30 miles."

I take another sip, enjoying the caffeine jolt, though it's probably only in my mind. I can't imagine the drug has taken hold that quickly. "So, a few hours in a hiding spot in your van?"

He nods. Luke puts his hand on my leg and I turn to him. He's stopped chuckling about my flexibility and looks completely serious. "I spoke to Gen. Maylee again this morning. He's willing to let you stay at the compound. He said he'd send a car to a location I request, if you want to go back there. You can either get in that car and go to the compound, or you can ride with us." He stops and closes his eyes for a second, as if debating whether to say the next part. "I know you want to help get our daughter back, but Kelsey, this is very dangerous — you coming back to FoSS. I'd really like it if you'd consider going back to the compound. I'd feel better knowing you were safe."

I'm surprised Luke is still trying to get me to go back. I look down into my mug, blow on the light brown liquid and watch it ripple. I take a second to remind myself not to be mad at Luke. He's not trying to keep me from helping; he's trying to keep me safe. I look up and see that Jasper is conveniently staring into his own coffee mug, as if the secrets of life's success are being explained inside it. I look back at Luke, who is still holding out hope I might change my mind. I shake my head. "I'll be fine in between the seat. I'm plenty limber."

Luke gives a resigned nod and Jasper looks up from his cup. "Then, let's go take a look at the van," Jasper says.

* * *

The van is in a small garage in the back of the building. We enter through a stairwell that pops out inside a cramped two-stall unit. There is a vertical garage door that would glide open and recede above us, I imagine, were Jasper to open it. He does not. It is dimly lit and there is just enough space for a person of average girth to slide between the door entrance and the van, which is parked very deliberately on its side of the garage. The three of us edge past it and go stand in the empty garage space, where I can get a better look at the van. It's a typical white cargo van: a little boxy on the front end, with only a driver's and passenger door in the front. The words Christensen Center are affixed to the side of the van.

Jasper climbs in and crawls toward the front of the vehicle. He arrives at the back of the front seat, a bench seat that goes all the way across the vehicle, then turns and motions for me to come inside. I join Jasper just behind the seatback, and he calls my attention to the fact that it is much wider than it needs to be. Jasper tugs on the bottom part of the seatback, the part touching the van floor and the leather panel lifts up revealing a space wide enough for a person to fit. The bottom of the area is lined with pillows. I'll have to lie down the width of the vehicle and bend my knees, so I can fit in the space.

"You think you'll be OK in there?" Jasper asks.

I can feel him staring at me. There must be a look of abject horror on my face. Ever since the holding facility, I haven't been a fan of being trapped in small spaces. A small part of me considers going back to the compound where I lived for the first few months I was in this country. The compound kept me safe, even if I was sequestered from the rest of the world, but then Penelope's face pops in my mind. Eyes screwed shut, tears dripping down her cheeks, her body convulsing from fear due to the inexplicable absence of her parents. I know I can't go back to the compound. I have to get my baby. "I'll be fine," I say, nodding my head, hoping to reassure myself as much as Jasper.

He nods, then crawls toward the open cargo doors, which I take as my cue to follow. Jasper excuses himself saying he needs to make a phone call, and Luke and I are left alone. Unfortunately, this feels too familiar. A tiny room, a helpful law-breaking doctor, a risky plan and too much at stake if the plan goes wrong. I sigh and breathe out.

Luke stands behind me and wraps his arms around me. "I can do this; I can bring her back if you want to stay with Maylee."

I'm second-guessing myself, wondering if I shouldn't just do what Luke asks. Last time I was in this situation, last time when things looked bad and Luke asked me to just go in for my marking surgery, I'd said no. But he'd been right. If I'd just gone in, I'd have been fine. None of this would be happening.

"Do I know everything?" I ask Luke. "Have you told me everything?"

He lets go of me and I turn to face him, "Kelsey, why would you even ask me that? I'm not keeping anything from you."

He's not. I can see it in his eyes, blue and steady, like the ocean. "I'm sorry," I whisper and lean into him. "I'm sorry. I'm just not sure. I feel in my heart I should go get her, Luke. But I was wrong before about what was best. When I was marked, I decided to run when I should've gone in."

"We're through keeping secrets," he says in my ear. "We promised that, and there's nothing I'm not telling you."

Only this time, it's me who's not telling him something. It's me who plans to give myself up if that's the only way to get our daughter back. "I want to go."

# 15

## SUSAN

The funeral service is long and boring. Too many people clad in either black or military dress uniforms saying kind things about a man I know to be a monster. My pale skin and nauseated appearance cause a lady sitting next to me to pat my shoulder and murmur something about how much we're all going to miss him. I simply nod and bury my head in Rob's shoulder, in the hope of not having to deal with further funeral goers lamenting Xavier Tisdale.

Rob and I greet his widow and offer our sympathies. This is the only time I feel bad, as the wife looks truly distraught: grey hair pulled back in a bun, sunken eyes red from tears and a general deer caught in the headlights expression, as if this is all too much for her.

There isn't much time for discovery at the ceremony, as everyone is huddled in their seats. I am beginning to think Lewis was right. I should have stayed home and attended to the details of my wedding. Lewis' wife, Haleema, didn't come. She is actually on her way to Georgia. It's a risky move, but Kelsey and Luke are going to stay at Belle Ruisseau. It's a Southern plantation Rob inherited from his grandfather. We're getting married there and people will be bustling about over the next few days to get things ready.

The caveat is the ceremony is outdoors and the bulk of the work going on will affect the grounds: lawn maintenance, tent set up, chair deliveries. The house should not get much traffic. Kelsey and Luke need to stay somewhere they can have access to her father without it looking suspicious. So, it's a good solution, at least for the next couple of days. I kind of wish I'd gone down with Haleema and ditched this death party.

We're in a room beneath the church for a post-funeral meal. People are eating and most of the guests are eventually finding their way to the widow to again express their condolences. Lewis is working the room, looking for answers from people he knows. Rob and I were assigned to look into Xavier's inner circle contacts. People Rob knew from his own interactions. Patricia, Rob's mother is also here. She, like Senator Reed is making a wide berth, chatting up lots of people in uniform.

Rob and I have just run into a sober looking man with several medals pinned to his uniform. He was a friend of Samuel, Rob's father, and he told us he was a good friend of Xavier's as well. Rob slips in a few probing questions about who was in charge of Xavier's final projects at work, but the man admits he retired six months ago and is out of the loop.

We excuse ourselves to grab a plate of food, then wind our way through the throngs of people who've come to pay their respects. There are at least 200 people in here, either at the buffet, or clustered in groups talking. "Listen," Rob says to me, as we approach the table covered with metal serving tins hovering over burners. "I want to check in with my mother. Do you mind if I leave you for a second?"

"Go ahead," I say, and give an encouraging smile. His mother never liked me, and at Xavier Tisdale's request, tried — but failed — to poison me. So I try to avoid her if I can. Despite my distrust of her, I said she can attend the wedding. Rob's nieces and nephews are coming, and it just seemed easier to shove her in the back than to make Rob's brothers explain to their children grandma wasn't there because she'd once tried to kill the bride.

The buffet line is moving well, the room loud with chatter of mourners. I pick up a plate — real china, no less — along with utensils and move forward toward a pasta salad and vegetables. In my right ear, I hear a familiar voice and a shiver runs through me.

"Ms. Harper, is that you?"

I try to compose myself, and then turn to see the face that matches that voice. It's a face I haven't seen in more than a year, but one I could go ten lifetimes without encountering and be happy. Now he sports stark white hair shaped in a buzz cut. I stifle my shock at the abrupt change in his hair, as if he's aged a decade in only a tenth of the time, and give him a somber nod.

"Yes, it's me," I say to Col. John Parker.

"I'm surprised to see you here," he says, in the matter of fact tone he always uses, as if everything in the world simply is and there is no way to change it. Despite my general dislike of Parker, who held me captive for six months under Tisdale's order, I've always appreciated his directness.

I step away from the line, clutching the plate in my hands and edging away from the crowd. The colonel doesn't question this. He simply follows along until we reach a semi-secluded spot in the corner.

The colonel gives me an expectant look, so I cut to the chase. "You're aware of the deal Tisdale and my colleagues came to after I left your care?"

A rueful smile crosses his lips at the way I described my captivity. "I am."

"I'm here because I want to know who inherited this agreement, now that Tisdale has passed away. And if it is, in fact, still intact."

The colonel turns and surveys those nearby. A woman on the right is weeping into a man's shoulder a few feet away, and there is a couple milling about eating some food to the left. Parker steps in closer to me, sticks an arm around my back and pulls me close, the plate pressed vertically in my hand between us. I feel a sense of déjà vu at the sudden embrace, though I'm certain the colonel has no plans to kiss me. "All FoSS citizens are still safe under the agreement," he whispers in my ear. "I can't say the same of fugitives."

I make what I hope is a sufficiently sorrowful moan and lean in closer, as if I need consoling. "Do you have Kelsey's daughter?" I whisper.

He pats my back, and I am stuffed further into his scratchy uniform. "I'm not at liberty to speak of that," he says softly. "What I can say is that if a man as deranged as his institutionalized wife has kidnapped a baby, I'd be very worried for the health and safety of that baby."

I pull back from him to examine his face. His black eyes are cold and clear, his mouth set in a rigid line. I am not sure what to make of it. "You didn't do this?"

"If there is a single suggestion that FoSS kidnapped this child, I can guarantee you that Greg Wilkerson, in his state of derangement, will hurt both himself and the child." His eyes bore into me, and I know that he has Greg and Penelope. When he sees my expression, perhaps a mix of shock and terror, he pulls me close to him again.

"If we can keep things discreet, the child could be safely returned to her father," he whispers.

My brain is zooming through a thousand things to ask. Why would he do this? Why would he hurt a child? How can we stop this? Is he bluffing? No, I know the colonel well enough to know he's not bluffing. He must be the person who sent the note to the senator. "So, we need to continue being quiet, not reveal she was taken?"

"Yes," he says, his voice triumphant. "Discretion is important. We don't want to hurt a child; we won't hurt a child if we can use the same discretion in these dealings as we've used in the past."

"We can be discreet, but what is it that you need to move things forward?"

The colonel releases me, cocks his head to the left a little, and I see Rob striding toward us. As my fiancé twists through the crowd, I feel the colonel's hand pat my shoulder. Col. Parker gives me a deadly serious stare. "We need what Mr. Wilkerson wanted. We need it sooner, rather than later, because at some point, the madness that drove Mr. Wilkerson to act alone and do this horrible thing might make him do something even more unspeakable. And I think it would be unfortunate if that happened."

The colonel takes a step back from me as Rob reaches us. "What did you say to her?" Rob growls. The sobbing woman to our right turns to see what we're up to, but the rest of the mourners seem not to have noticed. I touch Rob's arm. He can't draw any more attention to us.

"Susan and I were simply discussing how sad we are over events," he says, his eyebrows rising slightly and his mouth turning down in sympathy. "By the way, I heard you two were getting married. I think my invitation must have gotten lost in the mail. Given that I set you two up, I was certain I'd be invited."

Demanding that Rob seduce me and convince me to publicly urge people to revile Kelsey hardly qualifies as setting us up. I hand the colonel my plate, and thankfully he takes it without question. I quickly take hold of both of Rob's hands with both of mine. I figure if all our hands are occupied, neither of us will give into an urge to punch the colonel. At this moment, Lewis Reed walks up, his face blank, but his eyes darting between the three of us trying to figure out what is happening. "John," Sen. Reed says as he claps the colonel on the back. "It's good to see you again, even during these unfortunate circumstances."

I take this opportunity to excuse Rob and myself. I figure it's better if Lewis hears the threat directly from Col. Parker's mouth, rather than my retelling of it. He's also better at assessing the logistical matters involved in this. I tow Rob out of this mauve walled room and into the main chapel. We walk through it, passing a few mourners sitting quietly in the pews, perhaps praying, perhaps just needing a moment to themselves.

Rob has released one of my hands and we wind our way silently through the church, out its front doors and to the car. The sky overhead is gray and cloudy, and the air is moist, whispering of the rain to come.

Once we're inside the vehicle, I close my eyes.

"Are you OK?" Rob asks.

"I'm fine," I say. "But, we need to get home. I'm going to call Kevin again, see if he got my earlier messages and we can meet this afternoon."

# 16

## KELSEY

I am so happy to be out of that cramped van that I'm bouncing. Bobbing up and down on my heels, stretching, flexing and moving every muscle, now that I am able. The holding facility was nothing in comparison to that van ride. Two hours in that tiny area, stuffed and cramped with just a modicum of fresh air coming in through an air hole that looked inconspicuous to outsiders.

I reach my arms out and stretch. My bandaged wrists still tingle a little, but I don't care, as everything else feels uncoiled.

"Glad to be out of there?" Luke says to me, grinning.

I nod. "You'd be glad, too, if you'd had to ride that way."

He smiles in agreement, but then turns a tad serious. "It worked, though," he said. "They scrutinized my passport a little, but they didn't even search the van when we came across."

He's right. Crossing into the country was relatively easy, given how tight the borders are. Though, maybe it was easier because Jasper had crossed before, and Luke sounded nonchalant when he told the border guards he was simply catching a ride for a friend's wedding. I'm glad it turned out well, as crossing the border can be tricky, even with the right paperwork. My father's only visited me on two occasions due to the complicated nature of it. Perhaps, because I'm still a fugitive, they've made it difficult for him.

I turn and see Jasper has gone to the front door to knock. Haleema, who for years worked as my father's assistant, and who helped take care of me, married my father last year. She's supposed to be here to greet us, thanks so Susan.

Susan has been so incredibly helpful, I'm not sure how to thank her. Opening her home — hell, it's not even her home yet; they won't be married until Saturday. But she gave Haleema a key and told her to come meet us and didn't bother about the fact that I'm a fugitive. Or that helping me could land her in trouble. Helping me has already landed her in trouble. Six months held captive and almost murdered. Still, she helps again.

I look toward the house, part of an old plantation but refurbished a few years back. Susan went on in great detail about it — thank goodness it was in an email — I skimmed it. Her architect side can be a bit long-winded. But, looking at the house itself is impressive. It's two stories, stark white, with large pillars in the front and somewhat crescent shaped. There isn't a front porch, but I think Susan mentioned a patio or sitting area in the rear. I think she mentioned a cabin or cottage on the property, too.

Still edgy, I walk toward the side of the house, and in my periphery, see the front door open and Haleema pull Jasper into a hug. Seeing that makes me realize just how much I missed her. Haleema is a bundle of warm maternal love, willing to fold anyone into her arms, greeting everyone she's ever met like they're a long lost, more than welcome cousin. I think she's only met Jasper once or twice. One of the rare visits that Haleema and my father made to Peoria occurred shortly after Penelope was born. Penelope's premature birth and complications required a slew of follow-ups with Jasper, and Haleema came with me to a couple of them.

I blow out a breath. Penelope. I need my little girl safe and sound and with me. I head over to the front door, passing a row of azalea's that are starting to bloom. It's a colorful panoply of bushes: pink, red, and purple, all blasting the house with festive colors and I can't help thinking that Penelope would love it here. She would love these gorgeous buds and go wild when they actually popped open.

I climb four low brick steps to the front door. Luke and Jasper are already inside and Haleema is beckoning me with her hand.

The room I enter is a rotunda, with a winding staircase going up the back wall. The room is sparsely furnished with a decorative console table in front of the staircase, and to the right a two-seat sofa and a couple of chairs that look antique. Haleema looks at me, sorrow in her eyes. "Kelsey," she whooshes out, taking my hand and pulling me into her arms. "I'm so sorry. Your father and I are so devastated by this news. I can't imagine what you're going through."

I pull back from her, not wanting to discuss it right now, not wanting to examine the feelings I am going through or lay them out for the room to see. "Haleema," I say. "Is there any news from my father?"

She tucks a hair behind her ear and looks down at her feet. "Why don't I show you to your room?" she says. "Jasper you don't mind waiting here a minute, do you?"

Jasper nods and takes a seat in one of the chairs. I look to Luke. He appears just as apprehensive about Haleema redirecting us as I feel, but he just inclines his head for us to follow. She turns and walks through the room we're in, down a hallway and to a door on the right. We enter and find a large, dark room with a bed in the center and a few innocuous furniture pieces including a chair, chaise and dresser. Haleema flicks on a light and the room illuminates some, but it still feels dark. I look to the left and realize it's because there are floor to ceiling burgundy curtains made of heavy fabric drawn tight over the windows. I wonder if the windows are as tall as the curtains and go over to see, lifting the velvety window coverings and peering out. The windows are tall and have a great view of the grounds.

Luke clears his throat and I turn to see Haleema heading toward the door. "Haleema," Luke says, "You were going to tell us news from Sen. Reed."

Haleema, pushes the door shut, sighs, looks at us and nods. "You should sit down," she says. I take a seat on the chaise, which I realize is probably antique as I settle into the satin fabric and place my arm on the carved armrest. Luke, who is closest to the bed, just settles there, rather than joining me, and I wonder briefly why he's chosen to distance himself from me for this news. Not to hear it together. He says it's not my fault, but I can't help but feel he blames me for leaving our daughter in the car with Greg.

Haleema looks from me to Luke and then joins me on the chaise. She takes my hand and tells me that my father and Susan spoke with the man who has Penelope. As the words sink in, as the words wash over me, that they plan to kill my daughter unless they get what they want, Haleema gives me a hug and then excuses herself, saying she'll let Luke and I have our privacy.

When Haleema leaves, I feel my body convulse and hot tears burn my eyes as they stream out. The sobs come low and continuous, and soon I feel Luke's arms around me, his silent approach undetected.

"I shouldn't have gotten out of the car, Luke," I say. "I should have just gone with him and made sure he left her"

"It's not your fault, Kelsey," he says.

"I need to surrender."

"No."

"I don't want to live if she dies," I whisper

"She won't die, and neither will you. We'll figure out a way to get her back."

# 17

## SUSAN

We're at my apartment again. Rob and I debated where to meet Kevin. Rob suggested our house — or I guess I should say our house to be. I think Rob wanted to meet there as a territorial move, to show Kevin who's boss. But, when I said I didn't want Kevin just showing up there after we were married, Rob quickly agreed here was best.

We've gathered around the kitchen table again. I feel like it's my little war room. It seems we've done nothing but strategize in here the past couple of days. Kevin dressed more like a normal person today: slacks and a t-shirt bearing the image of my favorite band. Rob sits closer to me than necessary, so various parts of my body touch his. My arm brushes against his, our thighs graze each other, and his foot occasionally bumps mine. It's a bit annoying, but I can't blame him for feeling the need to remind Kevin of the obvious.

For Kevin's part, he seems unfettered by Rob's presence. In fact, he seems to relish the fact that my fiancé feels the need to be so territorial. Kevin is using a tablet to show us the original match results.

"Whenever they are looking for a donor, they do a DNA search for the best possible matches. The computer returns the top hundred best potential matches." Kevin's slender pointer finger taps the screen. "You're number 12 on the list, which is done by basic DNA profile."

I nod. Rob makes no movement. Kevin continues. "So, then they go in and do a detailed data analysis, looking at DNA and health factors. When they ran that analysis, Susan was number 93 on the list. She should not have been picked."

I look at the screen, which has my name listed next to the number 93. "So, who changed it, and how do you know this?"

He raises an eyebrow and gives me a cocky smile. "The data logs tell us everything," he says, turning the screen toward himself and tapping a few buttons. "Anytime someone makes a change, it's logged in the system. The person who made this change went and pulled the first back up, but…" he says smiling at me, eager as a puppy to be petted on the head.

"There's redundancy," says Rob, whose hazel eyes seem to have a little fire behind them. Rob leans forward resting his hands on the table. "Where is the second data backup?"

Kevin's eagerness fades now that Rob is interested, but he looks me in the eye and says, "Baltimore. They're stored in data banks. I went there, claiming to be a tech from Dr. Round's office and got the back-up. It shows who made the change. It also shows what was there initially, the file I just showed you."

Rob frowns and leans back in his chair. "There's no way to authenticate it, though," he says. "There's no way to prove what you took is the original."

Kevin shakes his head and gives Rob a superior look. From his bag, he pulls a small black box, about the size of a bar of soap and sets it on the table. Rob and I both look at it, but only Rob seems to know what it is because he picks it up, turns it in his hand and smiles.

"What?" I ask.

"The auto backup hard drives are all unique," Kevin tells me. "They have a serial code etched in the bottom. Once the drive is full, it is removed from the redundancy center and taken to the storage center, where it is shelved and catalogued. Each one typically holds four months' worth of data. I took two of them. Yours, which includes most of the four months prior to your marking — you were at the end of a cycle. He's got it in his hand. And I have Kelsey's too."

I smile. This is wonderful. "Thank you, Kevin. This is just what we need," I gush. "It will help immeasurably." I don't mention Kelsey's name because I don't think Kevin likes her after what she did to him. I don't say anything about Penelope, as I don't want the colonel to act on his threat over what will happen if the public is alerted to Penelope's kidnapping.

Kevin's face is hesitant, his cheeks a little too drawn, his eyes unsteady. He doesn't look like someone who has just received my praise, even though moments earlier he was salivating for it.

"This is incredibly helpful," says Rob, who seems to have forgotten his dislike of Kevin and has a look of awe on his face as he holds the little black box, as if it is made of gold. "This one and Kelsey's will prove it was all a lie. Where is Kelsey's drive?"

"It's in a secure location," Kevin says. Uh oh. That's not the answer I expected. I squish my eyebrows together, trying to decipher if that's good or bad.

Rob closes his hand tight around the black box with my data. "When can we get it from you?" Rob asks.

Kevin dips his head slightly, clasps his hands together in his lap. "Rob, would you mind if Sue and I had a moment alone."

I don't know where this is going, but it can't be good.

Rob shakes his head and gives a derisive snort. "I do mind," he says, hostilely. "I am not leaving you alone with her after what you pulled yesterday."

It feels like a powder keg in here. I want to cut the tension, but these two are at an impasse. Under the table, I slide my hand onto Rob's thigh and give a gentle squeeze. "I'd like Rob to stay," I tell Kevin.

He nods as if he was expecting this, but still doesn't look happy about it. "I spoke to Sen. Reed before I came over, and I was under the impression that you really needed any evidence related to Kelsey's marking."

Kevin pauses, bites his lower lip. "Well, he made it seem like the timing was crucial, and that being the case, I thought it might be a good time to negotiate for something I'd like." His eyes dart to the floor, then back to me. "Something I'd like in exchange for getting the evidence you want."

This is really unbelievable. I bite down on my lip, hoping the act of exerting pressure on something will make me feel better.

"And what is it that you want?" Rob sneers.

"I want to spend one day with Susan."

Rob stands, my hand sliding from his thigh when he makes the quick move. "That's not going to happen," Rob says. "You need to go, Kevin."

Kevin stands, too, and shrugs. "Fine," he says looking at me. "But the only thing left for your hacker boyfriend to find are the data logs. I have the original records. And trying to recreate them by tracking down the individual patient files and running them against each other is going to take you more time than you have."

Kevin lifts his leather satchel from the floor and places the strap over his shoulder. "Kevin," I say, reaching out to take his hand. "Please, don't do this. This is a life or death situation. There is a life at stake. Please don't keep this from us."

He shakes his head, his deep brown eyes catching mine and holding them steady. "Sue," he says, his voice soft, reassuring. "I'm not keeping it from you. I'll give it to you, I promise. Spend tomorrow with me and the drive is yours."

I feel a tug on my free hand as Rob tries to pull me away from Kevin. "You don't have to do that," Rob says.

But, he's wrong. We need this information. We need it as soon as possible. Penelope's middle name is Susan, after me. I can't let them hurt her. If getting this drive will give Lewis bargaining power, I have to help. "You swear to me?" I ask Kevin, ignoring Rob's pleading. "You swear to me on Fitzwilliam's life that you'll give it to me if I spend the day with you tomorrow?"

Kevin laughs. "Yes, I swear. May Fitzwilliam die tomorrow if I'm lying."

His easy laugh, his easy agreement leads me to wonder. "He's not already dead, is he?" I ask of Kevin's childhood cat.

"No, though he is 15, so he's getting close."

I sigh, knowing how important this is to Penelope, but also knowing that Rob is not OK with it.

"Susan, we can find another way," Rob says to me. "Don't agree to this. Not right now."

I don't look at Rob. If time weren't an issue, I'd agree that we could figure it out, but there's no time. "If I say yes, it can't be like yesterday," I say to Kevin, pointing my finger at him like a school marm. "If you do anything like that, our day is over. And you give me the drive right then."

He doesn't even pause to consider, just nods his head in agreement.

"Fine," I say, watching the grin break across his face. "Meet me here tomorrow at 9."

"It's a date," he says, though he looks at Rob, not me.

"It's blackmail," I respond.

He ignores me. "I can probably find my way out," he says, smirking. "I think Rob may want to chat with you."

With that, Kevin turns on his heel and disappears from the room.

I consider taking him at his word, but that's proved to be a mistake so far, so I follow after him, making sure Kevin exits and lock the door behind him. It's also a chance to delay, even for a few seconds, having to face my fiancé.

I turn around and see Rob standing in the doorway separating the main room from the hallway that leads to the kitchen. The hurt on his face is like a stab to my heart. "I'm sorry," I say, crossing the room toward him. "We need this information, and I didn't know what else to do."

I reach out to touch him, but he steps back. "Say no," he says, anger seeping out. "You could have just said no."

I shake my head. "I couldn't," I say. "I couldn't do that to Kelsey, to Penelope."

He runs his fingers through his hair and eyes me coldly. "Sen. Reed could have convinced him to give us the drive. You should've called Kevin's bluff, made him tell the senator he wasn't going to give it to us. Instead, you agreed to go on a date with him."

"It's not a date," I say, though there really isn't any other word to describe it. I try again to touch Rob, taking a step toward him, reaching out for his hand. "I'm just going to go with him, and ..." As I say the words, I realize I have no idea what I'm going to do with him.

"Uggh," Rob says tossing his hands in the air, and pushing past me. I'm not sure that he has an intended endpoint. He seems to simply want to move and let the anger that's risen up in him hiss out in a steady stream. He stops in the middle of the room and turns back to me. "You don't even know what you've signed on for here. You have no idea what he wants to do to you."

I shake my head. "He's not going to do anything. It's going to be strictly platonic. He knows I love you. Whatever he thinks he'll achieve, it's not going to happen. I love you, Rob. This is for Kelsey and Penelope. Me spending the day with Kevin doesn't mean anything."

"What about our wedding? Does that mean anything?" he asks pointedly. "Are you planning on coming? Because tomorrow, we're supposed to get on a plane for that."

My mouth opens in shock. "Of course I'm coming," I say, taking a step toward him. "I can reschedule my flight, or drive if I have to. I'll be there on time. I promise. If there are last minute things, I can ask Jane. She offered to come down early if we needed last minute help."

At this his eyes widen and he shakes his head in disgust. "So, let me get this straight: You plan to ask my brother's wife to leave her husband and children to come down early, so you can gallivant about town with your former fiancé?"

I take a deep breath. I'm not explaining this right. "OK, you're right," I say evenly. "While I think of Jane as my friend, it's more important in this context that she is your sister-in-law, so that's not a good idea. Actually, it was a terrible idea. I'll come up with something better, OK. I'll figure out a way to make this work. Please don't let Kevin blackmailing me come between us."

He takes a step back. "Kevin blackmailing you has not come between us. How you treated me today has come between us. You agreed to what he wanted, even though I was standing there asking you not to."

I take a couple of steps toward him, but this time he doesn't move away from me. "I didn't mean to ignore you," I say.

"Yes you did," he retorts, his voice rising. "You meant to ignore me, and that's why I'm upset, Susan. We talked about this. You don't get to make unilateral decisions like that. We can work it out together, but here, you just trumped me. You shunted me to the corner and dumped a load of quick-dry cement on me. 'There's Rob, the statue I like to have around to look at.'"

"Rob, please," I say, reaching out and putting my hand on his folded arms. "I'm sorry. I knew you didn't want me to, and I said 'yes' anyway. That ignored your feelings and I apologize. You're the last person I want to hurt."

He pulls back again. "You certainly have a funny way of showing it." He turns and walks to the door. Initially, I think it's just to put space between us, but as he turns the knob and pulls it back, I realize he's leaving.

"Please don't go," I say, my voice quavering.

"I need to be alone right now," he tells me, not looking back.

"Wait," I say, walking toward him. He turns back to me, and his eyes are moist and anguished. "Are you coming back?"

He shakes his head. "Not today, Susan," he says with a tone of finality, that makes me realize words won't change his mind. Instead, I move in quickly and wrap my arms around him. "I'm sorry," I whisper and then free him of my embrace. I wait a beat, and then he goes out the door, and closes it without looking back.

# 18

## KELSEY

Haleema comes back to our room a half an hour later and tells us that the house is going to be fairly deserted, but to keep the curtains drawn because there will be people coming tomorrow to set up tents and chairs for the wedding. She also brings news that her niece Zuri is on her way, per Luke's request. My interest is piqued, but I lack the ability to be hostile about it. My husband's ex, whose guile and beauty would give Scheherazade a run for her money, is well connected and may be able to help us to get our daughter back. I can deal with her flagrant attempts to seduce my husband if it means Penelope will be safe.

Haleema then hands me a note from Susan, and says she has to get back to her hotel. Luke and I hug her and say our goodbyes. As Luke ushers her out, not wanting me glimpsed at the door, I sit on the bed and pull the tiny slip of paper from the envelope Haleema handed me. The note is in Susan's script. Not a whole lot to it.

*K,*

*I'm so sorry about what's happened. I can't imagine how difficult this time must be for you. Given your situation, it's important that you keep out of sight. Obviously, a room with fewer windows and perhaps not so close to the hustle and bustle would be better. But I've put you here for a reason. In the closet on the right, above the top shelf, in the corner, you'll find a small black button. Press it. Explore. Now. Go there if you think you are in danger.*

*All my love. See ya soon.*

*S.*

Luke walks back through the door, a sigh on his lips. When he approaches me, I hand him the note and head toward the closet, opening the door. There are a few clothing items hanging and a hat-box on the shelf above the hangars. A step ladder is tucked in the left corner. I grab the step ladder, jerking it open, and climb until I can see into the upper right corner of the closet.

Luke is behind me now. "You find it?" he asks, slipping his hands around my waist, I assume because he thinks I might fall. I admit I'm clumsy, but even I can navigate a step ladder.

"I don't see it," I tell him. It doesn't help that the closet is painted black. Finding a black button on a black surface in a closet without any light is not the easiest thing. Or maybe that's the point. "Do you have a light?"

Luke releases one hand and I hear the rustling of fabric. He taps my leg with something hard, and I realize it's his phone. I take it from him, turn on its light and point the beam at the corner. There it is. A black button, barely visible. I press it and then hear a click followed by a creaking noise.

"We need a place like this," Luke says, awe in his voice. I step down from the ladder. A door has opened up in the lower rear wall of the closet. It's a perfect square, a little more than two feet high and two feet wide. Luke moves the step ladder out of the way, and gently guides me back with his hand. "Let me go first," he tells me, "to make sure it's safe."

I refrain from sighing. Susan told me to explore, so I'm sure it's not a bad place. But I hand him the light and let him have his way. It will make him feel better to protect me. He kneels down and pushes the door, which is only a couple inches ajar, all the way open.

He crawls inside and I kneel down to watch his progress, as best I can. It's dark in there so I can't make out much. Luke gives a little yelp, and I ask, "Are you alright?"

"Yeah," he calls back. "I just bumped into a step here."

All of a sudden light floods the tunnel. "Cool," Luke calls. "Come on, Sweetheart."

My curiosity piqued, I crawl through the doorway and find myself in a tunnel that lasts a few feet, before opening into a room with an odd, sort of curved shape. And I realize we are underneath the winding staircase in the main room. Inside the room is an aluminum chair, a small metal table, a cot and a square metal bin with a lid. I go over to the bin and open it. There are a couple of blankets inside, probably to go on the cot.

I turn to Luke, who is on his knees looking through a wall grate. I walk over and kneel beside him. "What is this?"

"Look," he says, moving aside and I peer through the slits and see the front door of the house.

"Is that the front room?" I ask.

Luke doesn't answer. Instead he starts toward the door, "Stay here," he calls out. I look after him, but he disappears back to our room. A moment later, he calls my name through the grate. "Can you see me?"

"Yes," I say, watching as he waves and squints at the grate.

"I can't see you at all. I wouldn't even know to look there," he says. "I never noticed the grate because it's under this table."

He gets on his knees and crawls toward me. "I can sort of see you now. But I don't think the average person would spot you. This is a perfect hiding place for you, Kelsey."

I nod, but I know he can't see me, so I say, "OK. Wait one second. Let me try something." I stand up, survey the room and look until I find the light switch. I flick the lights off. "Did you notice that?"

He hesitates. "Maybe. Do it again."

I flick the light on, then off, then on again. "Noticeable?"

"Yeah, when you turn it on or off, I notice the change, but it's not particularly noticeable if the light is on. It's just when you change it. I'm coming back."

I wait in the little room, sitting in the single chair, and wondering how long I could survive in here, if needed. Luke emerges a few moments later. "Susan put us in a good spot. If anyone comes looking, you come in here, and stay in here."

I nod. Susan's little room may be able to save me from detection. But, part of me wonders if I want that. If me being safe means Penelope won't be, I'd rather be found.

# 19

## SUSAN

It's been three hours since Rob left. My time alone has brought me to the realization that I really messed up. I panicked too quickly on this. Sen. Reed needs this; Kelsey is his daughter, and he has been good to Kevin, helping him after what Kelsey did. He can probably convince Kevin to give up the box. I need to give him a chance to do that, like Rob asked. If the senator can convince him without me acquiescing to Kevin's demands, we need to try that first. Rob didn't ask too much by asking me to say no, initially. If the senator can't convince Kevin, then maybe I agree, but that shouldn't have been my first move. I need to fix this.

I'm going to talk to Rob. I've thrown on a high-heeled pair of boots that Rob likes, emblazoned myself with cherry lipstick, and slung a purse over my shoulder. It should only take me 15 minutes to get over there, and if he's calmed down, maybe he'll listen.

I pull open my apartment door and find Kevin standing, poised to knock. He startles at my appearance. He's dressed the same as earlier, slacks, t-shirt and a brown satchel hanging off his shoulder. I stand in the doorway, stunned that he is here, but realizing maybe it's kismet. Maybe it's some cosmic orchestra directing us to this point, and I decide to blurt out what needs saying. "I can't go with you tomorrow," I say, looking him in the eye, trying to ignore his shocked expression. But I can't ignore it. I'm being too harsh. I soften my tone. "I would appreciate it if you would give us the drive anyway. That information is incredibly important to me, and I would be forever grateful if you would just hand it over."

He reaches into his shoulder bag, pulls out a small black drive and holds it out to me. I'm so shocked, it takes me a minute to process what he's doing before I reach out and take the device from him. "Really?" I say, clutching my hand tightly around it, knowing I wouldn't give it back if he responded in the negative.

"Really, Sue." he says, nodding. "May I talk to you, for just five minutes?"

"Yes," I stammer. I point him to the sofa, then excuse myself and take the drive to my bedroom, where I look around for safe places to put it, eyeing the empty dresser, the cleaned out closet and my bed. I quickly decide to shove it inside my pillowcase, although as I'm leaving I realize, that's no safer than anywhere else. When I return, Kevin is sitting at the far end of the sofa. I join him, taking the opposite side, leaving a full cushion of space between us. While I hadn't dared sit with him here earlier, I'm feeling less ambivalent since he's given me the drive without demanding anything in return.

"Why did you change your mind?"

He leans toward me slightly, but doesn't scoot any closer. It's as if he's erected a barrier in his mind that he doesn't intend to cross. "I guess you could say I had a crisis of conscience," he chuckles. "Or, maybe I realized I wanted to be the Kevin you fell in love with, the guy who helped you in your time of need. I wanted to show you that I had changed, that I wasn't the jerk who left you high and dry when you most needed his assistance. I'd wanted to show you that tomorrow on our day together, but I realized the way I was going about it, I was still being a jerk. So I just brought you the drive. I want to be the Kevin who helps you, not the guy who abandons you when you need him most."

I look down at the sofa cushion, a sunset orange colored leather, which is darker in some spots than others. His admission has taken us back to that deep, heavy place that I don't want to be. But I realize I should be the woman he fell in love with, not the defeated, lost, scared girl he left in the hospital. "The truth is you're both those guys," I tell him. "For a long time, I wanted to just call you 'that guy,'" I say, shaking my head, running my finger along the leather grain, still not quite ready to look up at him. "That guy who told me how he was feeling; that guy who told me he couldn't handle what had happened to me and walked away. That guy who hurt me. And when you were just that, it was easy for me to move on, to try to bury everything you were before then. But I realized today I can't bury that. You're both. You're the guy I used to share my secrets with, the guy who used to make me feel safe when I was wrapped in his arms, the guy I used to love with my whole heart. You're both. And I'm grateful that you're both. I'm especially grateful that today you were the guy I could count on to help me, just because I asked you to."

I look up at him, and his eyes are a mix of glistening regret and joyful memory. "You know, I'm sorry I wasn't ready to deal with it back then. I'm sorry I didn't handle it better."

"That makes two of us," I say. Shame flashes over his face momentarily, and I wish I'd been less candid. "It's all over. I've moved on. And... I thought you'd moved on, too."

Kevin threads his fingers through each other, takes a look at my stack of boxes, then finally finds me again. "I thought I had," he admits. "I was seeing someone until two months ago, and after the break up, I found myself thinking about you a lot. I remembered how easy it was being around you, how it never felt like work. How, I could spend hours holed up studying and you never complained or gave me a hard time. I remembered how much fun we would have together, how I could tell you anything, how you would always listen, how you would always see a solution to my problems that I hadn't thought of. I remembered good times, and I missed them."

I can tell my cheeks are reddening. My face feels hot and I want him to stop. It feels like he's talking about someone else. It's like he's remembering a different relationship. It wasn't a bad one; I just don't think it was as good as he remembers. "Kevin, I'm with Rob now," I say firmly, and he looks like I've thrown a bucket of cold water on him.

"I know," he says, looking down at the sofa.

"Just because your last relationship didn't work out, doesn't mean you won't find someone," I say, and I move a little closer to him, reach my hand out and place it on top of his. "Despite what happened to us, I still think you're a good guy, at heart. You'll find the right girl."

"Thanks, Sue," he says, smiling, looking at me from underneath his eyelashes. "I apologize. I was thinking a lot about you after the break up, then I found out about Dr. Rounds, and Lewis said something a couple of weeks ago that made me think I should try again."

"Yes, he told me what he said."

Kevin looks surprised for a moment, then his face softens. "I guess he must tell everyone that story: how he regretted not dating Haleema sooner, not telling her how he felt, even though she was always right there. 'Once you find someone to love, don't give up on them,' is what he said."

I nod my head as if this is what the senator told me, but it's not. I'm a little baffled on the inside about why the senator told me something different. I don't have much time to think about this, though, as Kevin stands; it catches me off guard. "I should be going, Sue," he says. "I'm sorry I've trampled on your last couple of days, but at least I've got no regrets now."

I nod and then stand too. Kevin heads for the door, and I follow along to see him out. As I open the door, he asks, "May I have a hug goodbye?"

I reach in and embrace him, he hugs back and it's nice, because it reminds me just how much warmer and better fitting Rob's arms are than Kevin's. "I'm happy, you're happy," he says in my ear, then lets me go.

"You'll find happiness too," I say, hoping it to be true.

It appears he's going to leave, but then he turns back and says. "If you ever need anything, I'll be there for you." With that, he heads out the door.

# 20

## KELSEY

I am in the secret room watching my husband meet with his ex, in the hope she can help Penelope. I'm sure she can't see me, so I'll get a real view of how she treats my husband when I'm not around. Luke insists she only flirts with him to get under my skin.

So far, she's greeted him with a hug that looks too tight and is definitely lasting too long. Perhaps hugging is a Nassorou family trait, but Haleema's hugs are friendly while Zuri's are more like foreplay.

"Thanks for coming," Luke tells her, as he pulls free of her and shuts the front door. Zuri Nassorou, all cascading ringlets of onyx hair, olive skin and curvy figure, takes a few steps inward and waits for Luke to come closer. He does, standing at an appropriate distance to have a conversation. Then Zuri decides to close the gap, wrap her arms around Luke and plant a kiss right on his lips. If Penelope's life weren't on the line, I'd storm right out of this room and rip every curl off her head.

Luke gently pulls away from her and folds his arms. "Zuri, you have to stop this."

She gives him a seductive smile and says, "While the cats away, the mice will play."

"I love my wife," he says with conviction.

She frowns and says, "You used to be more fun, Luke."

Taking a step back from her, he shakes his head. "I'm still fun," he says and then stares at her pensively. "I'm confused though. I have it on good authority that you are dating Jasper Christensen. Why would you want to mess that up?"

This is news to me. Jasper is too nice to date a harpy like her. But now it's starting to make sense. "Jasper has a girlfriend here" —

that's what Luke said. His comment to Jasper not to tell anyone that I was coming. Luke meant Zuri. And Haleema may hug lots of people, but that's not why she hugged Jasper. She embraced him like family because he's her niece's boyfriend. I wonder why Luke didn't tell me.

Actually, Zuri's reaction may be why. She narrows her eyes at him, points an accusing finger, and asks, "Who told you?"

"Who do you think?"

She furrows her brow in concentration. "There are only two people who know. Jasper and Haleema."

Luke shrugs.

Panic overtakes her face. "You haven't told anyone, have you?"

Luke shakes his head adamantly. "Not even Kelsey," he says. "But you don't have to keep it a secret once you leave Dr. Grant. He won't care."

Zuri shakes her head and begins to pace. "He'll care," she insists. "But he won't feel betrayed so long as he doesn't know how long it's been going on. And he can't find out I helped Jasper get evidence for his hearing. I told Dr. Grant last week I was moving on; a month's notice. He seems OK with it. I need to finish this month without any trouble. I don't want Stephen Grant for an enemy."

Luke shakes his head. "Don't worry about Dr. Grant."

She stops pacing and raises an eyebrow. "Clearly it's been too long since you've worked for him," she hisses. "He's the one person I do need to worry about it. You have no idea the vigor he pursued Jasper with, and he was angrier than a hissing cockroach when Jasper only got a slap on the wrist. I am not going to get on that man's bad side when we're almost through."

Luke holds his hands up in surrender. "Fair enough," he says. "I just meant that even if things didn't end perfectly, Jasper would still be there for you."

She throws a hostile glance at Luke. "I know that Jasper would stand by me. You don't have to tell me."

"Don't I? Because Jasper is into you, and from what I've heard, you're into him. So I can't figure out why you're still playing this little game of yours with me. You don't want me. And you know I love my wife, so why do you do this?"

Zuri turns, her cascading hair doing a seductive flip as her body spins. She takes a couple paces and plops down in a chair, then puts her head in her hands. Luke follows and kneels down in front of her.

"Zuri, are you alright?"

She peeks out from behind her hands. "I don't know, Luke," she says, her voice cracking a little. She takes her hand and, I think, wipes away a tear. "Jasper is great, and when I'm with him, it's perfect. But, I don't think it's going to work. I don't think I'm the right woman for him."

I can't see as well from this angle, but Luke shakes his head. "Zuri, why would you say that? You're a great catch for any guy."

"Am I?" she says, her eyebrows raised. "A woman who breaks the law on a regular basis. A woman who's on government watch lists, a woman who is only not in a holding facility through sheer luck and bribery."

Yeah, I see her point. Luke pats her shoulder. "Jasper knows all this, Zuri, and he doesn't care."

"Maybe he should care, Luke," she says, voice raised. "He's like you. He's a good guy and he doesn't deserve to be put at risk because of the things I do."

Luke takes Zuri's hand and guides her out of the chair, to the floor, where she sits next to him. Both of them face the wall where I'm hiding. I back away a little, lest I be seen. I can still see them well enough if I squint. Zuri lays her head on Luke's shoulder, yet this one time I don't feel even the slightest twinge of anger.

"I remember when I first met you," Luke says. "The thing I remember most is that you didn't take any crap from anybody. You stood up for yourself, you were confident, and you went after what you wanted. If you want Jasper, go for it. He is a nice guy. That's not a bad thing. And besides, it didn't stop you from going after me."

She pulls away and slugs him on the shoulder. Luke says, "Ouch," but it seems more for show, as it didn't look like she hit him that hard.

"I go after you because I know you'll say no. Then, I can feel good that you're still a nice guy." She gives Luke a half smile, which he returns, as if he's known this all along. I am a little dumbfounded, as it never occurred to me that she really didn't want him, even though Luke had insisted that was the case. "Jasper's a nice guy and he wants me, and if we keep on the same trajectory, it's going to be a forever proposition. I don't want him to commit to that and then have me mess everything up."

Luke puts an arm around her. "Jasper's a big boy," he says. "He can handle it. Don't push him away."

Luke gives her a little squeeze then a peck on the forehead.

Zuri seems astonished by this. "What would your wife think," she says in her deep seductive voice.

"That I was being a good friend," Luke says. "The way you've been a good friend to me. You've always helped me when it really mattered. And you and Jasper really matter, so I want to help you too."

She looks embarrassed, then stands hastily. "That's enough with the heart-to-heart," she says, as Luke stands up too. "You didn't call me over to discuss my love life."

He tips his head in agreement. "You're right," he says, giving her the bare-bones description of what happened, telling her I'm still in Peoria. "I need to find my daughter, rescue her, and get out without them realizing."

She gives him a you've-got-to-be-kidding look, then he gives her his full on dimple, please look. She relents and puts her hand under her chin in thought. She shakes her head. "Luke, you are the only guy ballsy enough to constantly ask me for the impossible and expect me to deliver."

"You're the only one I know ballsy enough to deliver each time."

She smiles. "That's not an easy task."

He nods. "I know."

"Would you consider giving up Kelsey," she says pointedly. "I think FoSS would hold up its end of the bargain, and give you your daughter back."

He gives her a harsh look.

She gives a half smile and says, "I was just kidding." Though I'm not sure she was. "Listen, I need time to think this through and see who I can call. But, I can't promise you a miracle."

"Just do what you can, please."

She nods, and with that, heads out the door.

# 21

## SUSAN

When Rob opens the door, I smile and hold up two empty teacups. "I was hoping I could interest you in a night-cap."

He raises an eyebrow, and I can tell part of him wants to smile, but he's still mad at me, so he doesn't. He slides out of my way so I can come in. Him not speaking isn't great, but he's invited me in, so I go with it. I walk past the entryway, through the house until I reach the kitchen, a spacious, open area with racks of hanging pots and premium appliances. Rob loves to cook and I love to eat, so we're a good match that way.

I set the two teacups on the table and then turn back to see that Rob has, as I hoped, followed. He's stopped in the doorway, so I walk back and stand in front of him. "I'm sorry," I say, looking him in the eye, meaning it.

"So sorry you're still ignoring my opinion and spending the day with your ex?"

I shake my head. "So sorry that I told Kevin I wouldn't go with him tomorrow."

He lets out a breath and pulls me into his arms. "Thank you, Susan," he says into my ear. "I don't think he meant what he said about not giving us the drive. I think if Lewis asks, Kevin will give it to him."

I'm so glad to be back in his arms, to be forgiven, that I don't tell him I already have it. I lean on him, enjoying the comfort of his biceps, drinking in his scent. I can even feel his heart thumping in his chest.

He pulls back from me and says, "Listen, not spending the day with Kevin is not going to hurt Kelsey or Penelope. I'll call Lewis and explain everything. I'm sure he can get the drive from Kevin. "

"You don't have to do that," I say, walking away from him, toward the tea kettle, which sits partially filled on the stovetop. I pick up the kettle, walk to the sink, pour out the stale water and fill it afresh. I can feel Rob's eyes on me as I carry the pot back to the stove and turn on a burner. I turn to him and admit, "Kevin gave it to me already."

His lips draw together tightly and his eyes narrow. "He gave it to you?"

"Yes, when I told him I wouldn't go with him tomorrow, he apologized for blackmailing me and gave it to me."

He walks over to me, a vein in his neck bulging. "I thought you weren't going to go see him by yourself." His tone is as tightly wound as he looks.

"I didn't go to see him. I was coming to see you, but he was on my doorstep when I went out. The second I saw him, I told him I wouldn't go. And that's when he gave it to me."

"Just like that?" Rob asks.

I nod. "He said he had a crisis of conscience."

Rob gives a quick eye roll, but doesn't say anything for a while, before reaching out and tucking a stray hair behind my ear. "Alright."

I turn back to the tea kettle. "Water will be ready in a minute," I say. Rob walks away from me and finds tea bags, cinnamon sticks and a box of sugar cubes. He sets it all on the table. I carry the kettle over and fill the cups with hot water, then return the kettle.

Rob and I sit and drink tea in silence for a few minutes. He looks up and says, "You remember the first time we had tea together?"

I smile thinking of that night, after a play, back in my room, telling him about how I loved cinnamon sticks in my tea when I was little. Ever since then he's kept cinnamon sticks around for me. "You kissed me," I say.

His lips curve into his own smile, as he nods his head. "Yes, I did," he says jovially, but then turns serious. "But, that's also the night you told me about your breakup with Kevin."

I swallow down the last of my tea, not wanting to hear more about Kevin, but feeling guilty about how I've let Kevin come between us in the past two days.

"You told me that you didn't hold a grudge against Kevin, that you were hurt, but let it go. Yet, I thought you were just saying it. I thought surely you hated him for walking out on you like that, and that's the reason you didn't talk about him," he says, looking into his own teacup, which is empty, save for the cinnamon stick resting on the edge. "Except when I saw you and him together yesterday, I could see it was true. You don't hate him. There is something there between the two of you, a connection I hadn't even fathomed. Seeing him look at you with such want and seeing you avoiding him, as if you weren't sure how you felt, it bothered me. Intensely."

I reach out and put my hand on Rob's knee. I shake my head. "I don't want Kevin," I say firmly. "I felt some unresolved emotion when I first saw him." I look down into my empty teacup, not sure I want to admit the truth. "Part of me had let go of what happened, but part of me was still stuck in that time frame with him, in this unresolved limbo, and I didn't want to deal with that or him. I just pretended that the past shouldn't matter to you. Today, I ignored your feelings when what you were asking me to do — to let the senator try first — wasn't unreasonable. I'm sorry for that. I love you and I want to marry you. I'm going to marry you, in just a few days."

Rob sets his teacup down and takes my hand into both of his, brings it to his lips for kiss. "I'm sorry I let Kevin get under my skin that way," he says. "I'm glad you have the drive, and I want you to know that if Lewis had failed, if you spending the day with Kevin was the only way to help Penelope, I would have been OK with it. I wouldn't have been happy about it, but I wouldn't have asked you not to go. I just didn't want that to be the first resort."

I squeeze Rob's hand, and he smiles at me.

"Let's just forget about Kevin," he says. I nod, and Rob tugs at my hand, urging me toward him. I slide to him, straddling him in his chair. He looks at me seductively, so I tip my head forward and kiss him. His hands slide up the back of my shirt and caresses my back, while his tongue probes my mouth. I know where this is headed, and pull back.

"I promised Dan I'd get there before 10," I say.

He looks incredulous. "You're really going to your cousin's house? You're really not going to stay here?"

I kiss him again, this time short and sweet. "I told you it's bad luck to live together in the marital home before you get married."

"But it's cool to come over, get your fiancé all worked up and then leave?"

I roll my eyes and look at my watch. "I can be a little late; but we have to hurry"

* * *

We did not hurry. Rob is nuzzling my neck as I try to read the messages on my phone. "Hold on, I have to figure out where I'm going to stay tonight," I tell him.

Rob stops. "You're really going to leave?"

"I told you; it's bad luck."

"I know, but you don't even believe in these crazy bridal superstitions," he says, exasperated. "Why are you texting your cousin and uncle instead of just staying here?"

I read the rest of Uncle Mike's reply telling me I can crash in the guest room, and to use the spare key. Since it's after 11, I can't go to Dan's; I'll wake his children. I text him that I'm going to stay with Uncle Mike instead.

"You spent the night at my apartment less than a week ago," Rob reminds me.

"And that was your apartment," I remind him. "This is our house, which you moved into to get a head start on moving, and that's fine, but I can't stay here with you."

He kisses my shoulder, his lips so soft and gentle on my skin. "I would really love it if you threw caution to the wind and stayed."

It's so tempting, but no. I sit up, pulling the sheet with me and exposing his toned abdomen. "I promise I'll be back in the morning. We'll grab breakfast, and then get our flight." I try to look perky, but my cheer does not appear to be infectious because he still looks like I'm wounding him by leaving. "Look, I'll be here every day after we get married. I don't know why you find it so strange that I want to uphold tradition."

He traces his pointer finger along my arm. Then he slides it down until his hand rests on top of mine. "It's not that you just want to hold it up. You're adamant about it, like if we defy this rule, we'll burn in Hell for all eternity."

I lie back down and turn to him, blowing out a breath. "You're right that I'm not normally superstitious, but I am about this, OK? I'll feel better if we just do the things we're supposed to do."

Rob reaches an arm around me and pulls me close. "You know, we weren't supposed to do what we just did," he says, kissing my nose.

He's got me there. "OK, you're right, but we crossed that bridge long ago. So let's just be traditional about everything else," I say. "Come on, just pretend I went to take a shower, and you fell asleep. When I come back in the morning, I'll crawl right into bed and you can pretend I spent the night."

He shakes his head. "You're impossible, Susan," he tells me. "Fine. If it makes you feel better, go stay at your uncle's."

"Thanks," I tell him, kissing him, then rising. "And if you don't fall asleep, maybe you can look at Kelsey's drive tonight?"

He nods. "As soon as I get back from dropping you at your uncle's."

"You don't have to do that, especially since you don't even want me to go."

He sits up. "I want you to get there safe and sound, so come on."

# WEDNESDAY

# 22

## KELSEY

Susan and Rob arrived a minute ago. My father will arrive shortly, though I'm not looking forward to it. Haleema stopped by last night and explained that I wasn't supposed to be marked, that my marking was someone's attempt to get my father to move me off the marking list. Only he didn't. At the time, I'd thought him too principled to do that, so it was a complete shock when Haleema admitted he wanted to move me, but didn't because he was worried about his career. She said he would explain more when he saw me, but that I needed to know the basics because Susan and Rob might want to discuss how best to use the information to get Penelope back, and they would arrive before my father. They have, in fact, arrived before him.

We're in the main rotunda and Susan looks great, so healthy, so happy. I'm glad to see her up and about. I'd seen pictures, but this is the first time I've seen her in person since I left FoSS two and a half years ago. It's difficult for single women of childbearing age to get permission to come to Peoria, and as a fugitive, I clearly couldn't go see her.

I'd like to get a moment alone with Susan, but she immediately goes to Luke and tells him there's something she'd like to show him about the secret room. She guides him away from me. I'm about to offer to tag along, when I see Rob coming toward me.

Rob approaches quickly and looks serious. He lifts his finger to his mouth, in a shushing motion and pulls a small tablet from his bag. He turns on the screen, and there is a picture of a woman in a hospital gown with wild black hair, crazed eyes and a face contorted in anguish. As I stare at it, I realize it's Emmie. I hadn't thought it possible, but she looks worse now than she did in the picture I saw on

Greg's phone.

"I think we've found Luke's sister," he whispers, "but I wanted to make sure this is her before I tell him. I wouldn't want to get his hopes up, if it's not her."

My eyes are wide with shock, but I nod. "It's her," I say. "Where is she?"

"Here," Rob says.

I step back, take a second look at his face. "What do you mean here?"

"I mean, about 90 miles from here, in Macon. Same facility where they held Susan. It's probably why Greg was so willing to come get you. We're only a few hours from the border, and he was probably here visiting Emmie."

I pull away and bite my lower lip. "So, she's basically close enough that we could drive over and get her?"

Rob nods, but then stills and slides the device back in his bag. I look up to see Susan and Luke return to the room, her laughing at something, Luke smiling for once. It feels like an eternity since I've seen him smile. Really smile like the world will be OK, like we haven't lost the only thing that matters. A genuine smile that edges from a place deep within that feels happy. As soon as he sees Rob and me, and our expressions, his smile fades away, replaced with that familiar worry I've seen before. Hell, that I've felt ever since Greg took Penelope.

He comes over to us, while Susan hangs back, and I suspect now that she was less interested in having a private word with Luke than in me having a private word with Rob.

"What's wrong?" Luke asks.

"I'm pretty sure I've found your sister," Rob says.

Luke's face is a mix of anguish and relief. "Is she alright?"

I take my husband's hand. Rob pauses, then shakes his head. "She needs anti-psychotic medication and they're not giving it to her. They do sedate her, but she's mentally … she's not well."

Luke's eyes don't leave Rob's. He is trying to appear strong, resolute. "You're sure it's her."

Rob briefly looks at me, remembering my ID of her, perhaps, then nods. "I'm sure."

"Where is she?"

Rob swallows and glances at me before answering. "She's in the same place Susan was held, but I imagine they're keeping her in one of the labs, someplace small they could pad, so she doesn't hurt herself."

Luke's eyes have a little spark, a little pep now. He takes a step toward Rob. "You know this place?" he asks, excitedly. "You could help me get her out of there."

Rob's face is grim. "I think we need to determine how to get her out Luke, without risking Col. Parker finding out and doing something to Penelope."

At this, my hand squeezes Luke's tighter. He can't do something to save his sister if it's going to risk our daughter. I know that's selfish on my part, but he has to keep Penelope safe. And the truth is, I can turn myself in and they can both be fine.

Luke nods. "Yes, you're right. We need to get them both out without jeopardizing the safety of the other. So, do you know anything else about her? "

Rob grimaces, and suggests Luke and I sit down. All of us go to the kitchen and gather round the table, Susan and Rob sitting across from Luke and me. Luke doesn't say anything but I can tell by his hunched posture and blank face, that he is dreading hearing what Rob has to say. Gritting himself up for the worst possible answer. I take my hand and lightly rub his back, but he tenses and leans forward in his chair, so I'm not touching him. I retract my hand and wait for Rob, who doesn't seem to want to speak.

"Your sister needs anti-psychotic medication and in the absence of that, she is not able to process basic normal functions like talking to and responding to people. She's hallucinating and I think we're going to need to actually get her some treatment before we can bring her out. That means we're probably going to need Greg's help."

Luke's shoulders fall and his hands, sitting on the table, ball into fists. "Greg," he spits. "You want Greg to help us?"

"From what I understand, he's living at the compound, waiting for her to be released. We just need to talk to him and get him to help us get Emmie out at the same time we're getting Penelope."

Luke stands up and walks to the French doors that open onto the back patio. He leans on the door, his arms folded. "He should be in a holding facility. He's a kidnapper. What makes you think we can trust him?"

"He wants his wife to get well, and if we can convince him we can do that, he'll help us."

Luke rubs his chin, the uncertainty over seeking help from his brother-in-law apparent. "You're sure it's her?"

Rob hesitates, then pulls the tablet from his bag again. "I had them send me a picture, because she's listed as Melissa Heath on the records." Luke walks back over, and stands next to Rob, ready to see the photo. Rob moves his hand to turn on the device, but stops just short, saying, "I have to warn you, Luke, she's not in good condition."

Luke nods and Rob turns on the screen. There is Emmie, or perhaps I should say, Emmie's body. A hollow shell that has the same exterior as the woman Luke grew up with, but nothing inside. Luke picks up the machine and pulls it closer to his face. He looks like he's been stabbed through the heart, his face contorting in horror as he realizes this woman on the screen, this woman who is so vacant, so wild, is the same person who used to sing him to sleep, tuck him in and tell him adventure tales. After a moment more, Luke sets the tablet on the table. "OK," he says. "We'll ask for Greg's help."

Then he walks out of the room without saying another word.

I get up and go after Luke, following him down the hallway and back into the rotunda. "Luke," I say softly. He stops and turns. I walk toward him and hug him. "Are you alright?"

His voice is a little hoarse when he speaks. "This is just a lot to take in Kelse," he whispers. He lets go of me and I nod. "I think I want to go for a walk, clear my head. You'll be alright?"

"Yes," I tell him. "I'm fine. Take the time you need. And, if you want to talk, I'm here."

He smiles. "I know," he grabs me and pulls me tight. "You're always here when I need you."

# 23

## KELSEY

It's been half an hour. I'm in our room and Luke is still out walking. I worry about his peace of mind. He doesn't want to let out how he's feeling; he wants to be strong and steely for me, but it's obvious he's completely anguished over his sister and Penelope. I wish he'd let it out.

I miss her so much, too. The way she used to play with my hair when I picked her up, her smile, her sweet adorable walk. Her being gone weighs on me so much. I feel the tears starting to come now, and say a silent prayer that she is alright, that she isn't as scared as I fear she is. That she isn't alone and miserable.

A knock at the door pulls me from my thoughts. I look up but don't respond. Susan said she'd announce herself when she knocked, and not to answer unless she did. While I don't really know who would be coming to this room if they weren't supposed to, I feel abundantly cautious.

"Kelsey, it's me," says a familiar voice. My father. I wipe the tears from my eyes and feel a wave of ambivalence. I want any news he might have, but I'm still reeling over the fact that this all could have been stopped if he had just gotten me unmarked two years ago.

I tell my father to come in. He walks straight toward me and wraps me into a hug. He kisses the top of my head and squeezes me tightly, as if I might somehow disappear if he lets go. "Kelsey, sweetheart, this must be so difficult for you," he says, loosening his grip on me, and pulling back slightly so I've enough room to breathe.

I extricate myself from my father and walk toward the four-poster bed. I lean a shoulder against a post as I look down at the cream-colored bedspread. "I'm holding up as best I can, Dad." I look up at him. "I miss her terribly. More than I ever thought possible."

He looks at me like I'm breaking his heart. "We'll get her back."

If I keep staring at him, the pity in his eyes — pity for me, pity for Penelope — will consume me and I'll start crying again. I can't do that. I have to be strong for Penelope. I have to be part of the solution, not a bystander to my own life. I straighten my back and ask my father, "What did the colonel say?"

My father threads the fingers of one hand through the other and taps his thumbs. "He's playing hardball," he says. "He insists he wants you, but I think he just wants this anti-Life First sentiment to stop. I've offered him a promise that you would publicly apologize for fleeing, that you would renounce your opposition to Life First and you and Luke would not speak publicly about it again. I also threw in Susan. She'll make whatever statement they want her to make about you, so long as it stops short of encouraging harm to you."

I take a few strands of hair and twist them around my finger. "What did he say to that?"

"He said he wants you," my father says solemnly. "I told him to think about my offer. "

Unhappy with that response, I walk to the window, its drapes pulled shut. I resist the urge to look out and turn to my father. "How long is he going to consider this? How much longer does my daughter have to be gone? We should be doing something more to get her back."

My father walks toward me, his arms outstretched as if he wants to hug me, but I glare at him, and he stops in his tracks. "I agree that this feels like a long time, but it's only been two days. Give me time to see if this will work. I'm trying to find out where they've got her; so is Zuri. We'll figure this out, and even though you can't see it, Penelope is fine. She's safe, OK. He's not going to hurt her."

"You don't know that?"

He looks me straight in the eye. "I do know that. He's got nothing to negotiate with if he hurts her. He has nothing if anything happens to her, no chance of getting what he wants, which is to stop people from parading you around as a symbol of a movement he doesn't like. I can get your daughter back to you. I will get her back. I promise you."

I walk away from him. Back toward the bed, stopping just short of it and resting my elbow on the dresser adjacent it. My father takes a step toward me, but stops halfway between the bed and window. He looks so guilt-ridden that I remember why he feels that way and the anger that was simmering over this situation, suddenly bubbles up, directed at him. "Haleema told me," I say, betrayal rippling through my voice. "But I want to hear it from you. Did someone really tell you that you could get my mark removed and you said, no?"

He straightens up. I hadn't realized he was slouching, but as he extends to his full height of six feet, it's noticeable. "Yes," he says clearly, but softly. "The person who asked about Susan, this person asked me again after you'd been marked. He said he understood that I thought it might be dicey to interfere for someone who wasn't family, but that he thought maybe this time I'd like to intervene. That if I did want to, he could put me in touch with a person who could get you removed from the list."

"And you said no?"

He is shaking his head in denial. But, his eyes say yes; they say it's true, even if his head gesture contradicts that. "I didn't tell him yes or no," he tells me firmly, as if there is some keenly important distinction in the fact that his first answer was ambivalent. His final answer was no, and that's all that matters. Despite my glare, my father continues, apology on his face. "First, I thought you had been marked Kelsey. The law said you needed to donate. It didn't seem fair for me to unilaterally decide you didn't need to do this. That I should pull strings in this."

"Even after what happened to Susan?" I say, narrowing my eyes.

He doesn't flinch. "Yes, even then. Susan's problems were so statistically unlikely that I couldn't reasonably see anything like that happening to you. OK? Not to mention, what he was asking was highly illegal. At the time, I wasn't into getting involved in illegal activity. We all know how far I went for you in the end. But back then, I hadn't been desperate, your life wasn't at stake and I wasn't ready to commit that level of subterfuge when I didn't even know that you didn't want to be on the list."

My lips pull together tightly and I point accusingly at him. "You didn't even ask me. You didn't ask because you didn't want to know."

He doesn't respond for a moment, simply staring at me. "I didn't want to be unfair, either," he says practically in a whisper. It's so unlike him to speak so softly, I'm not even sure I believe him. He stops looking at me and stares at the oriental rug on the floor. Déjà vu in reverse, I guess. I'd found myself staring at the pattern of an oriental rug when I attempted to flee the marking surgery he could have gotten me out of, but the chose not to.

I shake my head in disgust, "At some point you changed your mind, at some point you wanted to be unfair and then you just decided not to, because you were afraid about what it would do to your career if someone found out?"

I stare at him, wanting him to admit it, wanting him to say it out loud. But, part of me just wants my father to be telling the truth, to be that guy who was principled and didn't want to break the rules just for his family. To be the guy I thought he was when I ran from the surgery. To know that I wasn't a fool for thinking that. Instead, I know that Dr. Grant had been right all along about asking my father to pull strings.

My father looks up at me, shame lining every inch of his face. "Fine, Kelsey," he admits, defeated. "My first instinct was to be principled. To be a man of the people, to be like everyone else. But then I saw you, the only child I had left, walking around the house like a frightened dove. I saw that this surgery was stressing you to your very core. You were jumpy and skittish. The bags under your eyes were so big you could've packed for a six-week cruise. You slept late and lacked energy. Even though I asked you repeatedly if you were alright, you just put on that fake smile and said you were fine, then you'd start twisting your hair, and I knew you were scared. We all know that surgical complications rise five to ten percentage points if the patient is sick or stressed. I didn't want to increase your chances of risk, especially after what happened to Susan. So, I thought I could get you taken off the list, but as I was calling to get you moved, someone leaked the story to the papers. You'd been marked. You were a perfect match and the girl who was going to be first daughter of the state was going to make a wonderful contribution for society."

He slowly walks in my direction, taking a seat on the bed near a post. His blue-gray eyes plead forgiveness. "Gordon, my campaign manager, called within an hour of the leak and said my poll numbers had seen a wonderful upward blip with the news, but he'd need a day or so to see if it was anything that would stick around and help me in the final stages of the election. So, I thought, I just thought that if I could convince you it would be OK, that maybe it would be OK. If

I'd had any idea you'd run or that I needed to get you off that list, I would have risked it. I didn't know, and I'm sorry I let the prospect of the governorship outweigh your interest."

It's not an answer he's proud of, but it's the only answer he has. I shuffle away from him, making my way back to the window. This time I peek out of the curtain. Large white tents, some type of plastic or canvas, lay out front like blankets covering the lawn. Ropes and tent stakes are scattered between them, and the men are working in teams to pull each tent to life. I feel like one of those tents, laid bare on the lawn, waiting to be erected, given life again.

"Kelsey, I realized my mistake, and I stood by you during the trial."

Still looking out the window, I nod. He's right. Whatever plan he'd had to slingshot to the top by using my marking backfired. Instead, he stood by me and lost everything. At the time, he'd said he felt guilty for failing my mother when she needed him. She'd been pregnant and sick when she died. She'd asked him to help her persuade the medical board to offer treatment that would have meant death to the baby, but saved her. My father, away on business, said to wait, that he'd come home; only my mother and brother were dead before he'd returned. He led me to believe guilt over that alone was his motivator. Little did I know he'd gathered more recent fuel for his guilt fire.

I close my eyes and take a deep breath, so I can get some clarity in my own head. I have to let go of the anger and focus on going forward, on what needs to happen next, on how to get my daughter back.

God, Penelope. She has to be so scared and so alone and so confused as to why we're not there. I need her to feel safe and that can only happen if we get her back. I want to just sink into a pool of my own tears, but that won't do any good. I need to pull myself together. I have to, or my father won't listen to me. If he doesn't believe I'm in control, that I'm thinking straight, he'll ignore what I'm going to ask him.

I take a deep breath, release the curtain, making sure it has fully closed and no one can see in, and turn back to my father. "You did stand by me and I'll be forever grateful for that," I tell him as I head toward him.

"But?" he asks.

"There are no buts, Dad. I'll be forever grateful for that," I say, looking him in the eye, knowing what I say now is crucial. "I'm a parent now, so I understand that parents make mistakes. All we can do is do better the next time. I didn't ask you for help then. I didn't tell you what I needed, that I needed you to get me off that list. I know now if I tell you I need something, you'll help me. Right?"

He looks at me confused, wondering where I'm going with this. Taking hold of the bedpost, as if in need of support, he says. "I'll always help you, Kelsey. You know that."

I nod. "So, once we authenticate the drive, can you use the fact that I wasn't marked, that I shouldn't be a fugitive, to get Penelope back?"

"That's my hope," he says cautiously. "But we need to authenticate it first. While I feel really confident that he's not going to hurt her while we're negotiating, I'm concerned that if he feels like we've stopped negotiating or that we're going to double cross him and release information he wants contained, that he might not react well."

That's what I'm afraid of, too. "OK. Then I need your help, Dad." I look him in the eyes and he stares back at me, looking a little frightened by what he sees. I hope I appear as resolute as I feel. "If the negotiations don't work and you feel the colonel isn't reacting well, promise me that you will give him what he wants."

My father's lips part, as if to say, "no," but speech doesn't emerge.

I take a step closer to him, and he looks at me as if he's never seen me before. "I want this to work out, but Dad, you and I know things don't always work out. You have to promise me that you will do everything you can to get my daughter back, including giving up yours."

He sits down on the edge of the bed, unable to process my words and stand at the same time. I know he is digesting them, trying to figure out if he can convince me otherwise. I stare at him and hope he can see in my eyes that I am as unmoving as the pyramids. I shall not change my mind on this one fundamental thing. My contingency plan will be me, and no matter what he says, I'll find a way to do it.

"I love you, Kelsey, and I don't want to lose you," he says, looking at me desperately. Then he asks, "Is Luke OK with this?"

I hadn't expected that question, but I avoid showing my surprise. I take a deep breath and respond truthfully, "Luke and I want the same thing. We want our daughter back, and we want your help."

He looks down at the bedspread in silence. I feel a twinge of guilt for misleading him, but I need him to say yes to me. And I'm sure Luke will see the truth of what needs to be done, especially if this goes on much longer. Our daughter needs to be home.

Finally, my father looks up at me, meets my eyes, and says, "I promise you, I will give up whatever is necessary to get Penelope back."

The relief at having an ally floods through me, and I feel a slight unknotting of the tension my body has endured since Greg took my daughter. I give my father a hug and whisper thank you in his ear. It seems silly to thank him for being willing to send me to the gallows. It seems silly for me to wish to go to the gallows. But all I can think of is that my daughter needs to be home, away from the strangers who've stolen her. She needs to be with her parents. And if the only way to do that is for one of her parents to go away then so be it. I need my daughter safe. Not just for now, but forever.

# 24

## KELSEY

It's after midnight and I'm awake. Luke fell asleep and he deserves the rest; he's been up and trying so hard ever since this happened. I can't deny him peace, but I can't sleep and don't want to disturb him, so I quietly sneak out and head for the kitchen. Maybe I'll have a cup of tea or warm milk. Anything that might help me to sleep. Anything that will help me shut the world out for just a few hours. I need — for just a little bit — to forget my daughter is gone and that it's all my fault. Every time I close my eyes, I imagine that they're hurting her or mistreating her, keeping her locked away, bound, the way Greg kept me. The pain in my bandaged wrists flares up just thinking about it. I try to shake the images from my mind and walk faster.

As I near the kitchen, I hear the clacking of computer keys. When I turn through the doorway, I find Rob sitting at the table pecking away on his laptop. The little black box that holds the original marking records is plugged into it.

He looks up from his work and smiles. "Hey," he says, friendly.

"Hey," I say back, moving toward the table. "Couldn't sleep. Mind if I join you?"

He shakes his head and sighs. "No, please join me," he says. There's something a bit off in his face, an underlying hostility, though it seems directed more at the world than me personally. "I'm thankful for anyone who wants me to stick around my own house."

I pull up a chair cattycorner to Rob and sit. I don't want to go where he just went. I'm sure his statement has something to do with Susan, and I'd rather not be a part of their kerfuffle. "Are you making any headway with the data?"

He pokes out his lower lip and his eyebrows squish together. "It's the same as before," he says. "Everything points to Dr. Rounds switching the data, but I don't know of any motive he'd have for it. He had that letter but he never asked your father for anything. And Kevin suggested the data would point to someone else."

I roll my eyes. "I wouldn't count on anything he says."

He looks up from his screen, a little stunned, followed by a look of vindication. "Yes," he says. "So you get that vibe, too?"

I nod, a little uncertain why he seems so stunned. He knows I pulled some strings to get Kevin's acceptance to the prestigious Lazenby program revoked.

"Why does she trust him, then?" he asks me, as if I somehow have magic insight into this aspect of Susan. "Why is she so OK with him? Why doesn't she hate him and ignore everything he says?"

So, Kevin has reared his ugly head again. I lean in and say, "I'm sorry about what he did with the blackmail. I know Susan doesn't want to spend time with him. She just said, 'yes' to help me. Please don't be mad at her for that. I'll feel like it's my fault. And, frankly, on top of everything else that's going on, I don't want to feel responsible for you two fighting."

He rubs his temples a moment, then shakes it off. "Kelsey, I'm sorry. We are not fighting because of you. I'm just frustrated with Susan. She's not been herself lately."

I put my hand to my chin, poised to listen. Hearing someone else's problems will take my mind off my own. "What do you mean?"

He scans the screen for a second then looks back at me. "Well, she's suddenly become superstitious. We can't stay in the same house before we're married. And even the wedding itself. It seems like it's stressing her immensely, but I told her after I proposed, that I would be happy with a small, simple wedding. She insisted on this big wedding — which is fine — but it seems to be making her completely unhappy the closer we get to it."

I offer my best look of empathy and pat his shoulder. "I think I know what's going on," I tell him.

"Really? Then please clue me in."

"Kevin."

His mouth parts and he looks truly stunned, and even hurt. "You think she still has feelings for Kevin."

I shake my head vigorously in denial, as I realize I expressed myself poorly. "No, she absolutely has no feelings for Kevin," I tell him confidently. "But she does have feelings about what happened the last time she was engaged."

He cocks one eyebrow and gives me an inquisitive look. "Go on."

"Instead of getting married, she got dumped. The wedding didn't happen, and I'm pretty sure Susan planned to follow zero of the marriage superstitions. They were tight on time because Kevin had the Lazenby and had to be in New York in July. They wanted a small wedding, defying the norm, but the timing would best work out in August, so they were going to completely defy convention and stay in the Lazenby apartment until they got married. Susan also had decided white was too demure for a dress. She wanted bright red — to match her hair."

Recognition seems to be dawning on him. "So she's doing the exact opposite this time," he says.

"I think so," I tell him. "She's not superstitious, but she wasn't last time, and look what happened. I think she just wants to optimize her chances, even if it's silly."

He cups his hand on the side of his face and sighs. "I've been pushing back against it, and she's just getting more and more nervous." He closes his eyes. "God, I should've seen it."

I shake my head. "You didn't know," I tell him. "You never saw how she was after she woke up from the coma."

He nods, thoughtfully. "She doesn't talk about that time to me," he says. "I mean, she said it was a difficult time, but she never talks specifics."

I'm sure she wouldn't. I frown at the memory. "You know, she was OK after she woke up," I tell him, and his eyebrows rise in curiosity. "The paralysis would have done me in, Rob. It would have pulled me under, and I would've drowned if I'd woken up to a diagnosis like that. But it didn't do that to Susan. She's so strong." I pause at the memory of her sitting up in her hospital bed and assuring me that she would be alright, assuring me that she was alive and that was what mattered most. "Obviously, she wasn't happy about being paralyzed, but she had the attitude that she could persevere. She wanted to get back to life, to planning her wedding and figuring out how to make that move to New York. She even called the Lazenby people about her housing needs. The program had accessible facilities, and they were going to move Kevin to a first floor unit."

I stop here, choking back the pain that accompanies this memory, trying to convey to Rob what happened without actually reliving the anger and hostility I felt at the time. "And then he shattered her, Rob. It was when he told her they were through. That's when she cracked, that is when the strongest person I have ever known broke. He crushed her. Their marriage, their future was what she was holding onto to get her through this tough time, and he yanked it all out from her. She was despondent after that, like a zombie: vacant eyes, listless, barely eating, sleeping all the time. It was a nightmare that he brought about."

Rob's mouth has fallen open in horror as what I'm saying sinks in. Part of me wonders if I've said too much. Susan hadn't told him this, but I don't think she was necessarily hiding it from him. I don't know that she realized the state she was in until after it was over, and frankly, if I had ever been like that, I don't think I'd want to relive it, even in conversation.

Rob shudders. "I see why you pulled strings to get the Lazenby revoked. He didn't deserve it."

I snort. "No, he didn't, and truthfully, I didn't have to pull that many strings. I talked to one of my father's friends who was on the Lazenby board, but I also talked to the housing woman, the woman Susan had spoken to about changing their housing arrangements. She had spoken to Susan, gotten a rapport with her, and she hated what Kevin had done as much as I did. So, between her and me, yeah, we convinced Dr. Drake to revoke it, but I couldn't have gotten it done if Kevin hadn't been such an ass."

Rob nods. He pauses a moment, as if measuring his words carefully. "Susan said your father thought Kevin and I were a bit alike."

I wave it off. "Pfft. You're both interested in medicine; you're a doctor and he's in med school, but that's about it," I say. "I mean, after Susan's surgery, she thought she'd caught the flu from Dan's little girl, but it was really the spinal infection. Well, do you know what Kevin said to her — what that jackass had the nerve to tell her, when she was feverish and miserable and he should've been concerned about her well-being?" I raise my eyebrows in consternation and don't even wait for Rob to make a guess. "He told her he had exams coming up and couldn't afford to be sick, so she should really keep away from him. No, 'please feel better.' No, 'let me bring you some soup.'"

There is a look of complete incredulity on Rob's face. He cocks his head and asks, "What did she see in him? I mean, he's too lazy to even say her entire name."

I can't help but grin. "You're kinda snarky after midnight," I tease.

He smiles back. "Maybe. I just don't see how she could ever have been with him."

I sigh, trying to figure out how to explain them as a couple. "Kevin probably wasn't a bad guy overall, but he was selfish, and Susan has trouble seeing that. I mean, you know her aunt was an abusive shrew and while her uncle loved her, he put his needs ahead of making sure Susan was OK. And growing up like that, she doesn't necessarily see the selfishness in that. She sees that she ought to be grateful when someone loves her, because she doesn't have anyone to fall back on. Her parents are dead. She had to rely on her aunt and uncle. I wish I had realized how bad it was when I was a kid. I knew her aunt was cold, but not until I saw the recordings did I ever suspect it was that bad."

Rob doesn't say anything to me. He is silent and contemplative. I wonder if he is thinking of the recordings too. The videos FoSS forced Susan to make, where she supposedly described acts of torture perpetrated upon her by me. They were real stories, just not about me. About her aunt. About awful incidents of mental and sometimes physical harassment. I'd been Susan's friend and been too naive to see that her home life wasn't just routine family angst. That she spent her time at our place not just because we were friends, but also because she didn't want to be with that woman.

Rob blows out a long breath, gives me a nod. "Thank you for being so candid with me," he said. "I appreciate the insight."

I smile. "My pleasure," I tell him. "I love Susan and I want her to be happy. You make her happy, happier than I've ever seen her."

He blushes. "Susan makes me incredibly happy."

"And I'm sorry about any role I'm playing in her anxiety. It can't help that everything has gone haywire the week before her wedding. Kevin just showing up, her hiding me here because Penelope was kidnapped. But, I promise I'll help out. Tomorrow, she and I will talk wedding stuff, and I'll try to set her mind at ease."

Rob shakes his head. "Don't worry about it," he says. "You have enough on your plate."

I sigh. "Maybe, but reminding Susan that her wedding will turn out perfect seems more productive than thinking my daughter's eyes are swollen shut from crying. Or that she's catatonic from fear because she's with strangers and has no idea where her parents are."

Rob reaches out and pats my hand. "Kelsey, I'm so sorry about this. I'm trying to authenticate this and figure out who switched your data." He purses his lips and says, "You know, I should probably call Kevin and ask him what he did to hack into this thing."

He presses a couple more keys on his laptop, his face alight with frustration. "I've let pride and jealousy get in the way here. If he's better at this, then I need his help."

I feel a little confused. "You think Kevin is a better hacker?"

He frowns. "I don't know. He found a path that suggests someone other than Dr. Rounds changed the data," he says.

"I guess you're right. I'm just surprised he even knows how to do that. As far as I know, he didn't have any interest in the inner workings of computers or programming."

Rob stops typing and looks at me like I'm nuts. "What do you mean, he had no interest in computers or programming?"

"Umm, he didn't seem to have any special talent for network inner workings," I say. "He didn't seem to have a penchant for it. But, obviously, he's learned some new things in the past couple of years."

He looks at the keyboard and starts typing furiously and muttering, but it's so low I'm not sure the significance of his whispered curses. After a minute more of this, he pounds his fist on the table next to the laptop, and everything on the table shakes. "Kevin's not just an asshole, he's a liar," Rob says. "We need to get Susan. Now."

# 25

## SUSAN

I'll be honest, I thought the worst when Kelsey tugged me out of bed, saying that Rob needed me right now. All sorts of horrible things that could have happened flashed in my mind: accidentally impaled on a kitchen knife, the chandelier falling and crushing him, choking to death on a walnut. Awful, horrible things that made no logical sense.

But, this never crossed my mind. Luke woke up in all the commotion, and the four of us are huddled at the kitchen table digesting what Rob has figured out and his proposal to deal with it. There's been silence for a while. If anyone had suggested Rob would ever emerge with this plan, I would have said they were out of their minds.

"I think it's the best option we have, Rob," Kelsey says, before turning to me. "If you're OK with it, then I think we should do it."

Luke bites his lower lip and gives an uncertain look. "I know we need the information but it seems kind of cruel." He looks to Rob. "Maybe we do the first part, then you and I can have a talk with him."

Rob looks like he's considering this. "Maybe," he says, then stands, walks over to the French doors and peers out. "I hesitate because he lied to us about this drive. There is no way he tracked this down on his own. You said he didn't do anything with programming before this, right?" Rob turns back to us, looks at me intently. "Right? He didn't have any interest?"

"No, no interest at all," I say, softly, still having a hard time understanding why Kevin would lie and who he could be working with, who would've gotten him the drives.

"So, you're sure the data is fake?" Luke asks.

Rob nods. "These were easy to crack and the trail leads clearly to Dr. Rounds. He logged in and changed both the records, according to these drives." He shakes his head in disbelief. "But it was too easy. I went in and did a couple of tests, this data was all added. The drives are the real drives, right serial numbers, but the data is fake. It's a set-up. Anyone we give this data to will realize it's fake. They'll think we're trying to con them."

"And you're sure Kevin couldn't have learned this?" I ask.

"If he had no interest in tech and he's in med school, I don't see where he had the time," Rob says. "I know a guy who occasionally pulls stuff off the university servers and he pulled Kevin's transcript for me. Kevin didn't even take a device programming class. Anyone with even the slightest interest takes device programming, just to see how they could possibly tinker with the equipment. I can't say it with one hundred percent certainty that he's lying, but I truly don't believe he did this on his own."

"I still don't understand why this person Kevin is working with would want us to believe fake data or try to use it," I say.

Luke chimes in. "Maybe they wanted us to feel like we had some bargaining chip for Penelope, to lure us into a false sense of security so we would bring Kelsey back."

Kelsey frowns and shakes her head. "But they had Penelope already. Did they really need to lure us back with the drives since they had her? "

"But they didn't have her when Kevin got these drives," Luke says. "Maybe it was covering both bases. If Greg's kidnapping didn't work, they could lure Kelsey back with this false promise that she wasn't supposed to be marked, and then swoop in for the kill."

"Or maybe," says Rob. "Maybe they gave us the false lead because it's true."

We all pause and look at Rob like he's got three heads. Rob's been at this too long, I realize.

"Listen, I know it's one o'clock in the morning and it sounds crazy, but hear me out," he says. He looks to Kelsey and speaks pointedly. "Your father said people made overtures to him, to get you guys off the list, right?" She nods. "And let's face it, we've all taken statistics; the odds of both Kelsey and Susan being marked within a year of each other are phenomenally low, except it happened. When Kevin suggested it, Lewis didn't even question that it was a possibility. So if someone did this, and they were afraid they were going to get caught, what would be the best thing to do to make sure no one believed this happened?"

Luke's face mutates into a snarl. "Clue us in and make us show up with bogus proof. When we're shown to be liars, no one will believe the truth of it."

"Right," Rob says. "So, we need to know how Kevin got these drives and who he's working with. I think what I suggested is the best approach, but it's really up to Susan."

All eyes are on me. It's not a comforting feeling. "Can Rob and I have a minute?"

Kelsey and Luke nod and head off together.

Rob looks at me, and I stare at him like the stranger he feels like right now. "You'd really be comfortable with what you proposed?"

He grits his teeth. "I wouldn't like it, but I could accept it. Are you comfortable with it?"

I don't know. I lean back in the chair, close my eyes. "I thought we were through with Kevin, and," I pause, looking down at my hands. "I feel a little like Luke, like it's cruel."

He nods. "Maybe you're right. Maybe it is cruel," he says, walking over to me, kneeling in front of my chair. "Call him, now. You can sleep on the rest of it, OK. But, I think you have to do the first part. There's no other way to get him down here."

He's right. Kevin won't come unless I do this. I nod, rise slowly and head back to my room to get my phone. Once there, I consider going back downstairs to make the call, so Rob can watch. But I don't want an audience for this. If it's just Kevin and me on the phone, I won't feel like such an awful person. Rob's plan is simple: trade on Kevin's desire to win me back. Call Kevin and tell him I still love him and I need him to come to me, here in Georgia, as soon as he can. And tomorrow, profess my love and ask him to tell me the truth about how he got the drive. But I know Kevin wasn't faking. He wants me back and to pretend that I want him, too... it's not right.

I hold the phone in my hand and it feels too heavy, as the weight of the lie I'm about to tell settles in. I scroll through the recent calls, find Kevin's number, and send the call through. It rings and rings and rings, and finally he picks up. "Sue?"

I'm not sure I can do it.

"Sue?" he asks. "Sue, are you alright?"

"No," I whisper. "Kevin, I need you," I tell him, desperation in my voice. "I need you to come to Georgia, please. Can you come first thing in the morning?"

I hear rustling from Kevin's end, perhaps the clicking on of a lamp. "Sue, what is this about? Are you ok? Did Rob hurt you?"

"I'm... uh, Rob didn't hurt me," I stammer, trying to bring myself to say the lie Rob concocted. "I'm not hurt, but I need you to come."

"What's going on, Sue. You're not making any sense."

I can't argue with that. "I know," I say. "Can you please come?"

He pauses, and I can imagine him sitting up in bed, a look of complete confusion on his face. "Sue, you want me to travel across the country with no explanation?"

He'd come if I told him the lie, that I loved him. But I can't do that. My mind searches for another reason. I can hear his breathing, still heavy with sleep. "The other day, you said you wanted to spend the day with me," I remind him. "You said you wanted the time to show me how you changed. How you were a better person. That's what I want, too. I want to see the person you really are. Please come. I need you."

"And what about Dr. Donnelly?"

"Rob," I start, but don't know what to say next because I don't want to lie. I don't want to hesitate too long either. With no clue what else to do, I revert to the successful tactic of all the pretty, witless girls I've ever known and start crying. I sob into the phone, hoping to delay.

"Sue, please don't cry," he says.

"I'm sorry," I tell him. "I can't talk about it now. I just need you to come. Please." He doesn't say anything. I can tell he's weighing it in his mind. This is crazy. It's one o'clock in the morning and his ex is begging him to come to Georgia without any explanation. "Please, Kevin."

I see Rob come to the open doorway, lean on the frame. Kevin finally answers. "OK. I'll book the first flight out. I can drive there from Atlanta?"

"Yes," I say, wiping away my crocodile tears. "Thank you." I almost say he won't regret this, but I don't, because I know he will. I give him some barebones directions, and Rob silently makes his way over to the bed, where I'm seated and settles in next to me. I hang up and Rob rubs my back.

"You alright?"

"Nope," I say. "I can't pretend I still want to be with him, when I don't. But tomorrow I'll ask him to tell me the truth. If he doesn't, you and Luke can try to convince him."

He nods and gives me a half smile. "Sounds like a good plan," he says. "I should've known you'd come up with something fairer."

Maybe it's fairer, but it still seems less than fair to raise Kevin's hopes. Rob gives me a kiss on the cheek. "I know this is hard for you. Is there anything I can do?"

It's sweet of him to offer, but I can't think of anything that will make this easier. He and Luke can try to wheedle answers out of Kevin, but I feel like I've got the best shot of getting them. "No, nothing more for you to do. You already saved the day by figuring out the drives were doctored."

Rob rubs my arm. "You just look so sad. Do you want me to stay a bit or head down to the cottage? It's whatever you want."

I raise an eyebrow at his attitude shift. "So if I look sad, I get no arguments about me kicking you out?"

"Nope, it's not because you look sad," he says. "It's because you want it, and as your fiancé, it's my job to give you what you want."

"Can you stay for a little while longer before you go?"

He leans in and kisses me. "As long as you want."

# THURSDAY

# 26

## KELSEY

I talked to Susan a little while ago, and she said Kevin is on his way. His flight's going to arrive in Atlanta at 10:30, about an hour from now, and then he'll drive down. She's ditching Rob's suggestion that she imply Kevin has a romantic shot and just plans to convince Kevin to tell her how he figured out the drives and who he's working with. She's sure her plan will work, but Kevin has lied already, and I don't think her simply asking is going to convince him. Especially if she admits she and Rob are still together and he's got no hope of winning her back. Even though he stepped all over her heart without qualms, she refuses to do the same. It's probably the right thing to do, but I'm not particularly bothered by Kevin getting a taste of his own heart-stomping medicine.

Luke tried calling Zuri to see how she's doing at locating Penelope, but her phone goes straight to messaging. If he doesn't hear from her soon, he's going to call Jasper. We're running out of time to get this done. And I still haven't told my husband what I asked my father to do. I should. I know I need to, but every time I broach the subject of turning myself in for Penelope, he just says we still have other options so we don't need to discuss it. Plus, I don't want to fight with him. Our daughter has been kidnapped. I feel like we shouldn't be fighting. I don't have the energy to worry about Penelope and fight with him, so I haven't said anything. But, I realize I can't put off telling him indefinitely. It's already Thursday and my father hasn't brought any news. I worry it may come to what I've asked him.

I'm sitting up in the bed, pillows fluffed behind me, legs stretched out, supposedly trying to rest, as Luke instructed. But, that's hard to do when I have so much on my mind.

Luke is sitting on the chaise looking at a piece of paper he's been scribbling notes on. Ideas for plans we can use to get both Penelope and Emmie. It's all chicken scratch to me. Initials followed by a string of one or two words and more initials, with half of the items crossed out. Luke balls up the piece of paper in his hand. He's so frustrated. "Kelsey," he says to me. "Do you mind if I go for a walk down by the lake?" he asks, standing.

It's nice that he gets to get out of the house. I went for a walk last night when it was dark, but with delivery people coming in and out today, I can't leave the house. I'm confined to this room, preferably, though Susan said it's not a big deal if I go down to the kitchen, so long as the blinds are drawn.

"Wait," I say, and he walks toward me. I hear the doorbell ring. Luke stops midstride and listens. We don't hear anything out of the ordinary and assume it's a delivery. He continues toward me, sitting next to me on the bed.

"I don't have to go," he says.

I need to tell him what I asked my father, as I think it may come to that. But looking into his sweet, expectant blue eyes makes it hard. I know he'll be hurt that I went ahead and did this without talking to him first. "Yesterday, I asked my father to," I start, but have trouble getting the words out. He looks at me with patience.

There's a knock on the bedroom door, and I look toward it, thankful for this small delay. "Yes," Luke calls out.

The door opens. Susan pokes her head in, and looks at me. "Your father's here. He wants to talk to us all in the kitchen."

Luke gives me a look of curiosity and turns to Susan. "We need 30 seconds, and we're coming." Susan shuts the door, and Luke turns back to me. "You asked your father to what?"

I've lost my nerve, but I know it's essential to tell him in case my father actually did what I asked him to. I slide to the other side of the bed, get down and walk to the door. I turn back and Luke hasn't moved, but he is staring at me, confused. I say, "I told my father that if we can't figure out another way to get Penelope back, to tell the colonel I'd turn myself in."

His lips pull tight with anger, and he starts to speak but I cut him off. "They're waiting for us," I say, and turn and go out the door. OK, that was massively wrong of me, but right now I can't deal with the discussion Luke would want to have about this.

I walk quickly to the kitchen where I find my father standing near the island countertop. He is dressed in his usual work attire, a dark blue suit. Rob and Susan are seated at the oval kitchen table. I sit opposite of Rob and Susan. Luke stomps in a minute later and sits next to me. He's still smoldering, and refuses to look at anyone. Instead, he grips his hands together on the table and stares down at them.

"I have news," my father says. Luke lifts his gaze to my father. His stare is like a death ray, so cold that my father actually pauses a second and looks between Luke and me. I think he realizes Luke isn't on board with what I asked. "Zuri spoke to Haleema this morning, and she is not going to be able to find Penelope."

He says it so sure, so definite that I'm not sure what to make of it. "It hasn't been that long that she's been trying," I say.

"I know, but somebody has anticipated our moves, our helpers," my father says, slightly defeated. He sits on the edge of one of the tall bar stools poking out from under the island countertop. "She put out feelers to her sources and got nothing back. One person she trusts finally told her that someone has put out that Zuri is persona non grata at the moment, and if they do her any favors, they will suffer consequences."

Susan furrows her brow. "Who would do that?"

"She's not sure," my father responds. "The person wouldn't tell her who'd made the threat, but she doesn't think she'll be able to get anything." He looks at Luke and says, "She can't return your calls right now. If you need to get in touch with her, go through Haleema."

Luke nods, but is still giving my father such a contemptuous look that Susan and Rob are starting to stare.

Bringing attention back to himself, my father speaks again. "I, too, am getting nowhere with any queries trying to find out Penelope's whereabouts or any information on her. Someone has similarly talked to any persons they think I'd contact. Col. Parker wants us to deal with him and give him what he wants. As such, I did what Kelsey asked me to," he says, looking only at me, ignoring everyone else in the room. "I've negotiated Penelope and Emmie's release in exchange for Kelsey."

Susan gasps and turns to me looking for some type of reaction. I have nothing to give. Luke is reactionless as well. She looks back to my father for something, and he simply nods. Rob, smart man that he is, says nothing, but does place a comforting hand on Susan's back. "You can't be serious," Susan finally says.

"There's more," my father says, standing. He walks two steps to the table, turns to Rob and Susan. "Inform your caterer you'll be having two more guests." He reaches into his jacket pocket, pulls out a slip of paper and slides it onto the table. We all look at the block print letters that say: Col. John Parker. "His plus one will be," he says, sliding a second piece of paper on the table with my daughter's name written on it, "Penelope Geary."

I look at him and smile. "He's bringing her here?"

My father nods. "I've hired someone to follow him," he says. "As soon as he comes into contact with Penelope, we'll know, but it may not happen until Saturday."

He looks to Luke and says. "I know what I've agreed to, and I'm generally a man of my word, but I have no intention of letting that man walk out of here with my daughter. So, the five of us are going to come up with a plan that gets us Penelope and Emmie back but keeps Kelsey right here with us."

* * *

We filled in my father on the Kevin situation and spent the last hour or so strategizing on how to get my daughter and Emmie back without turning me over to the colonel. We've come up with the rudiments of a plan, but it's not going to work unless we get the information we need from Kevin. Susan and Rob just stepped out to deal with a wedding delivery to the small cottage in the rear.

My father looks like he might be ready to go. He's supposed to monitor the colonel Parker situation, letting us know if any issues arise. My father starts to stand, but then sits back down. "Luke," he says. "Would you mind giving Kelsey and I a minute alone?"

My husband, who seemed to have calmed down in the last hour, gives my father a look of complete incredulity and folds his arms across his chest before speaking. "The last time you and Kelsey had a minute alone, you agreed to sell her to Parker. So, I'll sit right here, if you don't mind."

I'm startled by Luke's refusal, and even more surprised when my father smiles at him, and says, "Fair enough."

Luke leans back in his chair and waits for my father to begin.

"Kelsey," he says. "When I agreed to this yesterday, you implied that your husband was on board with what you asked me to do, that he had agreed to it. While I understood his desire to get his daughter back, I was a little disappointed by how quickly he was willing to give up mine to make it happen. Only now, I see now that wasn't true."

My father frowns disapprovingly. If I could, I'd sink away. Being chided by my father in front of my husband is not my first choice of activities. My father maintains his shaming glare and continues to speak. "I had hoped to advise you privately, but I'll give you this advice with an audience. When you have important decisions to make, you shouldn't make them alone. Include your husband. Even if you think he'll disagree, include him. If you really need it, he'll help you because he loves you."

"Dad," I start to say, but he puts up a hand to shush me.

"I'm sure you'd like to say something about this being between you and me. I am your father, and you can always confide in me. But, ask yourself, what kind of marriage is that, where you confide in your father, but not your husband? "

He pauses to let his words sink in, and I feel even worse now. Out of the corner of my eye I can see that Luke is looking less hostile toward my father. "Especially when you think your spouse is going to disagree with you, it's worth getting his input."

He looks at Luke. "And it's incumbent upon your spouse to take your thoughts and concerns seriously. I remember when my wife called me as I sat in a Chicago hotel and told me she wanted help convincing the medical board to deliver a baby that couldn't live. I remember thinking that she hadn't assessed the situation accurately. That there must be a way for both of them to live. That if I could just get there and look at the situation with fresh eyes, I'd come up with a better solution, one that would save my wife and my son. Wrongly, I didn't listen to the truth of what she was saying because I didn't want it to be true. When I boarded the plane home, I was certain I would go to the hospital and come up with the perfect solution. Only, my wife and son were dead when the plane landed."

His voice is softer now, and the pain from that day almost twenty years ago is still evident in his face. He looks directly at Luke, and says, "Sometimes, we have to accept the truth of what we're being asked, even if we wish it weren't so."

I feel a lump rise in my throat, choked up and surprised my father is willing to bare his soul to us like this. "I would just like to remind you both that you have each other. In difficult times, you should rely on each other, listen to each other." He pauses, closes his eyes. "I didn't listen to my wife when she told me she needed my help, and I'll always regret that. But, I'd hate it more if she had never reached out to me for help. If she'd never sought my opinion and done something that ended up with the same result — her death — without even giving me a chance to register an opinion."

With this my father takes a deep breath and rests his hands on the table. After a moment of silence, he stands, straightens his suit jacket, gives a respectful nod to Luke and kisses the top of my head. "I'm going back to the hotel. Call me or Haleema, if you need anything," he says.

My father heads out of the kitchen and toward the front of the house. A minute later, Luke stands, the scraping of his chair the only sound in the room. "I need to think," he says, heading toward the patio exit from the kitchen. "I'm going for a walk."

I nod, and then I'm alone.

# 27

## SUSAN

I'd forgotten about the napkins. Rob & Susan, followed by Saturday's date inscribed in gold lettering in the corner. They were delivered separately, though the caterer, when she comes on Saturday is in charge of setting up the tables with them. Rob and I took them to the cottage on the property, and now I'm heading back to the house. I'd like to grab Sen. Reed before he leaves. As I wind my way to the front of the house, I see him descending the front steps.

"Lewis," I call. He turns toward my voice, and once he spots me, walks my way. "Did you have just a minute?"

He nods and we stop on the walkway when we reach each other. Birds are chirping nearby, and the tents, erected yesterday, hover like silent sentinels.

"Before I talk to Kevin, I just wanted to get some clarity about what you think is motivating him, or was motivating him. It seems like you're the person who's spoken most to him in the past couple of years."

Sen. Reed looks around at the tents, pausing for a moment to gather his thoughts. "I think it's obvious he wants you, Susan," he says. "He regrets what happened, and he thinks that maybe choosing you would give him the life he wants."

"But it's too late to choose me. He knew I was engaged, yet he came trying to woo me anyway," I say, still trying to figure it out. "He said you told him that you regretted not telling Haleema about your feelings earlier, and that motivated him."

He gives me a piercing look. "I guess I did say that to him. I apologize for not being more forthcoming earlier. I could tell I'd irritated Rob, and I thought coming clean about it being my fault was enough that I didn't need to further irritate Rob with specifics." He draws in a breath and continues. "The truth is, I told Kevin that it was never too late to try, but I thought your heart belonged to Rob. I think Kevin wants the happily ever after. I know the stereotype is that women alone want that, but relationships wouldn't work if that were true. Both people have to want it, and Kevin does. He thought he could have that with you when he proposed, but after your paralysis, he realized he wasn't able to cope. He moved on, met someone else, and then she left him, and now he wonders if he made a mistake with you. If you were supposed to be his happily ever after."

Gosh, Rob's plan would definitely feed into that. Maybe that's why Rob proposed it. He sees in Kevin that same desire the senator does: a yearning for the happy ending. "Do you think he'll tell me what I want to know if I tell him he's not going to have that happily ever after with me?"

The senator places his hand on my shoulder, and says, "Susan, I think you need to tell him the truth. He still has feelings for you, and he will appreciate honesty more than false hope."

I nod. "Yeah, I think so," I tell him. "But, I'm really afraid I can't pull this off unless he feels hopeful. I'm afraid he won't tell me the truth and you, of all people, know how important it is that we find out the truth about the drives. I want the truth, but can I really ask him for the truth while lying?"

He looks me in the eye and says, "Nothing good has ever come from me doing the wrong thing. If you do what's right, it may not work out perfectly, but I can guarantee you it will work out better than if you knowingly do something you believe is wrong."

He's right, I realize. I appreciate his moral compass. Even if it doesn't have a perfect record, it tends to be pointing in the right direction more often than not. I hug him. "Thank you, Lewis," I say.

"You're welcome, dear," he says, clapping my back gently. "I know you'll do fine with Kevin."

"And Lewis," I say as I release him. He smiles at me. "I know I was upset the other day when you said you didn't ask to get my mark removed." I take a deep breath, remembering the unfair anger I held toward him. "That was hindsight making me feel unduly upset. You judged the situation right at the time, and I had no cause for anger. I'm not angry. You've always treated me well, and I appreciate that."

He hugs me again. "Thank you, Susan. I've only wanted the best for you, and I will always do what I can to help you."

We separate and I watch as the senator goes to his car. Then I turn and head back inside. Kevin called a few minutes ago and told me his plane had landed and he was in a car headed my way. I need to get Kelsey and Rob into their places.

I decide to go around the back of the house and enter through the kitchen. Or not enter through the kitchen, if it looks like Kelsey and Luke are having a discussion. When I arrive in the back, I see Kelsey through the glass-paned door, alone at the table. When I open the door, Kelsey looks up and says, "Hey."

"Hey," I respond as I close the door, walk over, and plop down next to her in a chair. I slide my arm around her. "You alright?"

A sigh escapes her lips and she gives me a half smile. "Not yet, but if this works, if we get Penelope back, I'll be fine."

I scrutinize her face: full of false optimism. If we can get Kevin to talk and use what he says so we don't have to turn Kelsey over to the colonel, then everything will be fine. But, if this doesn't work, if we have to use Kelsey's plan, her daughter will be safe and she won't be. I can tell she is just holding on by a thread, so I won't push her on how she is. "How is Luke?"

At this, her face falls and she shrugs. "You should probably ask him," she tells me, defeated.

I take my hand from around her neck and put it on the armrest of her chair, which swivels. I give the rest a little push, to pivot her around so she's facing me. "What's going on with you two?"

She looks down at her hands folded in her lap. "I thought it was obvious to everyone."

"You didn't tell Luke your plan to turn yourself over to the colonel, and he's not happy with it?"

She looks up at me smiling. "See, it was obvious."

"I'm not happy with it either," I tell her. "Kelsey, as someone who grew up without a mother, you should know your daughter wants you a whole hell of a lot more than she wants some grand sacrifice in her name."

Her eyes widen at this, and her lips purse in anger. "As much as Penelope might miss me, I'm sure she'll be glad to be alive and well."

Kelsey's eyebrows are raised in challenge and her face is just daring me to say something contradictory. But I think it's best to just let the issue die on the vine. I nod and reach my hand up to scratch my neck. "Kevin is going to be here soon," I tell her. "I thought you and Rob could watch from the secret room. I'll start off talking to Kevin, and if he doesn't budge from his story, I'll ask for Luke's assistance convincing him. Kevin always liked Luke."

"Well, I have to admit, good taste in companions was never one of Kevin's faults," Kelsey says.

I lean back in my chair and scowl. "I'm over it," I tell her. "You should let it go, too, especially since we need his help to save Penelope."

She stares at me a moment, as if I've said the unthinkable. "If you convince him to help us, then I will change my tune about Kevin," Kelsey tells me. I smile. So does Kelsey, but then it fades away, as she looks toward the patio door. I turn and see Luke come inside.

There is tension in the room, and I am clearly a third wheel. "I need to find Rob," I say, standing, so I can extricate myself from their discussion.

"Actually, I just saw him," Luke says. "He's on his way up." He walks over to us, holds out his hand to Kelsey. She takes it and stands. "We'll get out of your hair," Luke says, as he tows Kelsey out of the room.

# 28

## KELSEY

Luke is leading me back to our room, his hand clenched tightly around mine. It seems like so long since we've held hands that it could have been another lifetime ago. Everything before this happened seems like a lifetime ago. A dream world where I had the most beautiful little girl with red curls and a honey smile, all sugar and spice and everything nice. And this is like a nightmare I'd like to wake up from, so I could hold my sweetheart again, and feel good knowing it had all been a bad dream.

We go inside our room, with Luke still holding my hand, as he guides me to the bed, where he sits and I follow suit. I look down at his hand, folded around mine, and wonder what he's thinking. If he's still angry or if my father's talk has caused him to have an epiphany of some sort.

My gaze wanders past his hand, up his arm, to his shoulder, neck and finally to his face. His jaw is clenched and his eyes somber.

"I'm sorry I went to him without telling you," I say to my husband, meaning it. My father was right about that. Luke is my husband and disagree or not, I should have told him before I asked my father to do that.

He squeezes my hand gently and gazes down at my hand in his. "I was hurt when I found out what you did," he says. "And I don't ever want you to cut me out like that. But, I think maybe I didn't make it easy for you to tell me what you wanted to do."

A soft chuckle escapes my lips. "No you didn't," I say.

He frowns. "Kelsey," he says, reaching his hand up to my chin and angling it so I need to look him in the eye. "If I kept trying to tell you I was going to throw myself in the lion's den, and there was nothing you could do to stop it, would you say, 'Hey, that's great Luke. Rest in peace'?"

I grimace. "Don't be flip," I say. "And this isn't what I want to do, Luke. This is what needs to be done if we're going to get our daughter back. In case you've forgotten, our daughter is only gone because of me. FoSS doesn't want her. It wants me."

Luke puts a single finger to my lips. "Please," he says. "I don't want to fight with you. I just want us to work together to get our daughter back."

I don't want to fight with him either. Something about him saying that, about his expressing his desire to not fight, to be the opposite of that — a team, makes me feel a sudden relief. Like a load of heavy sacks has just been lifted from my shoulders. I lean forward and rest my head on his shoulder. "That's all I want, too, Luke," I tell him, as I feel hot tears pour down my cheeks. "I just want us to be a team and get our little girl back."

Luke pulls me closer and rubs my back gently. He whispers in my ear that it will be OK, and I want to believe him even though I know I shouldn't. Everything might not be OK. We don't have any proof that I wasn't supposed to be marked. Our plan for getting Emmie out is weak, and we will only see Penelope on Saturday, when she comes here with the colonel. If we don't have something else to bargain with, something like proof of dishonesty in the marking process, then I have to go with the man who plans to kill me. Though, probably not before parading me before the world to say how bad I am. I lay there in Luke's arms for I'm not sure how long. There is no reason to look up and inspect the time, as being with my husband seems the most important thing, given the circumstances. But then Luke pulls away.

"I know you're scared for Penelope," he says, then swallows. "I'd love to say that I am strong and all-knowing and not scared. But I am. I'm scared that something bad will happen to our daughter. So, we're in the same boat, OK?"

I nod and wipe a few remnants of tears from my cheeks.

"If the time comes that you have to do what you proposed," he says, the words catching in his throat, as if he's not sure he really wants to say them. "If that time comes, you, um, you can do what needs to be done, but please don't pull the ripcord too soon on this. We still have time. And we still have options available."

Options. Time. Neither in the quantity I'd like to have them. There's a knock at the door. "Come in," Luke says.

I turn and see Rob. He realizes he's interrupted something, so he hangs back, just barely poking his head in. "Kevin will be here in 10 minutes," he says. "Susan thought Kelsey and I should watch from the secret room, and Luke, you can wait in the kitchen in case she needs you. I'm going to run to the restroom. I'll be back in one minute."

Rob turns and exits. I laugh. "You scared him away."

Luke laughs too. "No, that was definitely you who did the scaring." Then he strokes my cheek softly. "This is the first step of our plan working out. You watch and see. Susan will get Kevin to tell us what we need to know."

* * *

Rob and I are physically closer than we've ever been, our heads practically touching as we peer through the grate into the main hall to watch Susan and Kevin. We'd been sitting on the floor, on opposite sides of the grate, for the last five minutes. But the doorbell just rang, and he and I both turned onto our knees and stuck our faces near the opening so we could watch.

Susan answers the door, and there is Kevin, looking just as weasely as ever. He immediately grabs Susan and pulls her into a hug. Rob's entire body clenches. This can't be easy for him, even though he suggested Susan do this. Maybe it was a bad idea for him to watch.

Susan manages to detangle herself from Kevin. "What's wrong, Sue?" he asks. "What is going on?"

Her face looks grim and nervous, and I wonder briefly what Kevin makes of it. I know she is nervous because she has to do this right, because our plan depends on getting this information. But Kevin probably believes the nerves root from some problem that he can step in to and solve so that he can be her knight in shining armor.

"What did he do to you?" Kevin asks. "Did Rob hurt you?"

Susan shakes her head. "No, no. Of course not," she says, turning to the side and pointing to the chaise opposite the grate Rob and I are looking out from. "Sit down, and I'll explain."

Worry lines crease his forehead, but Kevin doesn't argue with her. He walks over and sits at one end of the chaise. Susan sits next to him and takes both his hands in hers. From the corner of my eye, I see Rob grimace. Yeah, it was definitely a bad idea for him to watch.

"Kevin, I need to talk to you about the drives," Susan says.

Kevin's shoulders are taut with tension, and he leans in closer to her. "The drives?"

"Yes, the drives," Susan says.

Kevin pulls his hands from Susan's and slides away from her. He looks toward the door, as if debating whether to bolt. "You called me in the middle of the night, telling me you needed me, crying, saying you couldn't talk about it but I had to come, making it seem life or death, and you just wanted to talk about the drives?"

Susan's face melts into apology. "I'm sorry, Kevin," she says. "I realize I should've been more forthcoming. I just didn't think you'd come, unless —"

He stands up and shakes his head in disgust. "Sue, the one thing I've always loved about you is your honesty. I can't believe you would tell me you wanted to spend time with me, see how I'd changed, when all you wanted was more info on those drives." He throws his hands up in the air and raises his voice. "And what is it that you don't have? I've given you the keys to the kingdom — everything you need to prove you shouldn't have been marked. That wasn't enough?"

Susan rises and puts her hand on his shoulder. "The data on the drives is forged," Susan says. "It's not what you said it was."

Kevin takes a step back from her, pulling himself free of her grip. He scrutinizes her face, as if he can ferret out whether she's lying.

"Somebody tampered with the drives," Susan says softly.

Incredulity pours out of him. "And you're accusing me?"

Susan shakes her head. "No, I'm not accusing you." She takes a step closer, looks at him all doe-eyed and says, "I know you would never do that to me. You would never do something like that, something that would hurt me like that."

Puh-lease. I see Rob rolling his eyes. Kevin hurt her in much worse ways than giving her a phony drive, yet the schmuck looks like he believes her. I've got to hand it to Susan; she gets how to talk to Kevin.

Kevin seems to soften. "I'm really confused, Sue," he says, reaching out and touching her cheek. She doesn't even flinch, which surprises me, and maybe even Kevin too, as it seems her reaction to his touch — or non-reaction to be more precise — puts him at ease.

"Sit down with me," Susan says.

Kevin sighs and goes back to the chaise with her.

"We did some looking at the drives, and they've been tampered with. There was a suggestion that you know something about that?"

"A suggestion?" Kevin scowls. "Let me guess: Blondilocks thinks I did it."

Susan gives Kevin a chastising look, and Rob grits his teeth next to me. Susan manages a direct, non-accusatory tone when she speaks. "Just tell me how you got the drives?"

"I told you already, from the storage facility in Baltimore?"

Susan gives him an exasperated sigh. "And how did you know to get them?"

"I told you, I found out where the backups were kept, so I went there."

Susan tucks some hair behind her ear, closes her eyes, takes a deep breath and opens them again. "When I asked you to come, I told you I wanted to see who you were, how you'd changed. I want to believe that you're the person you said you are, a person who's better than the man who couldn't come to my aid when I needed him most. I didn't lie to you when I said I needed you. I do. I need you. I need you to be honest with me about how you got these drives."

She reaches her hands out and takes his into her own. "I know you have never done much with computers, and the knowledge it would take to figure this out, based on finding a note in a drawer is beyond your skills."

At this Kevin looks wounded and tries to pull his hand from Susan's, but she holds on. She keeps steady eye contact, the kind of open, innocence on her face that anyone would feel bad lying to.

"I'm not judging you or saying you're a bad person. I'm saying, whatever happened with this letter and these drives up to this point is behind us. I want us to start fresh, right now, you and me. The past is the past. I just want the truth. A lot is at stake. Things you don't even know are riding on this. I need the information you have. I need it the way I needed you to be by my side after my marking surgery. I need you to show me that you can be here for me this time."

Susan so knows how to guilt trip someone. If he doesn't cave in, he really is a heartless bastard.

Kevin looks at Susan's face, and his resolve to stonewall appears to be disintegrating, but then some thought occurs to him and his face goes cold again. "What about Rob?"

Susan doesn't miss a beat. "Rob and I are getting married on Saturday."

"So, I came here for nothing?" His face colors and his eyes light with fury.

Susan waits a moment for his jaw to slacken and the burst of hostility to subside, then shakes her head and speaks gently. "You came here to show me you've changed. You came here to show me that you're a different person from three years ago. You're a different person from the man who abandoned me when I most needed him. I'd like to see that you are. I don't want you to abandon me again, not when I most need your help. Please don't do that to me again, Kevin."

Kevin looks down at Susan's hands holding his. He doesn't speak, just stares at her hands for a long while, as if having some type or internal debate. Finally, he lifts his head and says, "If I tell you, you have to swear to me that you won't tell him I told you." Susan is already nodding, so he continues speaking. "He's been good to me, and if there's some problem, I'm sure it's not his fault. He wants to see this error pointed out as much as anybody. He got me the job with Dr. Rounds, and he doesn't believe in the current marking system."

Susan gives another reassuring nod and leans in, as curious as I am about what Kevin is about to say. "Who is it?"

"Dr. Grant," he says.

# 29

## SUSAN

I hear Kelsey gasp, so I make a choking noise, praying Kevin didn't notice the sound from the vent. I'm shocked enough that I can't formulate anything to say. Finally, I sputter, "Dr. Stephen Grant?"

Kevin nods. "Yes," he says. "He said he'd always thought it was weird that you and Kelsey were marked so close in time to each other. Said that was the main reason he'd gotten involved in helping with your surgery. He'd contacted Patricia Donnelly when he heard about the spinal recalibration technique and even suggested you as the first patient."

I think I'm going to vomit. I put my hand on my stomach, trying to steady it, and take a deep breath.

"Sue, are you OK?" Kevin asks, leaning toward me. "Are you sick."

I shake my head no and try to pull myself together. Kelsey, Luke and Penelope are counting on me, but all I can think of is what Kevin said. "Dr. Grant suggested me as the first patient?"

Kevin nods as he tries to figure out what is going on with me. Why I look pale and stricken. He doesn't know. Very few people know that I didn't just find out about a surgery that could reverse my paralysis and then go in for it. I was kidnapped and held hostage by the people who wanted me to have it. And Dr. Grant suggested it? God, I can't even wrap my mind around it. Maybe he lied to Kevin about this. Maybe he didn't suggest me. But why would he lie about it? If he's telling the truth, that means Dr. Grant is responsible for my kidnapping, for me being held captive for almost a year and then nearly murdered.

"Sue, let me check you out," Kevin says, frowning with concern.

He reaches into his shoulder bag, and pulls out an LMS reader. It's a small rectangular device about eight inches long and two inches wide and deep. All doctors have one. "You really don't look good."

I need a minute to think, so I simply shove my arm in his direction, and he waves the reader over the LMS in my arm.

"Your heart rate's a little high," he says, looking at the readings. "Your blood pressure's good, cholesterol is fine, oxygen level is normal." He pauses a second, looking at the screen on his reader, then he scrunches up his face in confusion. "Sue, your medical file is locked."

I wish he hadn't said that. "I know," I say, deciding to tell him the story I concocted the other day. "Given that my marking file was tampered with, and we still didn't know who did it, I asked my doctor to lock it. She said it would unlock if a doctor declared it a medical emergency."

"That's true. I can unlock it by declaring an emergency override," he admits with hesitation. "But those are always investigated, so doctors prefer not to have to do that. Plus, most people leave it open so anyone examining them can have a look. I wanted to see if you had any conditions that might be contributing to your current problem."

I've got to focus, get him back talking about Dr. Grant. "I'm fine," I say, sliding my arm away from him. "I saw Dr. Grant a fair amount for pre- and post-surgery exams. He never said anything about his suspicions that my marking wasn't genuine." While it's true that Dr. Grant never said he thought something was wrong with my marking results, I barely saw him prior to my surgery. But I need to provide Kevin some type of explanation for the shock I'm not able to hide.

"I know," he says, and I look up at him, my eyes wide in astonishment. "He told me he saw you and the good doctor often. He didn't think Blondilocks was a good fit for you."

I look down at my lap. Dr. Grant has some nerve. He did this. He set Kevin on me. I ignore the dig about Rob and me when I speak. "So, he suspected for a long time? Why didn't he say anything? And how did you two come to be so close? I thought you'd only met him once." And that one time Kevin made a bad impression. Nothing as obvious as tripping over his words like a nervous Nelly, or insulting the good doctor. He'd just talked too much about himself, and I could tell that Dr. Grant had marked Kevin as conceited and written him off.

"It's the funniest thing," Kevin says, smiling at the memory, his perceived kismet of it all. "He was giving a guest lecture about a year and a half ago, and I spoke to him afterward. He remembered that you and I had been dating, gave me his card. We kept in touch and a few months back, he called to let me know Dr. Rounds had an internship opening up. Said he'd put in a word for me."

I nod. "He did this because he suspected Rounds was altering people's markings in exchange for political favors?"

Kevin tilts back, apparently surprised at the direction I'm going in. His smile wanes and he wags his head in the negative. "No, he just thought I'd like it. He didn't become suspicious Dr. Rounds was involved until later."

I nod my head yet again. I can't believe he doesn't see it. Dr. Grant played him. Completely and totally played him from their serendipitous meeting to this internship with Rounds. "So, you found the letter, and then told Dr. Grant?"

"Um, well," he looks a little sheepish. "I actually didn't find the letter. Dr. Grant did. But, because he didn't want anyone to know he was involved, he thought it was best that I say I found it."

I smile and try not to reveal my amazement at how he let Dr. Grant manipulate him. How does he not see what happened? "And Dr. Grant hacked into the logs?"

"Yes," says Kevin. "When he found out the actual information was on the backup drives, he sent me to Baltimore to get the backups. I did that."

"You did? You actually got the drives yourself?"

"Yes," he assures me, nodding emphatically.

"And they're the same drives you gave to me?"

He pauses. "Essentially," he says. "Dr. Grant had to verify the data on them before I could give them to you."

Of course. I can see the wheels turning in Kevin's head. Even to him this is starting to look fishy. "Listen, Kevin, thank you for being honest with me," I tell him. "I need some time to digest all this." I stand and wait a second for him to rise with me. When he does, I say, "Could you stick around till tomorrow. I can put you up at the hotel. It's the same one Sen. Reed is staying at. The Peachtree on Maple Ave."

He sighs and gives me an apathetic shrug. "I'm already here, and I hadn't booked a return flight, so it won't kill me to stay the night."

"Thank you," I say, glad he agreed to stay. I give him a hug and walk him to the door. Once it's shut behind him, I walk toward the grate, say, "Kitchen," and head in that direction.

Luke is standing in the hallway. "Did you hear?" I ask

He nods, his face grim. We head back into the kitchen and Rob and Kelsey wander in a minute later. Kelsey sits opposite Luke and I at the table. Rob closes the curtains near the French doors, then paces the floor.

"So, Dr. Grant knew this whole time?" Luke asks me. "Ever since you were marked?"

I give an uncertain heave. "I don't know. Maybe. It sounds like he suspected ever since Kelsey got marked."

Kelsey leans forward. "But, he never said anything to me," she says, looking to Luke, as if he might have some insight. "Why wouldn't he say anything to us? We could've used this then."

Luke's nostrils flare and his eyes are rock hard. "Maybe because he did it."

Luke's body is tense and hostile. "Did what?" I ask.

"Moved you and Kelsey to the top of the list."

I turn to him with a mix of confusion and disbelief. "But that doesn't make any sense, Luke. Why would he move me to the top of the list? He barely knew me at the time I was marked."

"But he knew you were close to Kelsey's father. He's been working pro-choice for a long time. He wants marked people to volunteer. What better way to get the public to support it than by showing that politicians can get their friends and loved ones off the list? He hated Kelsey's dad, and getting him to have you moved would have been the perfect way to bring him down."

I look at Luke, his face sure and unyielding.

"But my dad wouldn't," Kelsey says, cutting off her final word abruptly as she looks at me. She looks sheepish and starts again. "What I meant was, my dad didn't think it was necessary."

"It wasn't necessary," I say, trying to allay her concerns, but still feeling haunted by the memories of how my surgery went wrong.

Kelsey nods, then says, "So my father doesn't take the bait with Susan, she has the surgery, and it goes wrong."

Rob stops pacing and turns to us. "In August, three months after Susan's surgery, Dr. Grant contacts me and says he can be of help on the project I'm working on."

I'm trying to contain my emotions, but my entire body trembles. I'm not sure if it's the anger at Dr. Grant, or the terror at knowing that all this could have been avoided, that somebody has been playing God with my life. Rob sees my distress, comes over, and kneels at my side. "I had no idea, Susan," he tells me. "I thought he just wanted to be involved in this project, not that he felt guilty about causing your problems."

I close my eyes and take a deep breath. "I know you didn't know," I say to Rob. Nobody knew. I open my eyes and turn back to Luke. "So, when he failed with getting the senator to try to help me, he decided he'd try again, figuring the senator would surely help his own daughter?"

Kelsey balls her hands together in fists. "When he suggested I ask for my father's help, I just thought he was trying to be helpful. I just thought he cared." She pounds the table with her right fist. "He cared alright. He cared about furthering his own ends."

Rob puts his hand on my knee, and I turn to look at him. "You OK?" he mouths.

Nope. Not okay. But I nod that I'm alright, because my feelings aren't what's important now. "Rob," I say in a voice loud enough to carry across the room. "Is there a way to prove Dr. Grant did it, to prove he moved us?"

Rob stands and looks around the room at the three of us. He bites his lower lip a second and then says. "I think these are the original drives. They've just been doctored." Rob folds his arms across his chest. "But, if I were going to doctor the originals. The first thing I'd do is make a copy of the original hard drives in case something went wrong. The second thing I'd do is get rid of any incriminating evidence once I was sure I'd properly doctored the originals."

Luke blows out a breath. "He's too good to have kept them," he says, bitterness seeping out. "Our only proof is probably gone."

"What if it isn't?" Kelsey says. "What if he kept a copy?"

Rob shrugs. "We wouldn't be able to authenticate it."

"But if we got someone the copy, would it be enough to help us negotiate?"

I don't think it would, but Kelsey looks so desperate for a positive response, I say, "Maybe."

"Luke," Kelsey says. "Zuri still works for him. Ask her to search his office. See if he's got it there. Or something else that could be proof."

Luke nods. "OK, I'll go to the hotel to see your father and Haleema."

Luke heads off, and Kelsey goes with him. I go and get myself a glass of ice water. I'm still reeling over the most recent revelations. As I sit down at the table to drink, I feel Rob's hand on my shoulder. When I turn to look at him, his face is brimming with concern, and I wonder if something more is wrong.

"Are you sure you're alright?" he asks as he sits in a chair across from mine.

He's worried about me. It's sweet. "It's just a lot to digest. I'm fi-ne."

"I'm here for you, if you need me," Rob says reassuringly. "You don't have to deal with everything on your own. You can lean on me."

"I know," I say, touching his hand.

"You didn't have to go to someone else to lock your medical file?"

Actually, I did. Only my doctor of record can do it, and Rob isn't my doctor. I take another sip of water, trying to figure out the best way to respond. "With everything going on — the wedding, trying to figure out these drives — it just seemed like it was something I could get done on my own," I say, then smile. "It didn't seem like a big deal."

"A lock on your file is kind of a big deal. Most people leave it open, so they can get help in an emergency," he says.

"Dr. Peters said my file would unlock if my LMS sent a distress call; or if a doctor put in an emergency override request. Really, it's not a problem."

Rob studies me intently, as if he can tell I'm hiding something.

"If it bothers you, I can unlock it," I say casually. "I'm sure Dr. Peters can get it done once the weekend's over."

He studies his hands in his laps, then looks up at me, and says. "You can leave it locked. Just next time let me know. It's just one more thing Kevin's known about you before I have."

I stroke his cheek. "I'm sorry I didn't mention it," I say. "I was partly hoping to keep Kevin out of my files when I did it. I certainly didn't mean to make you feel left out."

He kisses my hand. "No problem. I know now, but know that you can always ask me for help, even if I'm busy with other stuff."

"I know, and I will. Promise."

He smiles, then adds, "You know, if you want, I can lock him out of your LMS."

I'm confused. "Just him?"

He nods again, smiling. "Yeah, you know, the LMSes we have? I installed a backdoor way in, so I could access them anytime."

Because LMSes provide tracking data, Rob and I removed ours when I escaped my captivity. But Rob felt the benefits of having an LMS in an emergency were important enough that we should get new ones. Only, he reprogrammed the LMS so it would only submit our location data if the emergency distress alarm went off. The rest of the time, the LMS Data Center, where most LMS info is tracked, isn't able to find it.

"What do you do with the backdoor?"

"Mainly, it lets me check the data that's been sent to the LMS Data Center to make sure they're not trying to ping your LMS for location information. It also allows me to do some remote reprogramming if necessary."

I shake my head. "I want to forget about Kevin," I tell him. "I'm getting married in two days and Kevin is the very last person I want either of us focused on." I lean in and kiss Rob. "I love you. So, let's just work on getting Penelope back and getting married, and nothing more to do with Kevin, OK?"

"Alright," Rob says.

# 30

## KELSEY

Luke hasn't come back from my father's yet, and I'm in our room pacing back and forth. It's hard for me to sit still, or else I start thinking about Penelope and then I start feeling helpless and weeping. I know it's not good for me, but I'm not sure anything else would be normal.

So, instead, I've been pacing the room, crawling through the tunnel into the secret room, going over the plan for the wedding in my head. Doing anything I can to keep my mind off my daughter, who is suffering right now, probably more than me because at least I can make sense of what is going on. She has no idea why she was taken from us. She must feel abandoned, like I just left her. And the worst part is that she's right. I did just leave her. I shouldn't have gotten out of the car. I go over the day in my mind again and again. I knew I shouldn't get out of the car. I knew I needed to lock him out. And when I couldn't, I made a stupid, split-second decision to flop out, to try to draw attention to us, when I should have thought about staying with Penelope. I should've thought about not leaving her side, even if it meant we were both stuck with psycho Greg.

The two-tone ring of the doorbell pulls me away from my thoughts. I know Luke would not ring the bell. Rob gave him a key to the back door, and he is to use that. This is a visitor. One of the many deliveries for the wedding. I am near the closet, and decide to go into the little room to watch. It will give me something to do, something to think about other than Penelope and my mistakes that led to her being taken.

At the grate in the secret room, I watch Susan open the front door. I don't have the best view here, especially with the bright sunlight streaming in, creating glare.

Susan closes the door slightly, a weird move, as no one has said anything. Then, she tilts her head so it just sticks out of the narrow opening she's left. "What is it that you want?" Her voice is terse and wary.

A loud, tough voice responds. "Ma'am, we have orders from Col. John Parker to deliver this package to Susan Harper or Dr. Samuel Donnelly."

Susan is unusually still, as if caught between uncertainty and fear. Finally, she reaches her hand through the crack. "Give it to me, please."

"Ma'am," the voice says again, in a clearly authoritative twang, "I need to see some identification."

I see Rob crossing the room, probably coming from the kitchen, to join Susan. "What's going on," he asks, pulling her aside.

The man at the door explains again and Rob produces some type of ID that is scanned. The man hands Rob a small square package, to which Rob responds, "Thank You," and closes the door. I watch a moment more; Rob and Susan look at each other, as if each expecting the other to offer up an explanation.

After a moment of silence, Rob pulls the brown parcel paper from the box, which fits in the palm of his hand. Susan moves closer to him to see, blocking my view. At this I decide I need to come out. I scurry back, and as I'm coming out of the secret room, there is a knock at my door. "Kelsey," Susan calls.

"Come in," I say, shutting the closet door. She enters and heads straight for me, her face drained of color, lips parted slightly and her hand outstretched, holding a sheet of paper that had once been folded into sections.

I take the paper from her. In tidy script, appear the words: "I look forward to seeing you Saturday. Sen. Reed wanted this as a token of good faith. Dr. Donnelly is welcome to authenticate it. It's genuine." It is signed, Col. John Parker.

"What did he send?" I ask, clutching the paper tighter.

"A chip," Susan says. "Rob is bringing something to watch it on."

No sooner does she say this than Rob breezes into the room, a little winded, holding up a tablet. Walking straight to the bed, he sets it in the middle, so all three of us can see as we stand at the foot of the bed.

He inserts the chip and a moment later, a video appears. There is a crib, and Penelope is sound asleep on the mattress. The camera zooms in and I can see the rise and fall of her chest. Next to her in the crib, is a flat screen, with a news program playing, the volume low. The reporter is talking, and as she heads into commercial, she mentions the time, 8 am and today's date. This video was taken to-day. And Penelope is OK. I feel solace in knowing that she's OK, that they do have her and that she is alive.

I pick up the tablet and lift it close to my face, so I can get a better look at her. Her eyes look puffy and the veins in her eyelids seem too pronounced. She's been crying. Bawling her eyes out because she thinks her parents have abandoned her. But she's managed to fall asleep and get a moment of peace, which is good. If she has to be gone from us, I want her to have peace.

Her little arm moves and she rolls from her back to her side, the side opposite me. Now I can't see her face anymore and it literally hurts. It feels like I've been kicked in the gut. And then, bam, the video cuts off. It's like someone slapped me to finish me off.

A circular arrow appears and I know it will replay if I hit it. I press the button. I watch again, the clip is probably only a minute long, but it's the only minute I've had with my little girl since Monday. I watch it again, and don't care that Rob and Susan are staring at me with pity. I just want to see my little girl and know that she is alive. For sure. Alive and breathing.

"Kelsey," Rob says, and I look up. "I'd like to take a look at that, just to see if I can authenticate that this is from today." The words sound regretted as soon as they leave his lips.

I pick up the tablet and pull it to my chest, wrapping my arms around it. "Let me look at it for a little bit more," I plead. "And you can check it out after."

Susan puts a hand on his shoulder and smiles at me. "Sure, Kel-sey, that will be fine. Rob and I are going to go and wait for Luke to get back."

I nod my head and return my attention to the video. I press play again and watch her sleep. I need to get her back. I'll do anything to get her back.

# 31

## SUSAN

Rob and I have gone outside to the back patio. Kelsey always stays inside during the day, so there's no chance she'll come out and overhear us. It's warm and sunny, and not too humid.

"I shouldn't have asked her for the chip," Rob says, after he's closed the French door to the kitchen. "I'm sorry. That was insensitive."

I shake my head. "No, you just wanted to help," I tell him. "I was hoping she would give it to you. I know it gives her comfort to know that Penelope is alive still, but I'm not sure it's healthy for her to keep watching it, to be so fixated. Or maybe it's fine. I just don't know. She was doing okay, I thought, until she got that. Now she seems so fragile."

Rob nods, "I know. She just needs time with it."

I take a seat on a patio chair and look up at Rob. "So what do you think you can tell by examining it?"

Rob shrugs. "Probably not a whole lot. But, I want to blow it up, look for any signs that images were cut together, that the flatscreen wasn't really in the room with her. Signs that this isn't some trick. Maybe see if there is a clue to where she is, though given how limited the footage was, and how thorough the colonel is, I doubt there's anything in there to help us locate her."

I hear labored breathing and footsteps nearby. Rob and I both turn to look in the direction of the noise. We see Luke jog around the corner of the house and into view. He slows when he sees us, and approaches apprehensively.

Rob's face or mine must betray something wrong because Luke looks as if he wants to ask what the trouble is, but Rob beats him to the chase, asking, "Were you able to contact Zuri?"

Luke takes a minute, his train of thought clearly interrupted by the question. "Umm, yeah," he says, after a moment. "She's OK with looking around Dr. Grant's office to see what she can find. He still trusts her and she has access to the office for most things anyway. He's out of town, so it shouldn't be too hard for her to snoop."

I smile. "That's good news," I say, trying to look optimistic. Rob seems to be looking at me, rather than Luke. I feel awkward, as I'm not quite ready to be the one to tell him that a video of his kidnapped daughter came, and that his wife has become unhinged watching it on repeat.

Luke stares, apparently sensing my misgivings. "Did something happen while I was out?"

I guess he needs to know. "Lewis requested proof that Penelope is alive and unharmed," I say. Luke's eyes widen with anticipation. "A recording came showing Penelope. It's very short and it looks to be from this morning."

"Is she alright?"

"She was sleeping in the recording," Rob says, not mentioning that she looked like she'd passed out of sheer exhaustive crying. "She didn't look mistreated."

"Is Kelsey in our room?" Luke asks.

I nod and Luke brushes past us into the house. With him gone, I look up at Rob. "I should go with you guys tonight," I say.

He shakes his head. "Susan, you don't want to go back to that place. They held you there. You almost died there."

True. But I still should go. "I think Luke will be less inclined to cross the line if I come," I say. "After today, after the video, after seeing what Greg did to his daughter, after seeing Kelsey so upset, I'm not sure he'll restrain himself if it's just the two of you."

Rob looks skeptical. "You think that your mere presence will stop him beating his brother-in-law to death?"

I frown at his sarcasm. "He's not going to murder anyone," I say, though I'm not entirely sure of it, as Luke was never crazy about the principles of Life First. And given that he lives in a country that abandoned those principles, I have to wonder what he'll do to Greg.

Rob runs his fingers through his hair and sighs. "OK, he's not going to kill Greg, but this is not going to be a pleasant meeting. And I think you'd be safer here."

I look at him genuinely. "I'll be plenty safe with you two. And, I think me coming will help keep Luke focused on the plan: saving both Emmie and Penelope with Greg's assistance."

Rob bites his lower lip, as he searches his mind for reasons I should stay. "Kelsey would probably like some company."

I shake my head. "No, we talked about it earlier; she'd like me to go, keep an eye on him."

Rob is silent, and looks as if he's going to suggest another reason I shouldn't come, but just says, "Fine." He pauses and speaks deliberately. "You can come, but you and Luke stay in the barn on the adjacent property. I'll go meet Fitzpatrick, the security director. He'll bring me Greg. I'll bring him down to the barn. If anything goes wrong, you and Luke just leave, OK?"

I nod.

# 32

## KELSEY

I am lying on my stomach, Penelope's monkey Mr. Giggles lying next to me, with the tablet propped on a pillow, watching Penelope in the video. I hear the door open, turn and see Luke enter, his lips a grim line as he crosses straight to me.

I smile at him, the motion feeling unfamiliar, as it seems like ages since I've smiled. "Look," I say, sitting up, grabbing the tablet and thrusting it toward him. "She's OK."

And as I say the words, it hits me that maybe she isn't OK now. That's just how she was a few hours ago. I don't know if they've done something awful to her since, and I won't know until we get her back.

Luke takes the device and sits down next to me on the bed. I lean my head on his shoulder as he watches the video. When the movie playback is over, he sets the tablet on the bed next to him. He wraps an arm around me and kisses the top of my head.

"You alright?"

I shake my head. "No," I say. "But, I'm better than I was before. It's good to know something, even if it's from a few hours ago, even if I don't know how she is now. I just feel better seeing her, even knowing she's not happy. Knowing they haven't lied to us about keeping her safe gives me hope that they'll keep their word about the rest, if that makes any sense."

"Yeah baby, it does," Luke whispers, giving me a gentle squeeze.

We sit there in silence for a bit, with Luke stroking my arm. I wonder what he's thinking. He hasn't said what he thought of the video. "You alright?"

With a gentle chuckle, he says, "I've been better." He releases me and I turn to look at him. With his hair shorn so short and the bags under his eyes, he looks older, tired, broken even. I wonder briefly how I've not noticed this rapid change in him, how this situation is wearing on him. I've been too wrapped up in my own misery and counting on my husband to be my rock, forgetting that he needs a rock, too.

"I'm sorry I've been a mess, Luke," I tell him, taking his hand into my own, looking into the depths of his blue eyes, though they seem to have lost their sparkle. "I appreciate how strong you've been for me these last few days. And I'm sorry I haven't been there to help you back."

"Kelsey," he says, his eyes seeming to find strength in my apology. "You've been everything I needed. Just knowing you're safe has been keeping me going. The only thing that's got me down is knowing this might end with me losing you."

I close my eyes, wishing he hadn't said that. Wishing he hadn't brought this up again. I don't want to look at that as a possibility, yet I am committed to trading myself for my daughter when it comes to that. And I mean when, because I don't think this plan they've hatched will work. But instead of saying that, I take a deep breath and smile, my lips feeling more forced than they did a few minutes ago. "You're not going to lose me," I try to inject the spirit of truth in those words, even though they are lies. "The plan is good, Luke."

He nods dispiritedly.

I stroke the hand cradled in mine with the top of my thumb, then crinkle my eyebrows as I remember where he's come from. "Did my father say something to upset you?"

"No," he says, his head bobbing back and forth adamantly. "No. He's really psyched about the plan."

And it sets in to me that my husband realizes my father's political ticks as well as I do. Dad can try a little too hard if he thinks something isn't quite going to work. It's not a rah-rah cheerleader enthusiasm, so much as a repetition of details, a drilling down into minutiae that should be irrelevant. His desire to show he's covered all his bases may reassure some people, but to me, it's always been a sign that he's worried he's forgotten something crucial and that by going over it again and again he hopes to see his error.

I love my husband, and I can't lie to him right now. I lean and hug him. Wrapping my arms around him feels so good, so familiar, so wonderful. I whisper in his ear. "The most important thing is she'll be back and safe on Saturday."

# 33

## SUSAN

Luke hasn't said anything since Rob left us here in the barn. My fiancé went up the hill to the compound where Greg is and will bring him back, so we can talk freely. The place was bugged last time I was there, so even if we could go in without arousing suspicion, it wouldn't be a safe place to discuss the plan with Greg.

Luke is standing in the corner, entirely too intense right now, with a look of complete concentration on his face. I'm hesitant to talk to him when he is like this: a bundle of explosives wound tightly into a little ball. Talking to him seems like it might set off the boom, but I don't want Greg to perform that detonation either.

"Remember, we need Greg's help," I say softly, hoping Luke will settle down a bit. That some of the energy he's keeping pent up inside will dissipate.

Luke runs his fingers through his buzz cut and strides across the room to me. He is no less intense when he says in a low and ferocious voice, "I know what we need from Greg. I won't jeopardize that."

I nod and offer a look of reassurance, but I don't believe him. He looks like he might strangle his brother-in-law. We both hear the creaking of the barn door and turn to see it open just wide enough for a person to fit through. In walks Greg, who I've only seen in pictures. He's a robust man, which is not captured in photographs. He's shorter than Rob, and burlier. His black hair is matted to his head, and he has a sort of deer in headlights look when he sees Luke and me.

As Luke walks over to him, Greg braces himself, instinctively knowing the wrath Luke is about to unleash. Greg doesn't even try to move when Luke closes in and slugs him in the stomach. Greg heaves forward, clutching his belly and staggers to the side. Rob, who has entered behind Greg, surveys the situation, but does nothing but watch as Luke walks over to a staggered Greg, and pushes him so he falls to the floor.

Luke's entire body is shaking with rage, and his breathing heavy. Greg rights himself to a sitting position and leans back against the barn wall.

"You bastard," Luke spits. "You leave my sister trapped with these people, and you don't ask for my help; you don't ask for my father's help or Chase's help; you don't even fucking ask for Sen. Reed's help. You just leave her there, and then you kidnap my wife and daughter."

Greg doesn't look up, nor does he make any response. He just sits there, his head down, staring at the ground. Luke towers over him, radiating loathing. "What do you have to say for yourself?"

Greg finally looks at Luke and I notice Rob edge closer. Like me, Rob must realize that if Greg gives the wrong response, Luke will have to be restrained. Greg appears to sense the tension as well, his face a mask of misery and remorse. "I'm sorry, Luke," he blubbers. "I was trying to help Emmie."

Luke's hands ball into fists at his side and he kicks Greg's foot. It looks for a moment as if he is going to move in and do more, but instead Luke takes a step back. "No, if you wanted to help Emmie, you wouldn't have done this. She's still in there, and my wife is in more danger than ever, and my daughter has been taken from us. My wife hasn't gotten a decent night's sleep since you did this, and God only knows what it's like for our daughter. You don't even know where she is, do you? You just gave them my daughter, and you don't know where she is or what they did to her, do you? Did you even ask?"

Greg's face contorts into a slobbering tearful mess. "No," he whimpers, "I'm sorry. I don't know where they took Penelope."

Luke shakes his head in disgust. "Look at me," he says. Greg wipes his eyes and looks up at his brother-in-law. Luke's voice is clear, resolute and deadly cold when he speaks. "You're going to help us. We're going to get Emmie out of here, and we're going to get Penelope back. You are going to help us do it, and if you mess this up by not doing everything we ask, or if you try to double cross us, I will hunt you down and kill you. Do you understand me?"

Greg nods and Luke shudders and walks toward the barn door.

He shoves the door open and it swings on its hinges until it bangs into the barn wall. Before he stomps out, Luke says, "Rob will explain what you need to do." He heads into the darkness.

Rob crouches over Greg, and offers to examine him, make sure he's alright. Rob generally does research, so I sometimes forget he is a doctor with an amazing bedside manner, until I'm confronted with him helping a patient. He uses a gentle touch and kind disposition now. It's more than Greg deserves. Part of me wants to sit and watch, but I need to check on Luke, so I make eye contact with Rob, incline my head to the doorway and mouth, "Checking on Luke." He acknowledges he's heard me, and goes back to his patient. I slip out the door, and into the dark night.

I look to the left and the right and don't immediately see him. I head right, toward the side of the barn, then take another right and spot Luke leaning on the barn's outer wall. I go over and put my hand on his shoulder. "You alright?"

He shakes his head, blows out a breath. "No, I'm not."

I lean in, put my arms around him, pulling him into a hug. "It's going to be OK, Luke. We're going to get your sister out, get Penelope and keep Kelsey safe."

I can feel his head bobbing on my shoulder as he moves it to disagree with me. "I don't know if this is going to work, Susan. I'm so scared I'm going to do something wrong and they're going to hurt my daughter."

Pulling back from our hug, I take a breath and look Luke in the eye. He seems so lost, a hollowness in his blue eyes that I've never seen before. "Luke, Penelope is going to be fine. She beat the odds during her delivery, and she'll do the same in this situation. She's like her godmother that way."

He cracks a smile. "Be nice if you were a fairy godmother and you could magic her away from captivity."

I press my lips together and breathe in through my nose, determined not to let myself sink into this emotional morass with Luke. He needs someone strong, and that has to be me right now. "I wish I could, Luke," I tell him, patting his forearm. "But, we're doing the next best thing. Greg will help us, and we'll get your daughter and your sister."

Luke puts his hands on his face, bringing them to a point at the bridge of his nose. "I don't want Kelsey to go with the colonel, but I know she will if it comes to that. I just don't know how I'll cope if that happens."

He looks so lost, miserable and confused. "What choice would you make, Luke, if the colonel said Kelsey could have Penelope back if you went with him?"

He takes his hands off his face, shoves them down into his pocket and kicks a rock near his foot. "I know I'd do the same, Susan. If there was any way I could swap places with her, if there was any way I could bear this burden instead of her, I would. That's why it's hard, because I know I would get Penelope back for Kelsey. The situation we are in right now is my fault. Emmie is my sister. Greg is my brother-in-law, and we wouldn't be here, if it weren't for Greg. She wouldn't even have opened the door if it hadn't been Greg. She would've trusted her gut; she wouldn't have taken Major Nelson outside if it had been anyone but him. She trusted him because of his connection to me. She shouldn't have to die because my brother-in-law is a miserable cretin."

Good point, but he can't focus on the why or he'll wallow in sorrow. He has to focus on the future. "Luke," I say, "It doesn't matter how we got here, OK? What matters is what we do next. The plan will work. It's a good plan. She won't have to go anywhere with the colonel."

Luke rebuts with a head shake; his eyes intent, his expression sober. "And if it doesn't work? If she goes with him?"

He's not going to let me Pollyanna this away. Part of me wants to try again, but the other part of me knows he doesn't want that, that he wants the Susan who accepts the bad and figures out a way to move forward. He wants the Susan that finally accepted her paralysis and decided to make her life work, not the one who pretended that marriage would make it all better and then had nothing left when that didn't work out. He wants the strength to accept a bad outcome. "I'm sure it will work," I say to him, and he looks desolate. "But, in the event that I'm wrong, be with your wife. Tell her you love her. Tell her anything you want to tell her that's important. Remind her that your daughter will be safe and with you by Saturday. So you two don't have to spend it worrying and scared. You two can spend the time remembering that you love each other. Have a great time with her so that however Saturday goes down, you have no regrets about how you spent these hours with your wife."

He closes his eyes, takes a deep breath and leans his head back against the barn wall. A minute passes and I wonder if I said the wrong thing, if I should've just assured him again that the plan would work and left it at that. But then he opens his eyes, looks up at the moon, and nods. "You're a good friend, Susan," he tells me, reaching out and pulling me into another hug. "We should go back, make sure Greg understands the plan."

We walk back around to the barn door. Luke pulls it open and holds it for me to go in first. I enter to find Rob pacing and Greg's face pale as a ghost. When Luke enters behind me, Rob stops and faces us. "We have a problem."

Luke and I hurry over, the worry on Luke's face deepening. "What is it?"

Rob squares off with Luke, looks him in the eye and says, "I don't think your sister went crazy. I think they're making her crazy."

# 34

## SUSAN

Luke staggers back as if he's been knocked in the gut. "I don't understand."

Rob puts a guiding hand on Luke's shoulder. "Why don't we sit down," Rob says, gently sitting on the ground with Luke. "I was telling Greg the plan, to place the replicator on Emmie so it would simply repeat broadcast the last two days of her LMS data. Then he could inject her with the antipsychotic and let her continue on the sedative until tomorrow night when he'd need to get her off so they could travel Saturday. That's when he mentioned another drug they're giving her. That's not normal for psychotic patients, and that drug tends to cause psychosis, not cure it."

Luke stares in disbelief, still trying to comprehend what Rob is saying.

Unable to contain my shock, I ask, "They're keeping her crazy on purpose? "

Rob shakes his head. "No, not keeping; they're making her crazy. People tend not to just go crazy like this in their late 30s. Usually psychiatric problems present in the 20s. Given the loss of rights that people undergo if they admit to needing help, most people try to hide the symptoms and self-manage until it's not possible anymore. I assumed Luke's family had done that with Emmie. But Greg told me that's not the case. Despite the family history, prior to this she's shown no signs of problems."

Luke speaks. "She's never had psychiatric problems before, but isn't it likely because of what happened with my mother? My mother went crazy after the stillborn."

"Your mother was always crazy," Greg says, his voice just above a whisper. "I was there. Your father did his best to manage it. Emmie did her best to keep it hidden, but everyone saw. Everyone knew. We just would never send someone to the state, reduce them to that fate. The stillborn was just the last straw. Emmie was never like your mother. Not that way."

Luke gives his brother-in-law a silencing stare and then turns to Rob. "So you're saying they did this to her on purpose, after the baby died?"

Rob nods. "Which means they made her insane to get Greg under their control. So, our original plan doesn't work. I was going on the assumption that the medical record my associate got me was accurate. If they're giving her something else, something other than sedatives, I need to know what it is."

Luke rubs his temples with his fingers. "How do we figure out what she's taking? And once you know, how do we get her off of it?"

Rob looks at Greg briefly, but decides to address his comments to Luke. "I have a proposal," he says, walking toward his medical bag in the corner. From it he pulls an LMS reader. It looks just like the one Kevin used on me earlier today. Rob walks to Greg and hands him the reader. "Take this back with you and wave it over your wife's LMS," he says. At this, Luke walks over to get a better look. Rob points to a touchscreen that runs much of the length of the reader. "Click 'menu,' and press, 'record data.' When that finishes, go back to the menu and select, 'medical record.' When you're done, bring it back to the security guard. Once I know what's in her system, I can figure out what to do. I need you to do this tonight. Can you?"

Greg nods.

Rob turns back to Luke. "Once I have the information, I've got to call someone. I'm not a psychiatrist, so I need to talk to one in order to figure out what to give her so she'll be able to leave with Greg on Saturday."

Luke musters a half nod, and Rob says he's going to take Greg back to the compound.

When Rob and Greg have departed, I go over to Luke, who has just sat down, back against the wall, knees up. I kneel next to him. "You alright?"

"Yeah" he says, though he doesn't sound it. "I just need a minute to think."

"Sure," I say. "I'm going to go out and call Kelsey, give her an update." I turn, walk out of the barn and wind my way toward the car. I sit inside, call Kelsey and tell her everything that has happened. Like me, she is shocked. When I finish, I start back toward the barn and see Rob heading down the hill from the compound. I wave at him, and luckily, he spots me, despite the darkness, and stops.

"Hey," he says softly when he reaches me. "Is Luke in the car?"

I shake my head. "Still in the barn."

He leans in and says, "Greg told me something in the barn earlier."

"What?" I ask, raising my eyebrows.

"Dr. Grant was Emmie's doctor," he says.

I gasp and pull my hand to my mouth. "Did he do this to her? Did Dr. Grant push her over the edge."

"I wish I knew," Rob said. "But my gut says he did. I mean, look at all the stuff he's done that we didn't know about. He set Kevin on us to get back at me."

I take a step back. "To get back at you?" I ask, a bit confused.

He sighs, nods. "I've thought about it a lot today, and I even looked up the date of that conference at the university. It happened within two weeks of an article that had a one sentence blurb about me working on an improved procedure to help paralyzed patients walk again. He wouldn't have had to dig hard to find out it was true. And he would've known my procedure, if successful would be preferred to the older one, one he holds a patent to. He set Kevin on this path back to you, out of spite toward me."

I'm speechless. I love Rob, but this seems a bit vain.

"Don't look at me like that," he says, wagging his head. "I've given this some thought. There are a thousand of ways he could have tipped us off to the switch that weren't traceable to him. Instead, he picked your ex-fiancé, and rather than simply orchestrate the internship from Dr. Rounds' end, he inserts himself into Kevin's life, telling him that we're not a good fit. He sicced Kevin on us, and he did it out of spite. Just the way he forced Jasper Christensen out of the Grant House. He's a mean and spiteful man."

I take a deep breath and mull over what Rob said. It still sounds extreme, but Dr. Grant has been different lately, if what Kelsey said is right. Pushing Jasper out so publicly was unusual for a man who likes to keep his battles private. If Rob is right, if Dr. Grant did this to be spiteful, that's not a good omen. "So you think he intentionally hurt his patient, because she's Luke sister?"

He nods ever so slightly. "I need to look at her complete medical record to see what I can decipher," Rob says. "I won't have answers until tomorrow, though." He stops and looks around in the dark, to see if anyone is coming. "Since there's a lot I don't know about Emmie's medical history or Dr. Grant's involvement, and since Luke is under so much other stress right now, I'm just wondering if I should tell him tonight. I want to be honest, but I don't want to burden him unnecessarily."

God. I need a hug. I step forward and wrap my arms around Rob. He reciprocates, standing there holding me for a minute or two. "Wait," I say. "Find out everything you can first." Rob pats my back and a moment later, I tense when I spot a shadowy figure walking toward us. Rob notices my stiffness and turns around to look, positioning his body so he's shielding me from the intruder. A moment later, Rob steps aside, and I see it is Luke.

"I thought I heard voices," Luke says.

"Yeah, we ran into each other. We were coming to get you," I say.

"Let's get out of here," Luke says. "I can't stand this place."

# 35

## KELSEY

I am sitting in my room waiting for Luke, Susan and Rob; they should be back any minute now. Susan called more than two hours ago, and I believe she said the place was only 90 miles away. It sounds like it's been a horrible night, given what they learned about Dr. Grant and Emmie. I wish I could have gone, but it's best I be seen as little as possible. And certainly, if I'd been seen by Greg, that would have been the worst possible outcome. He wants Emmie well, and would turn me over to FoSS in a heartbeat if he knew I was here.

My father and Haleema were here keeping me company for a while. Haleema made me tea the way she used to when I was girl. She even promised she'd do a tea party for both Penelope and me as soon as she was home. Her optimism made me feel better, though I hope it is not misplaced.

They've gone back to the hotel. I'm a little glad of the peace. It's the first time I've been alone, really alone since arriving here. There's a certain solace in the quiet of an empty house. I'm trying to make myself OK with the choice I've made. I've been so adamant about it with Luke and my father, with everyone really, that I haven't had time to really digest its ramifications for me. I keep simply looking at the golden apple at the end: Penelope back, safe and sound.

I've been pretty good at segregating my mind, focusing on the task at hand instead of slumped in a chair crying a pool of tears. The quiet is both kind and cruel. I've been slowly getting used to the idea of what might happen when I leave with the colonel. Till now I've only been imagining getting Penelope back, checking her over and seeing that she is fine. Sometimes I imagine walking out of this house with Col. Parker. But I never imagine what will happen afterwards. Where will he take me? What will he do? Will I even get a trial? Will I be publicly shamed and brought to justice or will there be a private execution?

Part of me hopes it's quick and stealthy. Publicity means I'll have to go back to a holding facility. I'm not sure I can take being cooped up like that again. Being stuck in a cell waiting until someone with a bad heart needs mine. The waiting drives people insane or catatonic. I don't want either.

Not to mention, my punishment could come long before my organs are needed for someone else. The guards, they... I shudder just thinking about what they do to the inmates. The last time I was in a holding facility, my father had enough clout to get me my own private guard — Luke — under the pretense I needed watching due to mental instability. But this time, there will be no such ruse available and I will be subjected again to men like Pig Face — a vile beast who tried to rape me on the last night of my imprisonment.

I shake my head at the thought. I can't go back to the holding facility, no matter what else happens. I just can't go back there.

I look down at Mr. Giggles sitting next to me on the bed and realize I shouldn't keep holding this little animal so close. He doesn't even smell like Penelope anymore. I pick him up, hop down from the bed and open the top drawer of the dresser. I'm going to retire him until I see my daughter again. Just as I close the drawer, I hear the bedroom door open. I turn to see Luke step in and shut the door behind him. I head toward him, and he's heading toward me, too, as we collide into each other, and I envelop him in my arms. "I'm so sorry about what they did to Emmie," I tell him. "I know that must have been so hard for you to find out."

He pulls free of my arms. "Emmie is going to be fine," he says, a conviction in his voice that he didn't have hours ago when he left. I try not to look perplexed, not to look at him like what he's saying is insane, because it's not. I just didn't feel like he believed it before.

"Of course," I say. "Rob will find the right medicine. They'll still get her out, and we'll get Penelope on Saturday."

He nods, takes a few steps closer to the bed, taking my hand and towing me along with him. "You're right," he says, though not as strongly as before.

He sits and I join him. He strokes my cheek gently. "I love you, Kelsey."

The words surprise me. Not that he's saying them, but the utter despair with which he says them. "I love you, too," I say, placing my hand atop the one he's caressed my face with. I pull his hand to my lips and kiss it. "You don't have to be sad about loving me."

He smiles and shakes his head. "I'm not sad about that. Never about that," he says. "I'm sad about what might happen on Saturday."

I shake my head, reassuringly. "It's going to be fine."

He doesn't respond. Instead, he leans in and kisses me on the lips, his mouth passionate, forceful, loving. I close my eyes and it's easy to melt into his kiss, to feel the love, the need, the want radiating from him as he kisses me with everything in him. After a minute, Luke pulls back slightly. I open my eyes and he stares deeply at me and whispers, "In case it doesn't turn out fine, I just want to spend the next day and a half loving my wife, OK?"

I swallow back the lump in my throat, his acknowledgment of what I've been trying to come to terms with tonight and just nod at him, because even though I hadn't realized it until he said it, that's what I want too. If this is it for Luke and me, I want to spend it with him, loving him.

# FRIDAY

# 36

## KELSEY

Luke and I awoke before the sun came up and scuttled down to the cabin on the property. It's ostensibly a guest house, and Rob is staying here until he and Susan get married. But, I'm to remain holed up here during the day because the bridal party is in town and will probably be roaming about the house.

The bridal party includes Rob's sister-in-law Jane, who has become good friends with Susan. She's going to be the matron of honor and has an entire day of relaxation planned for Susan. While Susan feels guilty for abandoning me, I've told her I'm perfectly happy away from the festivities. I've tried to reassure her that everything would turn out perfectly on her big day so she should just relax and not worry about babysitting me.

Luke went to see my father, as Zuri has information on Dr. Grant to deliver. This leaves me alone to think. I'm going over the plan in my head. I hope it works. The first part is getting evidence proving I was wrongly marked. With any luck, Zuri has it. It's strange how often my fate has come down to getting information from this woman who I so despised until recently. My luck is probably such that now that I finally get her, now that I finally don't hate her, she won't actually deliver the goods.

There is a knock on the front door, startling me. The little cabin is only three rooms — a main room sectioned into a living and eating area, a bedroom and a bathroom. Even though the front door is locked, I take a step back, wondering if I should dart into the bedroom to hide.

"It's me," I hear Rob say through the door.

I breathe out in relief, not realizing how tense I'd become just that quickly. I open the door and let him in. He's carrying a bag of food that has a large picture of a pig on it and smells really good.

"I thought you might like some Bubba's barbecue," he says, walking over to the table in the corner, setting the bag down.

I smile at him, "You didn't have to do that," I say, heading his way. "But thank you, I appreciate it."

"No problem," he says. "And Susan's really sorry about abandoning you today."

I shake my head. "She's not abandoning me; she's getting ready for her wedding. I'm fine. Please tell her I'm fine, not to worry. I want her to enjoy the day." The sweet, smoky scent wafting from the bag is irresistible. I reach inside and start pulling out small labeled containers: pulled pork, ribs, baked beans, corn on the cob.

"Rob, this is too much," I say. "You shouldn't have brought all this.

"It keeps well," he says. "And again, Susan and I feel bad that you've got to be holed up here all day."

As opposed to holed up in the main house? Either way, I couldn't wander, so this cabin is as good as the house. "I'm fine," I tell him. "It doesn't matter where I'm holed up. I just need to get through this day, so tomorrow we can get Penelope." My daughter's face flashes in my mind and the pain of her absence ripples through me.

Rob puts a hand on my shoulder, and says softly. "I know this must be hard for you, but hang in there. Susan and I are doing everything we can to help."

I offer the best smile I can manage, which feels weak. "Thank you. I appreciate that." I look down at the container of pulled pork with the steamy clear lid. "You want to join me for some lunch?"

"I ate actually," he says, "but I'll sit with you until Luke comes back."

I nod and sit down at one of the four folding chairs around the table. Rob sits across from me, as I take a plastic fork that was tucked inside the bag and start eating right out of the container. I shovel a few bites in my mouth. This is actually pretty good. As I eat, with Rob so close by, I realize now is a good time to ask him for a favor. I swallow what's in my mouth, and look up at him.

"Rob, you know, Luke and I have both had trouble sleeping recently," I say, trying to sound nonchalant. "I feel like we should be well rested. Is there anyway you could prescribe us something for tonight? Something to help us sleep. I've had Zandropan before and that's worked well."

He gives me an inquisitive look, then shakes his head. "I may be able to prescribe you something," he said. "But that's not what you want. That drug would really knock you out; make you too sluggish for tomorrow. And too much would be deadly."

I nod, trying to hide my disappointment in a bite of baked beans. He is staring at me too intently now, so I focus on the food in front of me.

"Kelsey, why do you really want that?" he asks. "Are you planning to drug someone?"

I shake my head. "No," I say, after gulping down beans. I wipe my mouth and look at Rob, wondering if I just tell him the truth that maybe he'll give it to me. "I want it for me," I whisper. "If they take me back to the holding facility, I can't do it. I just want to go to sleep and into the hereafter. I don't want to be tortured in that place first."

Rob starts shaking his head emphatically. "Kelsey, I'm a doctor," he says. "I'm not going to help you commit suicide."

I reach out and place my hand on his arm. He looks at it, then me. "Did Susan tell you what happened the night she and Luke helped me escape?"

When his face softens, I know she told him. "I'm sure what happened was traumatic," he says softly.

I raise an eyebrow and lean in closer. "Have you ever had someone rip down your pants, roll you on your stomach and tell you they plan to rape you anally? Have you ever had them tell you to hold still because it's gonna hurt? Have you had them say, if you don't lie there and take it, they're going to beat you in the abdomen so you miscarry your baby? I have. And I can't do that again. Do you understand, Rob? I can't do that again. And I am begging you to help me with that. Please."

Rob looks less resolved to say no than he did a minute ago. "Please," I say again. "Just give me the pills, so if I have to go there, I can just end things on my own terms. I'll go with the colonel to save my daughter, but do I really have to suffer that kind of abuse, too? Can't you just help me with this?"

He bites his lower lip, looks away for a moment. Then back at me, still unsure. "Is Luke OK with this?

"I don't know," I admit. "I was thinking about it last night, looking up what could help me if I had to go back to the holding facility. After everything that happened last night, I wasn't sure it was a good time to talk to him about it. But, I will talk to him. Just promise me if he's OK with it, you'll do this for me. You'll help me."

He stares at me for a moment, trying to discern something in his own mind, looking for some clue to help him make a decision, when we hear the door to the house creak open.

Luke comes in, looking a tad angry as he eyes us. "What's going on?" he asks.

"I brought you guys lunch," Rob says, pointing to the food on the table.

Luke stares at him icily. "Anything else?" he asks, and I haven't a clue where this hostility is coming from. Rob seems taken aback too.

"Luke," I say in my most soothing voice. "Rob is being nice. He's just trying to help."

Luke sneers, "If Rob wanted to help, he would've told me that Dr. Grant was my sister's obstetrician."

Rob stands up, a look of apology spreading across his face. "I just found out last night, when Greg mentioned it to me," Rob says. "Greg isn't trustworthy so I just wanted to check it out myself before I told you."

"You didn't think twice about asking Zuri to help you get a copy of Emmie's file though," Luke spits back.

Rob nods. "I saw the medical record on file for Emmie, but there was nothing strange in it. I wondered if Dr. Grant kept a private file on his office machines and wanted to find out more, so yes, I asked Zuri to see if she could find anything. I knew she could log in from inside the firewall. It would have saved me a lot of time if she'd found it. Again, I wanted to look at it before I talked to you."

Luke still looks irritated. "Well, don't worry about it, because now I know, and it doesn't even matter because Dr. Grant is gone."

Rob cocks his head, "What are you talking about?"

"He's gone," Luke spits. "Dr. Grant left. No one can find him. But he left Zuri a note, along with Kelsey's original drive. Seems the ones he gave to us were complete forgeries, serial numbers and all. Good forgeries, but forgeries nonetheless. The note said Kelsey wasn't supposed to be marked, and this drive would prove it."

My jaw drops. "He left my drive?"

Luke nods.

"And Susan's?" Rob says.

Luke shakes his head.

"Why?" Rob asks. "Why not Susan's?"

Luke looks at me, then reaches into his pocket, and pulls out a sealed envelope. "This arrived by messenger at your father's hotel," he says to me. I walk over and take the envelope from him. It has my name on it.

"What is it?" I ask.

"It's a letter from Dr. Grant. It came inside an envelope addressed to me. The note said I should give it to you, that it would explain everything. Then he made a jibe about how he knew I'd open my wife's correspondence, because I'm a thoughtless, intrusive jerk. I guess he knew saying that would compel me to just bring it to you."

I take the envelope and tear it open. I pull the letter out and it only contains an online address. I turn the paper so Luke and Rob can see it. Rob immediately goes to the bedroom, comes back with a small computer, and sets it on the table. The three of us gather round as Rob types in the address.

A video appears on screen, a still image of Dr. Grant; his hair is still a salt and pepper mix, yet he appears thinner than when I last saw him. He is sitting in a chair behind a desk with a blue wall behind him. Otherwise the room is nondescript. Rob opens another program, and says, "I'm going to record the feed." He takes a minute setting that up, then clicks the play button and the video begins.

"Hi Kelsey," Dr Grant says, his voice sounding clear and strong. "I wanted to leave you one last message. This is the last time you'll be hearing from me. I just wanted you to know that things aren't what they seem."

I can't help but roll my eyes at that. Things can't be other than what they seem.

"I admit that I have made mistakes. I've done things I shouldn't, done them out of anger. Frankly, I've never been a terribly forgiving person, when someone wrongs me or the people I love."

He pauses a moment, clears his throat, and I wonder who in the world he ever really loved. He's always seemed like a loner.

"I apologize for the role I played in your marking surgery. I let my hatred for your father get in the way of my better judgment. Of the duty I owed to you. You weren't there when your mother died, so you don't know how bad a shape she was in at the end. And I promised her then that she wouldn't die in vain. I worked tirelessly on a way to keep women alive when they were having pregnancy complications. But, in my own mind, I promised myself I would look out for you, because you were Maya's daughter.

"Instead of keeping my promise, I created a situation that I thought would hurt your father, but it only hurt you. And then I put my own interests ahead of yours, and when you called me on it, I treated you coldly, rather than apologize. For that I'm sorry. I hope the drive evidence I have provided makes up for my transgressions. I know you're not going to believe this, but Kelsey I truly want the best for you. And for Susan. I like her, and you two haven't deserved what you've gotten."

I shake my head as he says this, not quite understanding the point.

"I'm sure you're wondering where Susan's drive is, but the truth of the matter is that I don't have it. I did with hers what I should have done with yours: destroyed it after I made the fakes. For that I'm sorry. I guess I kept yours because I knew it might be important to you one day."

He sighs, looks away from the camera at something we're unable to see in the frame, and then back at the camera. "I realized last year that maybe my luck was running out, that I had ticked off one person too many. So, since then, I've been preparing to leave at a moment's notice, if necessary. But, I always intended to help you. Perhaps it's karma, or just universal irony. I've been a victim of blackmail. I thought Jasper was helping this person, so I drove him out. But, I'm not sure he was ever a part of it. I just know that I've done things I'm not proud of. I've tried to help out along the way, when I could. I got Kevin that job, I tried to clue him in, but that didn't work out the way I hoped. And then, with Emmie. Well, that weighs on me now, still. She's a good woman who didn't deserve what happened to her. Again, I'm sorry."

He grimaces as if he's truly pained by his actions. "I know you're probably wondering why I'm sending you this. It's because I want you to know that I have never forgotten my promise to you. Just because you were angry with me, just because you didn't understand, doesn't mean I haven't always tried to help you. I made a promise the day your mother died, and it's one I will always keep. Use the data on the drive to whatever advantage you can. And don't trust John Parker." The doctor stands and walks closer to the camera. "I have to go. Goodbye Kelsey, and good luck."

The video turns to black, then the window closes, and the computer shuts down. Rob grabs the laptop, hits a few keys, then the power button. Nothing happens. He hits a couple more keys, tries the power button again, and the screen remains black. "Damn him," he says, setting the laptop down with a hard thud.

"What?" I ask

Rob shakes his head. "I should have seen it," he mutters, and then looks toward me. "I figured he used a website to stream the video because he was going to pull it from the server the second it was watched. That's why I recorded the video as it streamed. Only he planned for that, and I'm pretty sure he streamed a virus to my machine."

"What kind of virus?" Luke asks.

Rob curses under his breath, and says, "A virus that has probably wiped the hard drive clean." Rob slams his hand on the table.

"I don't know what to say, Rob," I stammer. "I'm sorry about Susan's drive. I'm sorry he destroyed it."

Luke puts a hand on my shoulder. "What Dr. Grant does or doesn't do isn't your fault," he says, his voice wrapped in frustration.

We're all quiet for a moment, pondering the contents of the video that is now lost to the world. "Do you think he was telling the truth?" I ask. "That he was really being blackmailed?"

Luke scoffs. "No, I don't think he was telling the truth," he says with venom. "I think he's a liar who, for some reason, is fixated on the idea of you liking him. But, I do think he's ticked off someone big and making a run for it is his only chance."

"Someone big like Parker?" Rob asks. "You think Parker asked him to give your sister those drugs?"

Luke looks down at the table and bites his lip. "I don't know. I just don't know," he says, finally. "Of course, the only thing he gives us brings us more questions than answers."

That's for sure. I'm still stunned. That Dr. Grant would care that I know or understand what he did seems insane. That he still believes he's responsible for me somehow, that he needs to help me because my mother died, seems crazy. Yes, he was the attending physician when she died, and maybe he could have done something to save her. But I thought he felt he didn't owe me anything more, that we were done after Penelope was born. I'd told him I didn't trust him and that he wasn't my friend. It was a bad split that I believed left us on opposite sides. Yet, he still says he'll always help. I feel Luke and Rob staring at me, probably wondering if I can provide some insight. But I'm as lost as they are.

Rob closes the laptop and takes a deep breath, but when he finishes, there is still a scowl on his face. "Has anyone validated the data on the drive Zuri brought back from Dr. Grant's office?"

"Lewis hired a guy to do that," Luke says. Seeing further irritation on Rob's face, my husband adds, "He thought you'd be busy with wedding stuff, but you're welcome to take a look at what he has."

Rob clicks his tongue and says tightly, "I'm going to go over to the senator's and find out more." He starts toward the door, but turns back to face Luke. "I had no idea that Dr. Grant was leaving, and I would have told you about Emmie sooner if I'd thought it would make a difference."

Luke nods appreciatively and says, "I shouldn't have come in like that… It's just been a long day. Thanks for all your help."

Rob heads out the door and Luke walks over to me. "You alright?" I ask, standing and placing a hand on his shoulder.

He pulls me to him and clenches his arms around me as if he needs me in his arms or else he'll suddenly shatter. I feel his heart beating next to mine and his hold is so strong it's like he doesn't intend to ever let me go. "I'll be OK when this is over, and everyone is safe."

I pull back just slightly, but Luke doesn't loosen his grip. Talking into his shoulder, I say, "I know everything feels disjointed, and falling apart, but it's just because the news is a shock. What Dr. Grant did is all in the past right now. We're in charge of the future. Tonight, Rob will give Greg the meds Emmie needs so she's well enough to travel tomorrow. We'll go to bed and when we wake up, it's going to be the day Emmie gets out and the day we get our daughter back. Nothing else matters except those two things, OK?"

Luke buries his head in my shoulder and holds me for another minute. Finally, he releases me and sighs. "You're right," he says, as if he's now fortified to face the rest of the day. "We have to think positive." He looks at the food on the table, picks up a container, sniffs in the aroma and smiles. "Is this is as good as it smells?"

# 37

## KELSEY

Luke and I have eaten a fair amount of the barbecue. I am stuffed and my thoughts have left Dr. Grant and all the deception that swirls around him. Luke seems to have moved on too, his troubles temporarily forgotten as he enjoys a meal. He's polished off several ribs, and is adding some baked beans to his plate. I'm torn, because part of me wants to just enjoy this time where we seem to have achieved a moment of peace. To enjoy this quiet time, maybe my only time left with my husband. But the rest of me knows that I have to ask him something he's not going to want to hear. Something for my own peace of mind.

"Sometimes, I still have nightmares about Pig Face," I say, and he stops in the middle of a bite and stares. I have second thoughts as I see the horror on his face. "I'm sorry. I don't want to lay this at your feet right now, with everything that is going on. It's just that I realized I'm not as brave as I thought. I will make whatever sacrifices are necessary to save Penelope, but I'm not sure how well I can cope when they take me back to the holding facility."

Luke doesn't say anything. What's there to say to that? He can't protect me from that and neither of us can stop it if it's required to save our daughter. He pulls me into his arms and holds me, and it would be nice to stay there, but I have to tell him the rest. I speak softly, but I know he can hear me. "There's a heavy sedative Rob could prescribe for me. If I had to go with the colonel, I could take it and I wouldn't have to deal with that place. I could just be gone."

Luke squeezes me tighter, but doesn't say anything. I wonder what he is thinking. Finally, he releases me and then looks me in the eyes. He is shaking his head. "As bad as it may seem," he whispers. "You can't do that, Kelsey. Even if you go back to a holding facility, your father and I will fight for you. You can't give up just because you're in there."

I close my eyes. I can't be in there. I just can't. "Luke," I say, and I'm not sure what to say next. Only, the terror of that last night in the holding facility comes back, that night with Pig Face. Me imagining what would have happened if Luke hadn't come, what that man would've done to me if it had just been him and me. I shudder and hot tears well in my eyes. "I can go with the colonel. I will go with him. If he has some covert and quick end planned for me, I can do that. But if he wants to take me to a holding facility so he can make a public trial and capture, I can't. I can't go back in that place. I won't make it."

Luke wipes a tear from my cheek and says, "I have never given up on you, and you can't give up on yourself. You can do this. I swear to you, I will come for you, but you have to be there when I come. You can't decide to end things prematurely. Promise me you won't do anything to yourself, as bad as things might seem, as dark as you might feel. If there is a chance we can get you out, you have to give us that chance to get you. You have to endure." He stops; his voice breaks. "You have to endure whatever you have to endure so I can bring you back to our daughter. You grew up without your mother, Kelsey. If there's a chance Penelope doesn't have to, you have to make sure that happens."

What he's saying makes sense, but I keep seeing Pig Face in my mind, hearing his cruel laugh, knowing that the rest of the guards out there are like that. Knowing I can't take it. That I'm not strong enough for that. "Luke, what you find when you come for me may not be worth saving," I tell him, uncertain I want to say what I'm thinking. Knowing that if I do say it, it will hurt him. I look into his eyes, so full of resolve to save me, that I know by saying this, even though it will hurt him, it is the only thing that might sway him. The only thing that might make him see things my way. "What if the me you come to get is like your mother? You know how hard that was for Emmie growing up. Do you really want that for Penelope?"

He blows out a breath, closes his eyes. "Emmie loved our mother and so did I. Her stress came from having a father who was never home, a father who burdened her with the responsibility of a mentally ill woman whose illness he was trying to hide. I wouldn't do that to Penelope. And you are stronger than you think, Kelsey. You can do this. I know you can. You will do anything for our little girl. Anything. Do this for her. She needs her mother. Promise me you won't give up in there. Promise me you won't try to hurt yourself."

I can't argue with what he's saying, but I don't know that I can promise him. I can give myself up for Penelope, but can I endure for her? I don't know. I don't know that I can.

"Promise me," he says again, but this time it is a plea.

"I don't know if I can do that."

He draws in a deep breath, takes both my hands into his and says, "You just said you were willing to give up everything for her. I'm asking you to not give up on yourself. To do that for her, to do it for me. Promise me."

He's asking me to endure something I know I can't. For him. For Penelope. And all just to die anyway in that awful place. To endure torture on the crazy chance that he can save me, only to die anyway. But, when I look into his eyes, I see he has never given up on me, and for me to give up on me, would be a betrayal of him. I don't know that I can endure; I don't think that I can, but I say the words that will force me to try. "I promise."

He looks so relieved that I feel a pang of guilt for making a promise I don't think I can keep. I close my eyes and try to clear my head. I need some peace.

Luke is still clutching my hands, and it feels nice. "You haven't been sleeping well," he says. "You want to try to grab a nap on the sofa? We don't have to worry about anyone coming down here. Everyone's up at the main house."

He's right. I'm exhausted. Mentally, I need a break, the kind you can only get when your brain shuts down for a few hours. I go lie on the sofa, and Luke comes over a minute later with a blanket. I'm not even sure where he found the thing. But when he drapes it over me, it feels so warm and comforting, that soon I'm fast asleep.

# 38

## KELSEY

I hear noises, but my eyes are closed, so I can't see anything. I'm half aware that I've been sleeping, and that I'm on a sofa, but I'm not fully awake yet either. I know I will be awake and unable to get back to sleep if I don't fall back asleep right now. Only, there are voices and they're distracting. I roll over to my side, eyes still closed and hope sleep will wrap me in its arms again, when I hear Luke's voice.

"Shhh," he says. "She's had so much trouble sleeping, I don't want to wake her."

And for some reason, those words seal the deal. I'm awake now. I just know I'm not going to be able to go back to sleep. Still, I don't want Luke to feel bad for waking me, so I keep my eyes shut, hoping maybe I'll fall back asleep, even though it seems unlikely.

"Listen," I hear Luke say softly, "I'm sorry about earlier; it's been difficult for me with everything going on, but I shouldn't have taken it out on you."

"Really, it's fine," I hear Rob say in a low voice. "Everyone has been stressed, especially you and Kelsey. I can't imagine what it's like to have your child kidnapped."

There's a moment of silence and then I hear Luke speak again. "There's something I wanted to ask you," he says, pausing, and I can hear both their breathing. I wonder how close to me they are sitting. "If it's too personal, you don't have to tell me. It's just... I know your wife, Molly, passed away suddenly and I wanted to know how you were able to …"

"Luke," Rob says, his voice resolute. "You don't want to know this. Not right now. Your wife is still here. She's still alive. She's sleeping right there. Focus on what you have right now, not on what will happen if there are problems tomorrow."

Luke gives a morbid chuckle and sighs. "I don't want any of what I have right now, Rob. Not this man who wants my wife dead, not my daughter gone, not any of it, but it's all sitting here in my lap. So, part of me just wants to know if the worst happens, if it really is possibly to cope."

Rob breathes out. "Luke, just like you're dealing with everything now, you'll be able to deal if Kelsey…" He pauses, as if he's not ready to say it. "If she doesn't make it. You'll figure it out. I'm not going to lie to you. It's not easy. When it happens, it feels like you're never going to get over it, like everything in your world has collapsed and that you don't have a center, a home anymore. But, eventually, you get your center back. It takes time and there are weeks, maybe months, that you feel broken and lost, but eventually things seem brighter. Eventually they are brighter."

There is silence and I feel ashamed to be eavesdropping on this private conversation, where Rob is bearing his soul at my husband's request. I'm debating which is worse: to continue eavesdropping or making my wakefulness known and prematurely end a conversation that my husband wants and needs to have.

Rob speaks again. "Luke, you're going to get Penelope tomorrow. Even if your worst fears become real, you'll have a reason to keep going that I never did. Your daughter needs you to be strong."

"What am I going to tell my daughter?" Luke asks, blowing out a long breath. "What I am I going to tell her in a few years when she asks me why, why I let her mother die?"

"You haven't done that, Luke," Rob says, reassuringly.

"But if our plan doesn't work, that is exactly what I've done."

"If the plan doesn't work, then you tell your daughter that her mother loved her, and that sometimes bad things happen that we can't stop," Rob says. "It isn't your fault, and you can't hold onto that blame, especially if you want your daughter to grow up happy and healthy. You have to be strong for her, and you can't blame yourself. It doesn't help. Believe me, Luke, it doesn't. I blamed myself for not convincing Molly to give up her research; research I thought could end badly. Research that did end badly. But, in the end, it doesn't matter what I did or didn't do because she died. In the end, she was still gone. In the end, I had to accept that and move on. It's better for your soul, for your own peace of mind to let go of guilt, to never let it take hold."

Someone takes a deep breath, maybe Luke. I hear the creaking of a chair. "Kelsey is scared and depressed right now, and I feel like I'm letting her down," Luke says.

"I've seen the way she looks at you," Rob says. "I've seen the way her posture changes when you're in a room with her. You are what is holding her together. You are doing everything you need to for her. And everything you need to for your sister. I know that you're feeling dejected about the plan. But don't. It's going to work. I can feel it in my gut."

Luke chuckles. "You sound like Susan."

"Well, Susan is always right," Rob says jovially. "She told me that on one of our first dates. She even made me repeat it, 'Susan is always right.' And I think in this case she is. I think we'll get everyone home safe."

"I wish I could feel as optimistic as you."

"We all have moments of pessimism. This morning I stopped by the hotel to see my brother and ran into Kevin; he said something that put me on edge. It shouldn't have; but it did," Rob says. "Then, a little later, I got a piece of good news that made me realize just how insignificant Kevin is in the grand scheme of things. So, sometimes things can turn around, Luke. Even when things seem dark, they can suddenly go the other way."

I hear a rustling noise, a shuffling perhaps or readjustment, and then my husband sighs. I hear a clap on the back. "Listen, I've actually got to run and grab Emmie's prescription from the pharmacist. Are you gonna be OK?"

There is no spoken reply, so I can only assume my husband nodded, because Rob says. "Alright, I'll be back in a little bit and we can head up to Macon." A few seconds later, I hear the door squeak open, then bang shut. Rob is gone.

# 39

## KELSEY

I'm lying on the sofa trying to convince myself that I can survive a holding facility if I have to go to one, when I hear rustling at the door and look up to see Luke and Rob enter. They've just come back from the place Emmie is being held.

I sit up as Rob closes the door behind them.

"You can go back to sleep," Luke says to me. "I don't think Susan's coming for another half an hour. You should get some rest.

"No, I wasn't sleeping," I tell him, as I peek at my watch and see it's close to 11:30 pm. "Did you give Greg the medicine? Is he going to be able to give it to Emmie?"

Luke sits down next to me on the sofa, while Rob heads for a chair cattycorner to us.

"Greg has everything he needs and Jasper is going to monitor Emmie's LMS readings, the real readings. The rebroadcast ones are being sent to the monitoring center, but Jasper is getting what's really going on."

I turn to Rob, who looks bright and bushy-tailed for this hour. "She seems to be coming down already," Rob says. "When Jasper goes to get her tomorrow, she should be well enough to travel."

"And Jasper's going to take her someplace safe?" I ask.

Luke nods. "He and Zuri are going to take care of her, make sure she's safe. Then we'll get our daughter when the colonel comes."

I give Luke a pat on the leg, and from the corner of my eye, see Rob stand up. "I think I'm going to get some fresh air," he says.

I put out my hand to stop him and proffer a smile. "We'd like you to stay," I tell him, though I really don't have a clue what Luke wants. I only know that I feel like I'm kicking him out of his own home, and I shouldn't. He can't go back to the main house because Susan is finishing up her bachelorette party, after which, I'm supposed to return to the house unseen, so I'll be in place for the plan tomorrow.

"Sit with us a minute," Luke says. "The night air will still be there in half an hour."

Rob sits back down and smiles politely. "Sure, I can get some air later."

We sit in silence for a moment, Luke leaning back into the sofa, me doing the opposite, scooting up so I can speak to Rob. "I just wanted to thank you again for all the help you've been this week. Opening your home to us, not caring that I'm a fugitive, working on those hard drives, sneaking medicine to Emmie," I pause realizing just how long a list of things we have to thank him for. "I just want you to know how much I appreciate everything you've done."

His face is coloring slightly at the compliment. He waves me off. "You're like family to Susan, so you're like family to me. We'll always help you," he says looking at me, then Luke, "both of you."

I dip my head appreciatively, then flash a mischievous smile. "Well, can we at least do some bachelor-ish activities with you since you canceled your party to help with Emmie?"

A genuine smile pops on his face. "Thank you, but I'm fine. I've actually had one bachelor party before, and one is enough for a lifetime."

That makes sense, but I still feel bad about him spending the night before his wedding essentially running errands for Luke and me. Important errands, but still not his first choice of activities. There is a knock at the door. We all look at each other, eyes darting between the others and the door.

"Who is it?" Rob calls.

"It's me," Susan says.

Rob goes over and answers the door, while Luke and I stay put.

Susan pokes her head in and smiles at us. "I just need to see Rob outside for one sec, and we'll be right back."

# 40

## SUSAN

Worry lines mar Rob's forehead as he steps into the cool night air with me. "Is everything al —"

I pull him into a kiss. Despite being startled, he kisses me back with all the passion I'd expect from my husband-to-be, pulling me tight to him, his arms a perfect fit for my body.

We break free for air, and I tell him, "I just wanted to do that without an audience."

He chuckles. "Well, you are welcome to do that to me anytime you want. With an audience or without."

I lean in and hold him for a minute. I am so glad he is here. So glad we are getting married tomorrow, and part of me wishes we'd already done it. Wishes we'd just done it right when he asked. The anxiety I felt at the time seems silly now. I wanted to make sure we knew each other well enough outside my captivity, that we were going to be in sync in the outside world. Yet, there had been nothing to indicate we wouldn't be. Now we've spent an entire year together since, and I wish it had been a year we'd spent married.

Rob rubs my back gently and whispers in my ear. "What are you thinking?"

"That I can't wait until I am officially Mrs. Samuel Robert Donnelly," I say, choking up a little.

He pulls back to get a better look at me. "You alright?" he asks, hearing the deep emotion in my voice.

I smile. "I'm fine. Just becoming a bit of an emotional mess with the wedding so close."

He squints to take a closer look and appraises me in the dim rays cast off from the porch light. "It's normal," he says. "To be emotional now. I'm pretty happy myself."

The crickets are singing their night song and it seems like the perfect melody for the occasion. I lay my head on his shoulder once more. "How did it go tonight, with Emmie?"

"Well," Rob says, sighing. "The medication I gave her should counteract some of the stuff she's been getting. It's by no means perfect, but she should be OK to travel tomorrow when Jasper comes for her. I forged a release document for Emmie, and Zuri found someone who will encode it with the official military seal. Once we get word that the colonel is on the move with Penelope, Jasper will use the forged document to remove Emmie from the facility. That part of the plan will work."

A warmness courses through me as I relax into Rob's arms. This is good. Emmie's situation is falling into place, and I have a good feeling about tomorrow. That things will work out.

"I feel good about how things will turn out," Rob says. "So, don't worry about this. Everything this evening went just as planned. Now how about you? How was your evening — was the bachelorette party fun?"

Part of me hesitates at the change of subject, wondering if maybe there is something more to do or say. But, the truth is, we've done all in our power. All we can do is wait. I smile and answer Rob's question. "Lots of fun. A slew of games, and lovely little gifts." I chuckle thinking back on one gift in particular. "And, just in case you didn't realize, your sister-in-law adores you."

"Oh, I know," he says with a confident smirk. "Which sister-in-law would this be?"

"Jane," I tell him, remembering the barely there lingerie she gave me. "I think she's been getting shopping tips from strippers."

Rob grins at that. "Well, truthfully, she likes me, but she adores you." He takes a step back and looks more serious than he should right now. "You were really great when George had his setback."

I see his solemnity and can't help mirror his expression now. That was an awful time, one I am partly responsible for. Rob's older brother, George, ingested poison meant for me and went into cardiac arrest. He seemed fine for the first month of his recovery, but then he had another heart attack, probably because the poison had damaged his heart. Rob and I spent two months in New York, helping Jane, George and their three children. It was extremely stressful as doctors tried to parse out how weak George's heart was and how best to help him. "I'm just glad George is better now," I say, knowing that every day I spent helping out, watching the kids, making sure everything ran smoothly at their house so Jane could spend time with George, made me feel a little less guilty for what happened to him.

"Well, Jane appreciates how helpful you were, as do I," he says, leaning in and giving me a soft kiss on the forehead. "You are going to be a wonderful sister-in-law, and I can't wait until you're my wife."

He pulls me closer to him, his arms engulfing me in warmth and safety. I feel an overwhelming connection to this man who is going to be my life partner, and a sudden urge to confess. One I realize I should follow. I pull back from Rob and say, "There's something I need to tell you."

His lips part and he looks a little alarmed. I'd like to say it's not a big deal, but in the grand scheme of things, it is a big deal, and I should tell him now instead of waiting. I take his hand, walk over to the two-seater on the corner of the porch and sit with Rob.

His face is a mixture of concern and confusion when I open my mouth to speak. "I should've told you earlier, but when you asked me why I locked my medical file, I wasn't honest with you," I say.

I take a deep breath as I prepare to finish, when he surprises me and says, "I know."

It's my turn to part my lips in surprise. I narrow my eyes and stare at him. "What do you mean, you know? How?"

He looks down at my hand holding his, and then back up at me, a bit of shame in his eyes. "I'm sorry," he says. "I sort of broke into your medical file."

I can't help but frown. I hadn't expected that. While I wasn't sure he was entirely convinced by my lie about locking the file, I hadn't thought he'd break in to see it.

"I'm sorry," he says again. "Believe me, I felt like a complete jerk after I saw the file. I shouldn't have let Kevin get to me."

"Kevin?" I say, shaking my head in confusion. "I don't understand. What does Kevin have to do with why you broke into my file?"

He pauses a moment, as if debating what to say. Then he says, "You know I went to the hotel this morning to meet George, Jane, and the kids and make sure they'd checked in alright and everything?"

I nod, so he continues. "When I got there, Kevin was talking to

Jane and George. I went over to them, and George explained that they'd bumped into Kevin, who'd mentioned he was in town for his friend Susan's wedding. At this point, Kevin dropped that he was your ex-fiancé and that you had personally called to invite him."

Yeesh, that does not sound like a good scene.

"It was clear he was trying to cause trouble," Rob says. "So I asked if I could have a word with him alone. We headed off to a corner, and I told him that we didn't need his help anymore and he should go back to Maryland."

"How'd he take that?" I ask.

"He told me he'd go back when you told him to. That he'd come because you asked, and he would only go when you asked. Because I was annoyed, I told him that you didn't want anything to do with him, that you'd only locked your medical file to keep him away from you and your information."

Even now, Rob grimaces at the retelling of this story. "That's when he smirked and told me you'd actually locked the file last week, before he was in the picture, and that the only person you wanted to keep out of your file was me."

Now, I totally get why he looked at my file. Any resentment I was feeling earlier is fading away. I reach out and pat Rob's hand. "I'm sorry Kevin was such a jerk to you, and mostly I'm sorry that I didn't tell you the truth," I say.

"It's fine," Rob says, reaching out and touching my belly. "I understand."

"I just got it in my head that it would be so cool to tell you on our wedding night, but then Dr. Evans said if you looked at my medical file for anything, you'd see that I was pregnant. She suggested locking it, since it was less than two weeks before the wedding."

He smiles. "It would have made a nice surprise, and I'm sorry I looked."

I take a deep breath. "I'm not," I say. "It was silly to want to make a grand surprise of it. I realized that tonight. We shouldn't enter a marriage with secrets, even good ones."

Rob rubs my belly. "So, how are you feeling?"

"Fabulous," I say. "I wouldn't even think anything was different if my doctor hadn't told me." Seeing his hand on my belly, knowing we're going to be parents makes me smile. Then I notice the watch on his wrist. "Oh my God! It's ten till midnight. I have to go," I blurt out standing up.

He looks a little startled, then laughs. "Yes, it is bad luck for me to see you after midnight."

I give him a stern stare. "Yes, it actually is, and we need all the luck we can get tomorrow."

Rob joins me standing and wraps his arms around me. "I'm happy to do whatever will make you feel better, but no matter what else happens tomorrow, you and I are going to become husband and wife, OK?"

I smile, and I know he's right. "Yep, 'cause we're a team."

He releases me, looks at his watch. "You should go. I'll send Kelsey and Luke up."

"Alright," I say, as I turn to head off the porch. "I'll see you at the altar."

# SATURDAY

# 41

## KELSEY

I am ensconced in the secret room, the light on as it won't be noticeable to those coming and going. Susan didn't want me to be seen by any of the crew or people making preparations. I'm a bit nervous about the day's plan. I'm afraid the colonel will balk when he sees what we're doing. I want my daughter back more than anything and this venue makes sense, but I also don't want the colonel to do something to ruin Susan's wedding. Especially after everything she has done for us this week.

I am pacing the room because I'm too nervous to sit. Luke has gone to help Rob get ready and check in on his sister's health. Even though Rob isn't with Jasper, he'll remotely monitor Emmie's vital signs. More importantly, he'll see when her LMS signal cuts off.

Jasper is supposed to remove the LMS. Emmie has a newer model, like the one I had. It uses nanotechnology, shooting small nanobots, dubbed nanoparticles when used in an LMS, throughout your system. So, even if you remove the LMS, the nanotech is still floating about your body. With that kind of LMS, you can't really flee the government immediately because the nanoparticles send a signal indicating your location for the next 24 hours.

Rob figured out a way to remove the nanoparticles. He says it will work, so that should put Emmie out of the government's range as soon as Jasper removes the LMS. Jasper said he understood how to do it, and he seems a capable enough doctor to learn quickly. I just hope it goes as planned.

There is a knock on the door, and I hear Susan say, "Are you in there?"

I call out "yes," but no more, as I don't want to be overheard by anyone in the main hall. Though, I didn't see anyone, so I'm probably being over cautious.

I crawl through the tunnel and out into the main room, where Susan is standing next to the bed admiring a bold red dress, and holding a matching wide-brimmed hat with a netting veil. She is wearing a silk robe and smiles when she sees me. "Cheer up," she says. "You're going to see your daughter in just a couple more hours."

Ever the optimist. I laugh. "You're getting married in just a couple of hours," I say. "Your cheer is more than enough for all of us."

She holds out the hat to me, "I think it will be best if you put your hair up. And definitely angle this down so the veil covers your face."

I take the hat, but take her hand with my other and give a tight squeeze. "Are you sure this is OK?" I ask, looking her in the eye. "I know this is the plan we worked out, but I worry it's the wrong tactic. I know the colonel will want to see me before he makes the exchange, but..."

"But nothing," she says, laying her hand on top of mine. "What will make my wedding day perfect is if you will be in my wedding, and when the ceremony is over, go get your daughter."

I bite my lip in an effort to keep from speaking. She's made up her mind on this. I can see it in her eyes, but I worry that she's not thinking this through. They could point me out amongst the guests and the colonel will still have seen me. Walking down the aisle as a bridesmaid is like poking the bear. What if he makes a scene? "I'm just worried that he's going to get mad and..."

"And nothing," Susan says, cutting me off. "He's at a wedding, a wedding with a camera crew. He is not going to hurt a child, not with all those people around and not with it being filmed."

I let go of her hand and toss the hat on the bed. I walk toward the drawn curtain and peek out the side. There is a camera crew setting up. A last minute idea of Rob's. Ever since Susan's public surgery to reverse her paralysis, she's been a bit of a minor celebrity. Some broadcast show had asked about wedding interviews with Rob and Susan, which they'd declined, until we decided to make the wedding the drop spot for Penelope. Rob told the show they'd love to have a camera crew at the wedding. They'll be filming, and that's supposed to afford Penelope and me a measure of protection against the colonel's wrath.

But I don't know. If this colonel is as dangerous as everyone says, I feel hesitant to cross him. Even Dr. Grant warned me to stay away from Parker. Susan comes over to me. She looks so pretty, her face bare and hair pulled back into a ponytail. Her nails are painted a bright red that matches the bridesmaid dresses.

"Did you buy me a wedding gift already?"

Her question catches me by surprise, as it's completely off topic from our discussion moments ago. "Umm, not yet," I say, apologetically. "I know what I want to get you, but we were going to order it so it arrived after you got back from your honeymoon and with everything else going on…"

She pats my shoulder. "I'm not chastising you," she says. "But, whatever it is you were going to order, don't. I know what I want from you. I want you to believe." She looks me in the eyes, her green eyes gleaming brilliantly enough that I want to believe every word she says. "I want you to believe this plan is going to work, and I want you to enjoy this day. OK? Promise me you'll believe in this plan. Because you're going to get your daughter back today. And you're going to go home with your husband."

She hugs me, and I say, "I promise," even though I'm not sure I mean it. I'm making too many of these promises I don't quite mean these days.

After releasing me, Susan says, "Listen, I have to go upstairs to get ready, so I probably won't see you again until right before the wedding when we all come down here. It'll be me, Jane, my cousin Lily and the girls. Keep our flowers safe." She looks to the rows of bouquets set up on a small table the florist brought in this morning. I smirk and nod. I'm pretty sure there's nothing I can do to ruin the flowers. "The door to this room will remain locked. Only Luke and I have a key, so no one else will come in. I'm sorry you can't join the preparations."

I shake my head. "No, it's fine. No one who doesn't need to know should know I'm here until I walk down the aisle."

"OK, so I'll see you in a little bit." She flashes her brightest smile, her eyes lighting up with such confidence. "This is going to work."

Unfortunately, for all the confidence she seems to feel, it's how certain I feel something is going to go wrong. My gut is twisting inside, but I manage a smile and nod.

Susan heads to the door, and opens it just a sliver to look out. Then she says, "Lewis, can I see you for a minute?"

A moment later, she opens the door fully to let my father in. He smiles at Susan. "You look beautiful."

"A compliment pre-makeup and pre-dress! You're too kind," she says. "I have to go up and get ready, but feel free to hang out here as long as you want. Just lock the door after I go."

She gives us both a wave and heads off.

"She's really excited," I say to my father.

"She should be," he says. "This is a momentous day for them. She picked a good one in Rob."

I agree with him and plop down on the bed, looking at my dress. It's sleeveless with a v-neck, and it flows out from the waistline with lots of billowy red fabric. It's a very pretty dress, and very perfect for Susan's wedding.

"I have it," my father says, interrupting my train of thought. From his suit's breast pocket, he pulls a piece of paper folded in thirds. As he unfolds it, I see the official seal on it. He hands it to me, and I read it. What I wouldn't have given for a piece of paper like this two years ago. It's a pardon, but knowing that my daughter still isn't home with me makes it feel anticlimactic. I gingerly hand the paper back to my father.

"Thank you for getting this," I say.

"The drive did it," he says, smiling. "With that evidence, the governor felt compelled." I force a smile to mimic his happiness, but I still feel keenly worried something will go wrong. My father presses his lips together tightly and gives me a scrutinizing look. "The colonel won't like that you've been pardoned, that you're not a fugitive anymore, but he'll have to accept it," he says.

I look down at the dress again, not sure I want to voice my anxieties. Unfortunately, now is the only time I have to voice them, so I might as well. "You said earlier the colonel thinks of everything. What if he's thought of a way around this?"

My father shakes his head, and sits on the bed with me, the dress lying neatly between us. He raises both eyebrows and says deliberately. "He doesn't know about this. I hired a very discreet service to take me back to Maryland last night. I spoke with the governor in private. We had this witnessed and sealed, and he's not going to tell anyone about it, especially Col. Parker. There is no way for him to prepare for this, no way for him to know. You will not have to go with him."

Sometimes faking it is the best way to feel it, so I breathe out, smile big and say, "This will work." My father slides the dress out of the way and hugs me.

When he releases me, he smiles. He looks so happy, I decide that this is how I'll remember him. If things go wrong, this is a good last memory. "I love you, daddy," I say, embracing him again, squeezing him tight.

"This will work, Kelsey. This isn't goodbye," he says.

"I know," I lie. "I just want you to know that I love you. And I meant what I said the other day. You've been a great father. I'm not upset that you didn't try to get me off the list. You stood by me in every way that counts. And when Penelope comes home, it's going to be because of you. I appreciate your strength and your love, dad."

He pulls away and looks at me. "Stop saying your goodbyes to me," he says sternly. "You will get your daughter back, and you will not have to go anywhere with that man. I promise you. Once he sees this paper, there is nothing he can do. You're not the wrongdoer he can parade around as a bad example. You're safe."

He's so confident when he says it, that I almost believe him. "Has the colonel gotten Penelope yet?" I ask my father.

He shakes his head. "Not yet. My guys are following him, and as soon as they see him with her, we'll have Jasper get Emmie. No one will realize the permission to transfer Emmie is forged until after the wedding. The colonel won't know; he'll already be in transit with Penelope when it happens, and my private eyes are good. They won't let your daughter out of their sight once the colonel has her."

I take a deep breath and nod. This is going to work, I tell myself. Emmie will be safe and Penelope will be safe. "What if someone calls the colonel and tells him Emmie is gone?"

My father shakes his head. "It won't matter," he says. "I have two teams following the colonel. He won't go anywhere with Penelope without us knowing. The colonel wants this plan to work. He'll bring her here."

I nod again, more to reassure myself than him. This will work. Only, I still feel jittery. I think I'll feel better if I get a moment to myself. "Listen," I say to my father. "I should get dressed and everything, make sure I don't look like a hag standing up there next to Susan."

He looks like he wants to say something else, to tell me again that the plan will work. Instead he nods. "Sure," he says, standing. "And there is no way you could ever look like a hag."

Clearly, it's been too long since he's seen me first thing in the morning. I smile, then stand and hug him one more time. As I'm holding him tight, I remember something crucial and release him.

I say, "Mr. Giggles," take a couple of paces to the dresser, open the top drawer and pull out the stuffed monkey Penelope's had since she was just a month old. It's the first gift my father gave to her and he should give it to her again. "Be sure to give this to Penelope," I say, handing the animal to my father.

He looks at it, then eyes me skeptically and says, "I'm sure she'd rather you give it to her."

He thinks I'm still being pessimistic, still trying to make sure she'll be OK if I'm gone. But this time, I'm actually being practical. "Maybe she would," I say, "But if the plan works, you'll see her before the wedding ends. At the very least, she can hold it while she waits for me. She loves Mr. Giggles, and it might help her to have it sooner than when I can give it to her."

He nods and takes it. "I'll make sure she gets it when I see her."

I smile. "Thanks, Daddy," I say. "Now, I really should get dressed."

He gives me a goodbye nod, turns and leaves. I lock the door behind him.

# 42

## SUSAN

I am sitting on a stool in front of a mirror as Jane and Lily, my cousin Dan's wife, stare at me appraisingly. I feel like I'm on display, perched in my undergarments, my makeup done and my hair in loose curls that hang to my shoulder.

I feel like laughing as the two of them — so dissimilar in physical appearance — have that same serious, dedicated look on their faces. Jane, a statuesque, thin brunette with high cheek bones and Lily, a blue-eyed, blonde-haired petite woman endowed with all the curves you dreamt you would be lucky enough to get when you were pre-pubescent.

"You look beautiful," Jane says, as she moves a hair on my head, which must be out of place.

"Agreed," Lily says. "So, in about 15 minutes, we'll put on your dress and then we'll head downstairs."

At the words downstairs, Lily throws Jane a significant look. I cast my eyes down, as I don't want to be questioned again. The ladies want to know who my last minute addition to the wedding party is. I've told them they'd find out right before the ceremony. Only, that answer has satisfied neither woman.

"Annabelle, Colleen," I call to the two flower girls. They come over, squishing their way between their mothers to reach me. "Let's have a look at you two in the mirror."

I step away, so the girls, ages 5 and 7, can admire their ankle length red dresses and matching wicker baskets that soon will be filled with flower petals.

"You two are perfect," Jane tells them. "Can you girls head out-side and stand guard? I think Rob may want to sneak a peak, which is absolutely not allowed."

The girls giggle and happily agree. Lily doesn't look so sure about this plan, and offers to go out with them. I think she's worried they're going to somehow ruin their dresses (and given Colleen's love of cartwheels and mud, that is a distinct possibility). With everyone else leaving, I'm certain Jane is going to make an effort to get me to spill the beans once more. I suck in a breath and place both hands over my tummy, hoping it quells the flutter of nerves inside. I hadn't anticipated being this topsy-turvy today. Wedding jitters will do this to you, I suppose, but I've got a lot more going on today than just wedding jitters.

Jane watches the door close after the girls leave, then turns back to me. "Are you going to be okay," Jane asks, frown lines setting in. "You look like you're going to regurgitate."

I look up at her, with raised eyebrows. "Regurgitate?"

She breaks into a huge grin, her brown eyes sparkling. "I knew that would get your attention," she says. "Maybe you don't look like you're going to vomit, but you do look pale." Jane takes a step closer to me and gingerly places the back of her hand on my forehead. "You're not hot," she says, then walks over to the makeup table a few feet away and grabs the compact. She takes a little powder brush and slides it across my forehead.

Satisfied that she's cured any ill caused by her checking my temperature, she folds the compact shut with a snap, and puts it back on the table. She comes back to me, takes a deep breath, pauses a moment, and finally says, "Susan, I thought you and I were friends, good friends, but I feel like you're shutting me out." Her voice is low with an undercurrent of sorrow, and I feel bad.

I shake my head adamantly "This has nothing to do with our friendship," I tell her. "I would tell you if I could, but I can't right at this moment. Just know I appreciate all your help. Especially throwing the bachelorette party and helping plan everything. You've been a godsend."

A smile that doesn't touch her eyes appears on her face, and for the first time, I worry I've offended the one family member of Rob's who I've grown close with.

Banging on the door breaks my train of thought. Jane and I both turn to look at the closed door, but she's the one who takes action, walking over and opening it. I take a step back, hoping not to be seen, as I'm only in my brassiere, panties and stockings.

Lily pokes her head in and says, "Sen. Reed says he needs to see you. That it's urgent. That Col. Parker is here."

I walk over, grab my robe and slide into it. "Yes, send him up," I say, then pause, finding the courage to say the next part. "I'm really sorry, Jane, but this is a private matter. Would you mind leaving us while I take care of it?"

Her mouth drops open and the silence before she walks out makes me feel like the absolute worst friend in the world. Within two minutes, Sen. Reed and Luke are inside the room with me.

"Is she here?" I ask them. Luke raises, then slumps his shoulders in an 'I don't know' motion.

Lewis speaks. "He called from his car and told us to meet him up here in five minutes."

I start pacing the bedroom, which feels smaller with the tension of the situation.

"Susan," Luke says. "I'm sorry to do this on your wedding day. Please don't upset yourself."

I half laugh. "I love pacing, Luke," I tell him. "So don't worry about it. My wedding day will be perfect if you get your daughter back."

A quick nod lets me know he heard me, but his face looks completely drained of color, and I can tell he is on pins and needles. The senator, under pressure more often, I suppose, looks fairly free of nerves. He adjusts his cufflinks, but there is no other sign that he might be worried.

Another knock on the door. Senator Reed and I stand frozen, but Luke, who is standing right near it, reaches over and opens it

Col. Parker, clad in a military dress uniform, walks in, Penelope ensconced in his arms, her head on his shoulder.

"Peanut," Luke says. The girl turns to see him, and immediately stretches out her arms to grab her father. Luke reciprocates, pulling his daughter from the colonel's arms and taking a few steps away from him. She looks well. Not too thin, dressed in a long-sleeved, pale pink dress with matching Mary Jane shoes, and a pink ribbon tied in her hair. Yet, the way she clings to her father, as if she will never let go of him, makes me wonder how traumatic this experience has been for her.

The colonel shuts the door behind him, and walks toward Sen. Reed. "I've kept my part of the bargain," Parker says, his voice cold. "Where is Kelsey?"

The senator glances at Luke, who is holding Penelope and rubbing her back, then he scowls at Col. Parker. "You'll get Kelsey when the ceremony is over."

"That wasn't our bargain," Parker retorts.

Sen. Reed places a hand on the colonel's shoulder. Parker looks momentarily revolted, like he might back away. He doesn't. The senator says evenly, "Our agreement was that you would get her at the wedding. Not at a specific time. We'll conclude our agreement at the end of the ceremony."

The colonel takes a step back, allowing the senator's hand to fall away. "Fine," he says.

The senator's face morphs into surprise. I feel how he looks. I didn't think it would be that easy to get him to acquiesce. He's given us the only leverage he has — Penelope. We'd expected him to put up more of a huff at the possibility of a double cross.

Suddenly, Luke erupts. "What is this?"

I look over, and he's got Penelope's sleeve rolled up. He walks closer and shows us all the white bandage on the girl's arm, between her wrist and elbow.

"LMS," the colonel says plainly.

Luke's face is red and a vein in his neck is bulging. Penelope is clinging to him, tightly, and he seems to be using every ounce of effort to speak calmly so he doesn't disturb his already-traumatized child. In a low voice, he says, "You had no right."

The colonel scoffs. "I suspected you would try to double cross me and had this implanted yesterday. Seems it was a good call as I just learned Jasper Christensen removed your sister from a treatment facility using a forged order. That was not part of the bargain," he spits. Then he smiles. "It's not a big deal, though. I'm sure there won't be any other problems with our agreement. If there are, I'll have to exercise my insurance plan."

Luke bites his lower lip. "Insurance plan?"

"Yes. Your daughter's LMS isn't like other ones," the colonel says, "It's one of the prototypes we've been working on."

"A prototype," Sen. Reed says. "What kind of prototype?"

The colonel turns to him, a wicked smile on his lips. "Well, LMSes are a great warning system that can bring help to a sick patient. But, our researchers wanted to look into whether we could use an upgraded nanoparticle to help start medical aid, say, to stop further damage from a stroke, or even start repairing damage while paramedics were en route."

The senator looks nervous now. "That's not an answer, John. What does the prototype do?"

"I'm getting to it," the colonel says, his voice calm, the smirk of victory on his face. "I had my team determine if they could cause a problem, rather than just fix it. Turns out, we can induce a stroke with the click of a button. We will induce a stroke if there are any further double crosses."

I think Luke would be ripping the colonel limb from limb if his daughter weren't in his arms. Luke takes a step back, gripping Penelope tighter to him.

Sen. Reed, on the other hand, takes a step closer to Parker. "You would hurt an innocent child?"

Parker brushes at his sleeve, as if removing a bit of dust, and then says, "I'm sure you won't have to find out, because I'm certain you are going to deliver your daughter, as promised. Just as I've delivered your granddaughter, as promised."

Then Parker turns to Luke. "And don't even think of having your doctor friend try to remove her LMS. I'm sure he fancies himself a whiz at this kind of thing since he prevented us from tracking himself and Ms. Harper. However, he doesn't know this LMS system. It uses three nanoparticles and you can't remove the LMS and nanoparticles without triggering an alarm."

Luke is glaring at him, but the colonel seems to relish this. "Let me explain, just so you don't get the idea that you can outsmart me. At any given time, one nanoparticle is charging at the LMS while the other two float through the body. One nanoparticle must be in the bloodstream at all times, or else the LMS will send an emergency alarm to us. If that happens, that single remaining nanoparticle will be directed to induce a stroke. If you try to change our agreement further, we will implement our insurance policy and your daughter will die. You have your daughter. I suggest you do what is necessary to keep her safe."

With this, the colonel turns on his heel and heads out the door.

The four of us are alone now, and with Luke trying to comfort Penelope, I turn to the senator. "What are we going to do?"

The senator's lips barely part when he speaks, his words almost inaudible. It takes a few seconds before my brain processes what he said: "We have to give him what he wants."

"The hell we do," Luke says. "Lewis, come with me." He turns and heads out the door, with Sen. Reed following close behind.

* * *

The senator and Luke left a few minutes ago, and I'm pacing the room, my stomach in knots. When the door opens, I expect to see one of them has returned with news, but it's Jane.

My expression must show my disappointment because her lips pucker like she's just sucked on a lemon as she walks over to me. "What's wrong?" she asks, a mix of sympathy and irritation.

I turn and run toward the bathroom. Just barely, I make it to the toilet to vomit.

I hear Jane follow after me. She puts one hand on my shoulder and uses the other to hand me a damp wash cloth. I wipe my mouth with it and say, "Thank you."

I flush, close the seat lid and sit down on it, leaning forward, so I don't feel so shaken and ill at ease. How quickly the day is changing for me. I felt good vibes all morning, and now I feel nothing but bad vibes.

"You can tell me what's bothering you," Jane says soothingly. She pauses a second, takes a deep breath, and then says solemnly: "I know your ex is here. If you're having second thoughts… If you don't want to marry, Rob… You shouldn't. If you're having doubts, I'll go explain to Rob, to everyone. Don't worry. I'll stand by you. Just tell me, and we'll figure this out."

I'm momentarily both too stunned to speak and incredibly touched. She is truly my friend, whether I intend to marry Rob or not. But I must dispel her notion as to the source of my distress. "I'm marrying Rob, Jane," I say vehemently. "That is absolutely happening today."

She looks relieved, but confused. "This isn't about your ex, who happens to be staying at our hotel? The ex who seemed to be succeeding in gloating about something to Rob the other day."

I shake my head. "No, Kevin's reasons for being here have nothing to do with the wedding or any lingering feelings I have for him. I love Rob, and the one thing I want is to get married today. There's just another situation going on. It's adding stress to the day."

"Maybe I can help," she says. "Two heads are always better at solving a problem than one."

But, there is nothing she can do to help this situation. I decide to go ahead and confide at least some of what is going on to the woman who will be sister-in-law, but who'd planned to stand by me even if I wasn't. "I'm pregnant," I say.

Her lips part in shock, at first, but then widen into a grin.

"Promise me you won't tell anyone," I say. "Only Rob and I know."

She puts her hands over her heart, and says, "I swear."

I nod. Rob and I didn't talk about telling anyone, but Jane is a secret keeper, if anyone is. I take a breath and tell her a very simplified version of the truth, with maybe a few stretches. I say Kelsey's father managed to get permission for her to attend the wedding, and Rob surprised me with the news yesterday, but now Kelsey's daughter has a medical problem that needs immediate attention, and may cause a bit of delay. She takes it in stride, and I'm glad I have someone to talk to.

# 43

## KELSEY

I am all ready, clad in my red dress and the matching hat with a short veil. Hopefully it will hide my face. The wedding should start shortly, so I'm not surprised when I hear the key in the lock and see the door open.

Only, when Luke enters, my heart fills with dread, my mouth parts, and I say, "What's wrong?"

His face is pale, and his expression worried, but the minute he looks at me, he forces a smile, and says, "Nothing." He walks over and looks me over from head to toe. "You look pretty in your dress."

"Thanks," I say, as I stare at him, trying to figure out what's wrong. "I thought you were going to wait for the colonel, for Penelope."

"I am," he says, with a reassuring nod. "It's just that the colonel is running a tad late. He has Penelope; he'll be here shortly, but I just wanted to come and check on you, make sure you're alright."

I scrutinize him a moment more and know there is something more to the story. "I'm fine," I say. "What is it you're not telling me?"

He smiles again and insists, "Really, there's nothing I'm not telling you. I just wanted to check on you, tell you, I love you."

I can't help but smile at that. "I love you, too, Luke," I say. "I'm sorry if it doesn't seem like I'm glad to see you. I just worry that something's wrong. Why don't you think he's here?"

Luke purses his lips. "He's on his way."

"My father's detectives have seen him?"

Shock plays across his face that I've asked this question. After a moment, he responds, "Yeah, of course," he stammers. "Everything will be fine. I just came down so you wouldn't worry about the delay."

Ha. I wish it was that easy not to worry. Luke takes off my hat, tosses it to the bed, then pulls me close to him. "It's going to be OK," he says. "Just remember that I love you and Penelope more than anything in the world. I won't let the colonel hurt either of you."

I wish that were true, that he could protect us both from the colonel. But, if something goes wrong, if the colonel has something else up his sleeve, he might not be able to protect me. I blow out a long breath. I can't think like that. I promised Susan I would believe. That's my wedding gift to her. I have to believe this plan will work.

I pull away from the embrace. "You should go," I say to him. "You need to be ready for when the colonel arrives with her."

He nods. "Right."

"And my dad has Mr. Giggles. So as soon as you get her, be sure he gives it to her."

Luke stares at me, his expression one of disbelief. "You gave your father Mr. Giggles?" he asks, as if my doing so has mortally wounded him.

Maybe it has. Maybe he feels the same way my father does, that me parting with Mr. Giggles right now is a sign that I'm giving up. It's not. I put my hand on his shoulder, take a deep breath and try to put his fears to rest. "This is not me giving up hope," I say. "I know my father didn't want to take it, that he thought me giving it to him, was just me admitting defeat. But that's not it. I want her to have it so she can have back some of what was stolen from her. She'll get you and Mr. Giggles immediately. That's all. I didn't do it as a goodbye to her. I just thought it would be nice for him to give it to her again."

Luke is still staring at me like he's not quite comprehending. Then, he pulls me to him and squeezes me tight. "I know you weren't saying goodbye. I'm glad you gave your dad Mr. Giggles. It's right that he gives it to Penelope again."

He gives me another squeeze, draws in a breath, and then chokes out, "I just want you to know that I love you… And your father loves you... And I would never do anything to intentionally hurt you or Penelope. Always, I want to protect you two."

"Luke," I say, pulling away. His eyes look wild and frantic and his face is a mask of sorrow. "You're scaring me."

He closes his eyes, opens them, clearly trying to look more reassuring, but he doesn't. "I," he starts, but then closes his mouth. Eying me piteously, he starts again. "I've been trying to be strong for you, and just in this moment, everything sort of caught up with me. The cost of what we're doing, the cost of what happens if we do it wrong. I'm not trying to scare you. OK. I just felt overwhelmed for a minute."

I reach back in and hug him. I've wanted him to confide in me and now that he has, I realize I won't be much help to him. "It's OK to be scared," I say to him. "I'm scared too, but I think we have to try to push that out of our minds for now. And besides, we're almost there. He'll be here soon with Penelope."

Luke wheezes out and then releases me. His eyes look moist and I feel bad for him. I'm about to tell him to sit down for a minute, when he says. "I need to go, to make sure I'm available when the colonel arrives."

I nod. He starts to turn and go, when I notice his shirtsleeve has a red spot on it. "Luke," I say. He stops, turns back to me, and I look at the spot on his sleeve. It looks like blood. I take a step toward him, reaching out my hand to touch his sleeve, near where the bloodstain is. "What's this?"

He snatches his arm back. "Nothing," he says, eyeing the stain menacingly. "I just cut my arm trying to grab a ball one of the flower girls accidentally tossed behind a rose bush. Thorns. Little cut. Thought I got it cleaned up. I'll be wearing a jacket, so no one will notice."

Something is weird. "You were outside and the girls were playing ball?" I ask. "In their dresses?"

He has this deer caught in headlights look for a moment, but then shakes it off. "See, they're not supposed to be outside playing ball in their dresses," he says with a smirk. "So I was kind enough to get their ball, and promise not to tell their mothers. You shouldn't either. They're kids. At a wedding. That is delayed."

He's right. Kids will be kids. I force a smile. "Go on, then, in case he's here."

"I love you," Luke says, as he walks backwards to the door, never taking his eyes off me. "Don't open the door for anyone, OK?" I nod. "Penelope will be safe, and so will you. I promise."

With that, he leaves. I'm alone again, and more anxious than ever.

# 44

## SUSAN

I felt better after my confession, and Jane's been a great help. Shortly after I fessed up, my uncle came and told us that Rob had some type of patient emergency, and we needed to delay the wedding for a half an hour. Lily went on about how this is Rob's wedding day and wasn't there a doctor who was filling in? I told her I didn't mind. I'm pretty sure Rob is trying to sort out the LMS problem. If anyone can figure it out, I know he can. If half an hour will give Rob the time he needs to get that chip out of her arm, so be it.

Jane, given what I told her, has been sitting by my side stalwartly. I'm glad I told her, because she's been a buffer between Lily and me. While Dan is my favorite cousin, his wife can be grating at times. I'm trying to recall now why I felt compelled to include her in the wedding. Lily is scowling in the corner while Jane is trying to convince her this is a quite normal part of being a doctor's wife. "Susan might as well get used to it upfront," Jane is saying. I'm just thankful that Lily hasn't thought to bring up the fact that my soon-to-be-husband works in a research lab and doesn't actually have patients right now.

I look at the clock. The wedding was supposed to begin at 3 o'clock, and it's already 3:35. Despite sitting still and trying to appear calm, I'm starting to get antsy. Starting to worry that Rob won't be able to help. And I'm also feeling like the worst host ever as this is our event and we've got 200 people down there waiting for a wedding that should have started already. I take a deep breath and will myself not to get up and pace. I actually feel better when I pace, but doing that will start Lily ranting again.

There is a knock on the door and Lily answers it. Luke comes in. I immediately head straight for him.

His nerves still look frayed, his face pale. "Were you guys able to…" I start to ask, but I'm not even sure what they were trying to do. "Did you fix the problem?"

Luke nods solidly. "She's going to be fine."

"Who?" asks Lily, butting in. "I thought this was a patient of Rob's."

Gee, I wish she'd stop. "Rob's patient is Luke's — " I'm saying when Luke cuts me off.

"My sister," Luke says. "My sister is Rob's patient."

I stare at him for a moment and then realize he's right. Lily, of all people, doesn't need to know Penelope is here. I nod.

"Rob wouldn't have delayed the wedding for just anyone," Luke says. "I just wanted to come up and apologize again to Susan for causing this problem on her wedding day."

Luke turns back to me. "I really am sorry, Susan. I want you to have a beautiful wedding. You've always been such a good friend." Then he leans in and hugs me.

"It's fine Luke," I tell him. "I don't care about the delay so long as she's going to be alright."

"She's going to be fine," he says loud enough for Lily and Jane to hear. Then he whispers in my ear, "I told Kelsey the wedding was delayed because the colonel was late. Don't tell her anything about Penelope's LMS. Please."

We let go of each other. I look Luke in the eye and nod.

"Rob is ready," Luke says. "So, let's get you two married."

# 45

## KELSEY

I am sitting on the bed, my hands in my lap, trying not to wrinkle the dress. It is so pretty and fits surprisingly well given that Susan had to get it last minute, when I hear the key turn in the lock.

It's almost forty minutes past the wedding start time, and I can't help but thinking that the colonel hasn't shown up with my daughter. I take deep breaths and try to calm myself. Tell myself it will be OK. I promised Susan I'd believe. That's supposed to be my wedding gift to her. I can at least try to do that properly.

I turn to see the door open and Susan walk in. All my anxiety melts away when I see her because the look on her face says nothing is wrong. My breath catches in my throat. She is literally breathtaking in her strapless white gown that flares out in a full-bodied hoop skirt. She looks just like a Southern Belle, the princess of this plantation, if plantations actually had princesses.

"You're gorgeous," I say, walking over to take a closer look at her.

She blushes and is about to respond when I hear a gasp and peer behind Susan to see a well-endowed blonde, Lily, covering her mouth with both hands. "What are you doing here?" she says as she pulls her hands away to reveal a face pinched with venom. "You're a fugitive."

The woman next to her, a tall brunette who was moments ago fiddling with Susan's train, making sure it had fully gotten through the doorway without snagging, straightens herself out and gives Lily a harsh look that immediately silences her.

A second later, two girls, also in red, with flower wreaths in their hair, walk through the door. The tall woman smiles at them, and says, "Girls, I need you to wait outside for just two minutes."

I recognize the smaller girl as Colleen, Dan's daughter, and I can only assume that the bigger girl is the daughter of this woman who's taken charge. The girls give a put-out look, but turn tail and exit. Lily shuts the door.

"Kelsey being here for the wedding has been cleared by government officials," the tall woman says coolly and authoritatively.

"How do you know, Jane?" Lily asks.

"Susan explained that's what Sen. Reed was doing when he interrupted us earlier: telling Susan he'd gotten final permission for his daughter to attend."

Lily gives me a suspicious glare and folds her arms across her chest.

To this, Susan says, "It's fine, Lily, really."

Lily shakes her head. "I have three children and no desire to be in a holding facility."

Jane narrows her eyes at Lily and says. "You are not at risk of that, but if it will make you feel better, you can wait outside with the girls. You can pretend you didn't see her."

"But she's in the —" Lily starts.

"It's my wedding day," Susan says. "Please, just let it go, for now."

A small breath escapes Lily and she scrunches her lips to one side in internal debate. Finally, she says, "I'll be out helping the girls get ready."

She turns on her heel and speeds out the door.

Susan breathes out. Jane smiles. "Thanks," I say to Jane.

"Jane, Kelsey; Kelsey, Jane," Susan says by way of introduction.

We exchange pleasantries, but then I turn my attention to Susan. "Col. Parker came?" I ask.

She smiles brightly and says, "Yes, of course. Don't worry about anything. Everything is going according to plan, only a little delayed."

I blow out a breath of relief. "That's good," I say. "Did you see her?"

Susan nods. "She was holding on to Luke, so she's fine."

I almost can't believe it. My daughter is here, and she's with Luke. It's going to be OK. "You were right," I admit. "It's going to be fine." I look toward the door and think of Lily's reaction to my presence. "Hey, the way Lily reacted," I say. "I worry other people might feel the same way. So, if this is going to cause you an iota of ill feeling on your wedding day, I don't have to walk down the aisle with you."

Susan is shaking her head before I can finish. "I want you in the wedding," she says. "And we need to hurry. We're already behind."

Jane heads over to the flower table, grabs a bouquet and a clear bag brimming with flower petals, and heads out the door, presumably to dole out the flowers to Lily and the girls.

Susan looks lovely in her dress, but I worry I'm ruining what should be her perfect day. I'd like to offer to bow out again, but that would just raise her ire. I plaster my public smile on my face. "You really look beautiful," I tell her again.

And she really does. She's even got a veiled tiara, the veil flipped behind her for the moment.

"So," I say "You ready to become Mrs. Donnelly?"

Susan's face beams. "More than you know," she says.

There is a knock at the door, so I turn and walk to the bed, pulling the hat over my head and tipping the netting on the front so it covers as much of my face as possible.

The door opens and I hear the voice of Susan's uncle Mike, but don't look back at him, for fear he'll recognize me and want me gone, like Lily. Only, I don't think a harsh glare would make Mike acquiesce as easily as Lily.

"You ready?" he asks.

"Just one second," Susan says and I hear the door shut.

I turn back to Susan. "I can stay here," I remind her.

She shakes her head. "Get us our bouquets, please. It's time."

I grab the large bouquet of pink and white roses and hand it to Susan. I take my smaller bouquet as well as the remaining one for Jane. At that moment, she re-enters the room.

"You ladies ready?"

"Yep," Susan and I say in unison, and then laugh. I hand Jane her bouquet, tuck my head and go out the door, past Mike. He starts to say something to me, but Jane comes out right behind me and says Susan wants him.

I hear the processional music start and Lily is already at the house's front doors standing with the flower girls. She doesn't look back at me. At some point that she knows, and has already rehearsed, she sends the girls out, with their baskets full of petals. A few more bars play, then Lily herself goes out. Jane gently presses her hand in my back, she urges me forward. "I'm next," she says. "You start after I reach the back row of chairs."

She goes out the door, walking at a perfectly timed pace out into the yard where the chairs are assembled on either side of an aisle of white silk. I can make out Rob and his brothers at the altar, along with a minister. I hear footsteps behind me and know it must be Susan and her Uncle. I see Jane walk past the marker and head out the door and into the sunshine and the waiting crowd.

I try to keep my head down as I walk down the aisle, and there are a couple of gasps as I pass. Seated along the aisle, I see Col. Parker, whom I recognize from his photo. He gives a short head shake and smiles lamentfully. Then, two rows ahead, near the front, I see Luke, with Penelope in his lap. She is nestled in his arms, sound asleep, and she looks perfect. I almost stop and pick her up when I reach him, but I realize I can't. That would ruin the wedding. I've paused, though, and I notice everyone is staring at me like I'm making a mistake. I take a deep breath and keep walking, past my little girl and up to the altar, where, Jane, Lily and the girls already stand. Suddenly, I realize I don't know where to go.

Jane inclines her head to the right and I step into the space next to her, putting the three of us directly across from Rob and his three brothers. The music halts, and then the first chords of Mendelssohn's wedding march play. We all turn to see Susan, accompanied by her uncle, begin her descent down the aisle.

# 46

## SUSAN

I'm nervous, but not in a bad way. It's more an excited nervous, a flutter of the tummy, my heart beating in excess. Walking down the aisle on uncle Mike's arm, walking toward Rob, toward the man I am going to spend the rest of my life with, fills me with joy..

When we arrive at the altar, with Kelsey, Jane and Lily and opposite them, Rob, George, John and Paul, I realize I've never been happier to be arriving at any place in the world. I smile from ear to ear. Rob lifts my veil, then offers the crook of his elbow, so I can slide my arm into his.

The minister, a silver-haired man named Reverend Dobbs, who has known Rob since he was just a boy, bades our guest be seated and welcomes everyone. He is saying a few words about the importance of marriage, and two people being partners in every way, and I know how right he is. I know that this is the beginning of a new chapter for us, one that bonds us together forever.

"Rob," the reverend says. "You have some words you've prepared for Susan."

Rob slides his arm out from mine and we turn to face each other. He takes my hands in his and says, "Susan, the day I first met you, the thing I remember most, the thing that made me know right then and right there that I wanted to find out everything I could about you, is that you faced new things head on, with curiosity, optimism and an open mind. You didn't know who I was or why I'd come to see you, but you didn't let that frighten you. You faced me, you heard me out, and you even challenged me.

"Since that day, I've learned that's how you face all things, head on. And it's one of the things I love most about you. So, today on our wedding day, I promise to love you always, to be your partner always, and to face the rest of our lives, each day, no matter what it brings, good or bad, with you, bringing the same optimism, curiosity and straight-forward view that you faced me with on that very first day."

He squeezes my hand, and then the reverend turns to me. "Susan, you have words you wanted to share with Rob."

As he says it, my throat suddenly feels dry and scratchy and I wonder if I will be able to do this, to say what's on my mind, in front of all our guests. But I look into Rob's beautiful hazel eyes and the jitters fade away. I give my throat a gentle clear before starting. "Rob," I say, softly. "I actually planned to say something a little different, but all day today, in my mind, I kept thinking about last night." I turn my head and see George grinning behind Rob. "For those of you who weren't there, we had a late night chat. And when I realized it was almost midnight, I ran out, declaring I couldn't stay because it was bad luck. I guess I was half worried I'd turn into a pumpkin or doom our lovely outdoor wedding to non-stop thunderstorms. But before I left in an insane bride-to-be haze, our talk made me feel better. I think the evening keeps coming back to me because it represents what I want our marriage to always be: honesty and sharing."

I take a deep breath and squeeze Rob's hands. "The thing I've learned most since I've been with you is just how much I want to share my life with you. I think really, that's what marriage is about: sharing everything together. The good, certainly. The average, of course, and unfortunately, the bad. The bad always comes, but it's not so bad when you spread it out over two people, when you're there to support each other.

"Me, I've always liked independence, taking care of myself, so sharing my sorrow and letting you support me was an adjustment in the beginning. But, I've learned so much from the times I have. I've learned that you are there for me, when all else seems doomed. That you will support me when I need it, that you and I can agree to disagree, but that we'll always face things together.

"So, today, I am promising to share my life with you, to bask in the glow when you share with me, to support you whenever you need it and to face everything together as a team: the good, the bad and the ugly. Doesn't matter so long as we've got each other."

Reverend Dobbs smiles and clasps his hands together. "What heartwarming pledges Robert and Susan have made toward each other. If they uphold the sentiments expressed today, theirs will be a long and happy union. At this point, we would like to exchange the rings."

Rob turns to George to get the ring. When we face each other again, Reverend Dobbs speaks. “Rob, place the ring on Susan’s finger, and repeat after me.”

Rob slides the gold band on my finger, and it feels almost magical. “With this ring, I thee wed,” the minister says and Rob repeats it. Then, I turn to Jane who has the ring for Rob, which I slip on his finger and say those six wonderful words.

Reverend Dobbs says, “I now pronounce you husband and wife. You may kiss the bride.”

# 47

## SUSAN

As Rob and I retract from our kiss, I realize I am happier than I ever thought I could be. Husband and wife. Simple words, but infinitely, wonderfully complex in meaning. I'm so grateful for this moment.

Rob and I turn back to our guests, who have risen and are gently applauding. I'm surprised there are so many of them. I think my smile would creep past my ears, if that were humanly possible. I look toward Kelsey, who is beaming at me, and then remember that now is action time. It is now that we must save Kelsey.

The gentle hum of applause has died down, so I look to Rob and he speaks, just as we rehearsed it. "I want to thank you all for coming today. It's been such a special day for Susan and I to have you all here. We are so glad you ventured out to join us. But, in addition to that, we have other happy news. I'd like to let our good friend, Lewis Reed, Senator Emeritus from Maryland, tell the good tidings."

At this, Sen. Reed stands and the crowd looks to him. He smiles and says, "First, I want to congratulate Susan and Rob, as I know this will be a good and strong union. I've seen them grow as a couple and the two of them, I'm sure, will have many fine years of happy marriage ahead.

"As to the news: I know Susan because she has been my daughter's best friend since they were in kindergarten. In recent years, however, my daughter has been a fugitive for failing to show up for her marking surgery. I learned earlier this week that my daughter was never supposed to be marked. She was not the best match for the man whose surgery she'd been scheduled to donate for."

There are a few murmurs and gasps in the crowd. Senator Reed waits a moment for silence then goes on. "I learned that my daughter was moved up on the list in some sort of bid to get me to use my influence to remove her name from the marking roster. This new evidence was presented to Maryland's governor yesterday, and after reviewing it, he has issued a full pardon for my daughter. So, our other happy news is that she too has returned to witness Rob and Susan's union and wish them a long and happy marriage."

I grab Kelsey and pull her toward me. "I am so honored and glad my friend, Kelsey could be here with us today as a fully legal FoSS citizen," I say, as Kelsey forces a smile to her face. I see she is nervously eyeing Col. Parker, whose face is reddening in silent fury. I look at the camera crew now and smile, knowing that the colonel will not do something to hurt anyone, not with everyone watching. "So, thank you all for coming."

Reverend Dobbs looks to me and, assured I'm done, announces that we'll be receiving guests and that the reception is off to the side tent. I whisper in Kelsey's ear. "It's going to be fine. Go get your daughter."

I take a step closer to Rob, but watch as Kelsey heads toward Luke and Penelope. Rob says, "I have to go."

My head whips around. "What?"

"The only way to take it out of Penelope without causing her to have a stroke was to put it in someone else," he says.

"Someone else," I say. I see Luke ready to hand Penelope to Kelsey, and I gasp. I think back to that night in the barn, where he said he'd trade himself for Penelope if it meant Kelsey would be safe. And today, he made me promise not to tell Kelsey about the LMS. Not so she wouldn't worry about Penelope, but so she wouldn't realize what he'd done. I open my mouth to speak, to ask Rob something, to find out what to do, but no words come out.

"I can get it out, I think," Rob says, seeing my distress. "I just need a tool Jasper has. Hopefully, he's here now."

"Hurry," I tell Rob, and he kisses my forehead, turns and rushes away.

# 48

## KELSEY

I wade through the crowd and find Luke standing next to a tree. He hands me Penelope and smiles. Her little arms grab hold of me and she buries her head in my neck. She smells just like Penelope: sweet and fresh and perfect.

"Right where she belongs," Luke says.

It feels so good. "Mama's here, Sweetheart," I say. "Mama's so sorry I wasn't there for you. I'm never going to leave you like that again." She doesn't say anything; she just clings to me, and I to her, and I am so glad.

My father comes over and stands beside Luke. "I told you this would work out, didn't I?"

I nod. "Yeah, you were right," I say. But, then the expression on his face sobers, and I notice he is looking behind me. I turn and see Col. Parker approaching us.

"Stay here," Luke says. "I'm going to talk to him."

He walks toward the colonel, meeting up with him about 15 feet from us. My father puts his hand on my shoulder. "You're safe and Penelope is safe, OK? You don't have to go with him."

I don't intend to. I don't think my body could let me leave this little girl who fits perfectly in my arms, this little girl who trembles with fear that I'll abandon her again. I watch as Luke and the colonel speak in low, furtive tones. I don't know what is said, but after a minute, Luke takes off, at a jog, in the opposite direction. I'm not sure where he's going.

My father looks at Luke's sudden departure, furrows his brow and takes a step toward Luke, as if he wants to follow. But, he sees Col. Parker continue striding toward us and instead straightens his posture and stands protectively beside me.

"So, this is you at your word, Lewis?" the colonel asks when he reaches us.

"I've kept my word," my father says. "I told you I respected the laws of our nation and I would turn over my fugitive daughter. She is not a fugitive, and I am not turning her over to you."

The colonel scowls. "And the girl's life means nothing to you?"

At this, I perk up my ears. I know what they're saying is important, but I don't understand it. I look to my father, begging with my eyes for an explanation.

The colonel sees my reaction and smiles. "So no one told you?"

I wish I didn't have to admit I am in the dark, but I want to know the answer more than I want to hide my ignorance. "Told me what?"

The colonel reaches out like he intends to touch Penelope, and I jerk away. He holds his hand steady, not coming closer, and says, "We gave your daughter an LMS."

I look down at her and then reposition her, so that I can roll up her sleeve without dropping her. With her sleeve up, I see a bandage on her left arm. I look to my father. "Daddy?"

"It's OK, we took it out."

The colonel smiles. "I knew you would," he says. "I'd been trying to figure out how Dr. Donnelly got his and Susan's LMS tracking beacon off, when I bumped into one of the guys who works in LMS tech, and he told me he was a friend of Rob's. I told him Dr. Donnelly would call today to ask about the best solution in removing one of our new LMSes, and that he should suggest putting it in someone else."

My father's eyes widen in shock and he mutters, "You bastard." I'm still not sure what exactly is going on.

"What is he talking about?" I ask. My father just stands there, staring, his lips parted. The colonel responds to me.

"The LMS we put in your daughter was initially designed to deliver treatment to patients, but we reengineered it to cause damage, a stroke, to be exact."

I can't hide my alarm as what he is saying is starting to sink in. This seems to heighten his pleasure. "I told Rob you couldn't remove it without triggering the stroke, only that wasn't true. Just like I thought, Rob called his friend, and it appears my plan worked perfectly. Rob put it in someone else. My guess was that he'd move it to you, and I'd get to kill you anyway. Only, it looks like he didn't use you. It looks like your husband was the guinea pig, and now, Mrs. Geary, he's going to die because of you."

My mouth falls open in shock. I look to my father, and the stunned expression on his face is enough to let me know the colonel is telling the truth. I remember the blood on Luke's sleeve. How he said he wouldn't intentionally hurt me, how he said he loved me. The colonel was never late. My husband was getting a deadly LMS implanted in his arm to save our daughter.

"No." I say to the colonel, and I reach out and touch his arm. "Please, you can't do that to him. Luke hasn't done anything wrong."

"That's too bad, because he will pay the price for your double cross." The colonel turns and walks away. From the corner of my eye, I see Luke, flanked by Jasper and Rob, heading toward us. The colonel is getting further away, and I realize what I have to do to stop this. I do something I wouldn't have thought possible just a few minutes ago, and I pull my clinging daughter from my arms and give her to my father.

"Kelsey, no," he's saying, as I run toward Parker.

The colonel is a fast walker, but I catch up with him. "I'll go with you," I blurt out as I get near. "Don't do anything to my husband. Please."

He turns to me, and grabs my arm, squeezing tight, like he doesn't intend to let go. With ferocity in his eyes, he says to me. "We all make choices in our lives, Mrs. Geary. You could've chosen to come with me, to honor your agreement. You could've chosen to help me show this country that people who reject Life First get what they deserve. Instead, you chose subterfuge, lies and betrayal. Those choices have consequences."

"I'm sorry," I whimper. "I am. I made a bad choice. I'm trying to fix it now."

He sneers and releases me. In his opposite hand he holds up a small portable electronic device. "It's too late," he says, then tilts the device so I can read the screen. One word is scrawled across it: activated.

I want to slap him or grab him or kick him, but instead I turn to see a crowd has gathered not far from where I'd just stood with Penelope. Oh my God. I know Luke is at the center. He's collapsed, I'm sure. He's dead, or dying.

I turn and sprint back, the crowd parting for me like the Red Sea.

And there in the center, is my father.

# 49

## KELSEY

Daddy," I shriek, as I see Jasper slice open my father's arm where his LMS should be. Rob and Jasper are standing next to him on the right. Haleema is sitting on the ground on the left side of him.

"I need everyone to back up, give us some room here," Jasper says loudly to those gathered nearby. As the others back away, I move closer and kneel near Haleema, who is near his knees. My father's shirt is ripped open and his entire body is limp.

Rob takes a wire attached to an electronic tablet and sticks it into the incision in my father's arm. "This nanotech was originally programmed to fix things," Rob says, glancing at me and Haleema. "I'm hooked into the LMS and I'm going to reboot it to it's original factory settings, and that should get the nanoparticles to repair some of the damage. An ambulance is coming."

As Rob works on this reboot, I see Haleema is holding my father's hand and saying softly, "Lewis you're going to be alright. Just stay with us." But my father's face appears lifeless, and he is not responding to her words. I back up slightly, worrying I'm in the way, even though I'd like to be close to my father.

I feel a hand on my shoulder and look up to see Luke holding Penelope. He kneels next to me. "Your father is going to be alright," he says. I hear a siren in the distance, and I try to turn back to my father, but Penelope has leaned forward and grabbed hold of me. I take her from Luke, and press her against me. She buries her head in my chest, which is just fine, because she doesn't need to see this.

I have no choice but to calm my racing heart with Penelope clutched around me. Still, I don't know what I'm going to do if my father dies. If he doesn't pull through, it's because of me, because he was trying to save me, save Penelope, save Luke, save us all. I close my eyes, open them again, and then look at Rob, who seems to be finishing up.

He nods. "I got it rebooted, and the nano is starting the repair," he says, knitting his brow. "I went ahead and pulled the LMS, just to make sure they don't try to reprogram it remotely. You can't reprogram the nano once the LMS is out. It should just do its intended job."

I nod, though I don't know if I understand or really want to understand. I just want my father well. The siren sounds like it's closer. Luke says, again, "He's going to be fine."

"How did this happen?" I whisper.

"I'm sorry," Luke says, placing his hand on my back. "I told Rob I'd take it. Rob had even started to make the incision, but your father stopped us. He said I should talk to you first. Not about doing it, but just to make sure that you were OK, explain about the delay. He also suggested I get Mr. Giggles to make the removal easier on Penelope. I thought he had a point, so I left to check on you and get the monkey but when I talked to you —"

"You realized I'd already given him Mr. Giggles, that he'd sent you on out on…" a fool's errand, I start to say, but I don't. My voice is monotone as the events of the day finally start to make sense.

"Once I found out he had Mr. Giggles all along, I realized what he'd probably done. That's why I told you I would never do anything to intentionally hurt you. I wouldn't have agreed to let him do this. By the time you and I had finished, by the time I got back to the room, the LMS was already in your father's arm. I asked Rob to take it out of him, to put it in me. I told him I was younger and had a better chance of surviving any problems, but your father insisted on leaving it there. Rob said it wasn't safe to keep trying to move the thing from person to person."

Paramedics approach with a stretcher. One of the medics says, "We need everyone to step away, so we can get him transported."

I stand up, back away, as the medics move my father onto the stretcher and slip an oxygen mask on his face. I watch as they take him to the ambulance.

Rob comes over and hands Luke a set of keys. "Take my car," he says.

Susan appears at his side, her makeup smeared by tears. "Kelsey, go ahead to the hospital, and as soon as we get all the people out, we'll come by."

I look around and there are still tons of guests milling around. This is supposed to be a joyous occasion. I pat Penelope's back and then look up at Susan. "Please stay, and try to salvage your reception," I say. "There's nothing you can do at the hospital. We've got Penelope and I'll have Luke with me. Stay and enjoy your wedding. You and Rob haven't even danced."

She shakes her head. "That's fine. We want to be there for you," she says.

"No," I tell her. "I'll feel worse if you come. Please stay." I see the ambulance drive away. "We should get to the hospital. I'm sure my father will be fine." I force a smile. "Stay and enjoy your wedding."

Before she can offer again, I start walking away. Luke joins me. We have to get to the hospital. We have to make sure my father is alright.

# 50

## KELSEY

I'm sitting in a chair in my father's hospital room and Penelope is asleep in my arms. Haleema is sitting in the chair on the opposite side of his bed, and there is an empty chair next to me, where Luke had been sitting. He went to get me something to eat. One of us should probably go home and get some sleep.

But, I feel too terribly guilty to leave my father right now. He did this so that I could live, so my daughter could live. He made a promise to me, a promise I thought he couldn't keep; a promise that Penelope would be safe and I wouldn't have to go with the colonel. That promise wasn't supposed to cost him his life.

Luke comes back, and he's got a bag in one hand and a drink holder with what looks like two cups of coffee. He smiles when he sees us, and sets the drink holder and bag on the adjustable wheeled table in the corner of the room.

"Here," he says to Haleema as he hands her the coffee. "I grabbed an extra sandwich in case you change your mind and want something to eat."

Haleema, her mix of silver and black hair pulled back into a bun, smiles back at him and takes the coffee. "Luke," she says softly. "Thank you, but my nerves are too frayed right now. I can't eat anything."

Luke nods, then brings me my coffee. He grabs a sandwich from the bag and brings it to me. It's going to be hard to eat with Penelope draped across me like this. Recognizing my dilemma, Luke attempts to take Penelope. She wakes up with a start, opens her eyes and looks momentarily dazed. She sees Luke, taking her from me, and breaks into a full wail.

"Shhhh," I say, pulling her back to me and patting her back.

"Momma's right here. It's going to be alright." Penelope shoves her little body as close to mine as possible and refuses to move. But she stops crying. I shake my head, wondering what this past week has been like for my daughter.

"You can go home," Haleema says. "You just got her back. This isn't any place to try to bond, to make her feel secure again."

She's right, but I don't want to leave. "I know," I say. "I just," I start. "I want him to know I love him and I don't want to leave after everything he sacrificed for me."

Haleema looks at me, her brown eyes warm and penetrating. "Kelsey, your father sacrificed so you and your husband could take your daughter home, not sit in a hospital waiting for him to wake up."

I close my eyes. "Haleema," I say, "I'm really sorry. If he dies, it will be my fault. I'll have cost you your husband and Penelope her grandfather."

"Lewis is not going to die," she says to me with a conviction I'm not sure I've ever heard in her voice before. "No matter what happens, you did not cause this. Col. John Parker did, and he is solely to blame."

I nod. She's right. It's his fault. All his fault. Penelope has fallen back asleep, just that quickly, nestled in my arms. Her breathing is steady and peaceful, but then she whimpers. Maybe she shouldn't be here. Yes, here in my arms, but maybe I should take her away from this hospital. I look down at her, tiny, helpless and fragile, then up at my father. He too is helpless and fragile. I look at Haleema, staring at him, devotedly, and wonder if maybe we should leave for a few hours, and we can spell her relief in the morning. "If we go," I say to her, "you'll be OK here by yourself?"

"I won't be by myself," she says, patting my father's still hand. "He was reading a biography of Jerry Maylee. I might read it to him. He'd probably like that."

My father looks so helpless, connected to tubes and monitors, his eyes closed, skin pale and wan. I see the rise and fall of his chest and know he's still breathing. I look at Haleema. She's so good for him, she believes in him, loves him. "We probably should take Penelope back, let her get a good night's sleep." I look at Haleema, then at Luke. "Could I just get a moment in private with him before we go?"

Haleema looks down at my father, strokes his cheek, and says, "sure."

Penelope is still nestled in my arms. I make one more attempt to put Penelope in Luke's arms. She wakes up, during the transfer, but I move around so she can see me and say, "momma's right here." She looks at me a moment, and closes her eyes again. Luke and Haleema leave the room and I am alone with my father. I step in close to him, and give him a kiss on the forehead. I notice my lipstick has left a mark on him. I'd half forgotten I was still gussied up from the wedding.

"Daddy," I say. "I just want you to know that I love you, and I appreciate beyond measure what you did for me today. You kept your promise and you made everything right. For that, I'll be forever grateful."

I take a deep breath and use my thumb to wipe the lipstick off his forehead. "Part of me wonders if you did this because you felt guilty about not trying to get me off the marking list. When I told you before that I wasn't upset with you for that, I meant it. You've always done your best for me. I love you so much, and more than anything, I want you to get better. You've done so much today already, but I want to ask you to do one more thing. Don't give up on yourself. Fight to come back to us. Haleema needs you, I need you and Penelope really needs you. You're her pop-pop. Please come back to us all."

I lean down and give the best semblance of a hug I can offer given that he's hooked into tubes and lying on his back. Then, I head into the hallway where Luke is standing talking with Haleema. He stops speaking when he sees me. I walk up to them. "Thanks, Haleema," I say.

She smiles, and says, "I'm going to get back to him."

"I will be back in the morning," I tell her.

She nods, then goes back to my father's room. I look at Luke, with Penelope snug in his arms. "You alright?" he asks me.

I shake my head. "Not really, but Penelope is here. So that's the most important thing."

Luke looks behind me down the hallway and raises an arm to wave someone over. I turn and see Jasper and Zuri walking our way.

"Hey, how's Emmie?" Luke asks, as Jasper arrives.

"Checked into the psych unit here," Jasper says. "They're going to evaluate her, but like I said earlier, they're not going to want visitors until they finish the evaluation."

Luke nods.

"Is there any change with the senator," Jasper asks.

I shake my head. "Same."

Jasper nods solemnly, then says. "I spoke to Rob a few minutes ago. I told him Lewis was still unconscious. He said the wedding guests had pretty much cleared out, and he wanted me to let you guys know you are welcome to come back to the house, stay in the guest cottage."

I'm so exhausted I can't think of anything that sounds better. I turn to Luke. "We can get a good night's sleep then come back tomorrow and check on Emmie and my dad."

"Thank you for all your help, Jasper," Luke says.

Luke and I are about to go, when Haleema rushes from my father's room. "He's awake," she says. "He's awake."

# 51

## SUSAN

I am exhausted. Mentally, I'm completely zonked. Thank God for Jane and George, who corralled our guests, convinced them to eat the food and then leave. We talked to a few people, but given what happened we sent the band home and tried to shorten the affair.

The cleaning crew is here, and it's starting to get dark out. I can see well enough due to the temporary lights that were set up. They're reminiscent of torches but use electric lights inside. I can still see the layer of silk fabric that was my aisle today, the place I walked to meet my husband. My husband. It sounds weird to me still, but I know it's true, as I hold out my hand to look at the ring on my finger. The gold band seems shinier in the low light, the metal casting a bright reflection. I head toward the house, to look for Rob, who was going to check in with the hospital.

"Susan," I hear Rob say, and I turn to the see him coming from the side of the house. "I found you." He is carrying two champagne flutes in one hand and a bottle in the other, as he approaches me.

"Hey there," I say, smiling, as he holds out a flute to me. "What's this?"

He lifts up the bottle, which I see is some type of sparkling cider. "I just wanted to share a toast with you, before you the evening was over."

That's sweet. Everything felt so rushed. Despite Kelsey's plea to enjoy ourselves, it was fairly difficult to carry on when a guest had a stroke and was carted off by ambulance. My husband then had to call the hospital and explain the LMS problem that caused Lewis' stroke, so he was gone from our reception for a good 40 minutes. I'm glad for the people we did get to see, but even gladder the day is winding down.

Rob pours me some cider, then some for himself. "What should we toast to?" I ask, as he sets the bottle of cider on the ground beside us.

"May we have a long and happy marriage with very few days with as much excitement as we got today," he says, with a grin.

I clink my glass with his. "Yes," I say, taking a sip. "I never want another person to have a stroke in front of me again." I remember George's heart attack, and now Lewis, and try to shake off the thought. "Did you find out about Lewis's condition?"

Rob nods. "He's still not conscious, but his vitals look pretty consistent. We can stop by in the morning, if you want."

"I do," I say. "I still can't believe it was him. When you said you had to put it in someone else, I thought for sure it was Luke."

Rob shakes his head lamentfully, looking into the distance. "It was supposed to be Luke, but then the senator told him Penelope needed her stuffed monkey and sent Luke to get it. As soon as Luke left, he pulls this monkey out of his jacket and tells me to put Penelope's LMS in him." Rob sighs, looks down at his foot. "I don't know, Susan, I wonder if I did the right thing. I wonder if I shouldn't have just waited for Luke to come back, let him decide."

I set my glass down on the ground, then wrap my arms around my husband.

"You did the right thing," I say. "Lewis is an adult. He knew what he wanted to do."

Rob blows out a breath and rubs my back. "I know he did. In my head, I know that he wanted to do this for her because he felt like he was partly to blame for the entire situation, going all the way back to the marking. But, he's still older than Luke. And with the age and health factors considered, I knew Luke had a better chance of surviving, but I still did what he asked."

I pull back slightly and look up into his hazel eyes. "Hey," I say, "You did what he asked you to do. It was also the right thing to do. Luke and Kelsey and Penelope deserve to be together and Lewis made his own choice. Most importantly, you saved a Susan. That's always the right choice."

He laughs, a hearty laugh that shakes us both. "Is this another rule about Susans that I don't know?"

"Yes," I grin. "In addition to us always being right, you're always supposed to save a Susan, if possible."

He squints at me. "Really?"

"Truly," I say, then give him a peck on the cheek. "You did the right thing."

He nods and squeezes me tight. I'm so glad to be here with him, now that the day is done. And I get to stay this way for the rest of our lives. I stand there with him for a moment more, and I realize my feet are killing me. I slip off my heels, and knock them aside.

"Tired?" he asks.

"Yep. Long day," I say, breathing out. "I'm incredibly happy that we're married, but everything else was a bit draining."

He takes my hand, turns and leads us to the front steps of the house. He sits on the top step and I sit beside him. Probably not the best place to sit in a wedding dress. But, I don't care. It's just a dress.

Rob wraps an arm around me and we sit quietly for a bit, staring up at the evening sky. It's dark enough you can see a few stars, and it's still fairly warm out. May in Georgia really is a beautiful time of year. Rob pulls his phone from his jacket pocket and opens the music section. "Did you want to have one dance before we call it a night?"

Ahh, my husband thinks of everything. "Sure," I say. "What song?"

"Well," he says, "Given our names — and by our, I mean my brothers and I — on our wedding day, all of us have danced to something by one of the Fab Four, either when they were together or solo."

Rob's father was a huge Beatles fan, so he named his sons George, Paul and John. Only Rob's mother was not alright with Ringo, so he's named Rob. But his brothers call him Ringo. My husband tilts the screen toward me and I see a bunch of Beatles and solo album names. "How did I not know you guys did this?"

Rob grins and says, "Because the song is chosen by the brothers not getting married, so it's supposed to be a surprise."

Hmm, I'm not sure how well that would go over. The Donnelly brothers have the spirit of pranksters. I raise an eyebrow. "You trust them to pick a song?"

He nods. "They're actually very sentimental. When Molly and I got married, they actually wrote new lyrics for *Ob-La-Di Ob-La-Da* and had a cover band perform," he says, smiling at the memory. "Molly was a doctor at the psyche ward," he sings to the tune of the song. "Robert programmed devices medical."

He stops singing, and I lay my head on his shoulder. That is sentimental. "Well, I think we should definitely uphold the tradition, then," I tell him. I look at the list of albums and click on Ringo's Greatest Hits. I admit I wasn't familiar with the Beatles' catalog, and certainly not with Ringo's best solo titles before I met Rob. I was, in fact, doubtful that anyone named Ringo could produce hit songs. But the more I learned, the more Ringo became my favorite. Not just because my husband was supposed to be named that, but also because, by all accounts, he was an amazing guy. He was a brilliant drummer, who never cared if he was in the limelight, but who did amazing things with his craft. And most importantly, his contemporaries said he was a guy who was a good friend to those around him.

I smile as I look at the list of song titles and point. "That looks appropriate for the day we've had." Rob laughs again, and I know that he is the perfect guy for me. That despite everything else happening, this was the perfect wedding day for us.

Rob starts the music, then stands, helps me up and pulls me to him. It's not a slow romantic song. It's actually a bit peppy, and rather catchy. I lay my head on Rob's shoulder, the two of us more sway than dance as Ringo sings, *It Don't Come Easy.* I have to agree. Nothing worth having in life ever comes easy — love, success, happiness — but once you've got it, it sure is worth savoring.

THE END

# EPILOGUE

## SUSAN

Kelsey is still rubbing her hands together to warm them when she enters my room. I'm sitting in my bed, which is where I've been for the last four weeks. Bed rest is not a pleasant thing, though I won't complain if I have healthy babies because of it.

"So how are you, little momma?" she asks

"I think big momma, giantess momma or humongous momma would all be much better descriptors," I tell her.

She rolls her eyes. "How about beautiful momma?" she asks, revising. She comes and sits in a chair next to my bed.

"So, did Luke and Penelope come with you?" I say, looking toward the door.

She shakes her head. "No, the two of them and my dad were going to make a snowman. So, I thought it was a good time to pop in."

"How is your dad?" I ask, knowing his recovery has been long and tough. He suffered partial paralysis in the stroke.

She bobbles her shoulders. "Given how bad things were, he's doing much better. With physical therapy, he's gotten a lot of movement back on the right side, but it's still not the same range as before." Kelsey pauses, bites her lip. "Truthfully, he told me he's been in better spirits the past couple of weeks, now that Col. Parker is gone."

Col. Parker is dead. Shortly after Rob's and my wedding, Col. Parker was arrested, tried and convicted of Penelope's kidnapping and attempted murder for his role in the senator's LMS-induced stroke. The swiftness of FoSS judicial system always amazes me. His appeals ran out and a couple of weeks ago, they harvested his body for organs. I hadn't expected Lewis to be the type of man who would enjoy vengeance, but perhaps it's something less sinister than that. "Did it give him closure?"

Kelsey nods "I think so," she says. "It may have even given me closure, too. I don't know. I hated him for what he did, but I also felt being put in that place, being subjected to the guards of the holding facility meant he would be punished. He would know what it was like to be at the mercy of others, others who were cruel and mean and had no regard for his humanity. He was probably wishing for death by the time it was over."

I nod, as I know what Kelsey is talking about. I saw what almost happened to Kelsey in the holding facility. I saw how rotten that place really is. I don't know that I relish anyone being exploited, but I certainly felt justice had been served when they led him away to that holding facility. Tisdale is dead, and now so is Parker. The only person who hasn't seen any legal repercussions is Dr. Grant. "Do you know, have they any leads on Dr. Grant?"

Kelsey pauses a moment, probably struck by my subject change. "No," she says. "People still don't know where he is. It's like he vanished into thin air." Kelsey sighs, then uses her palm to smooth my blanket. "But, I don't want to talk about Dr. Grant or Parker or anyone else who caused us pain," she says, then smiles at me. "Let's move on."

"Agreed," I say. I look at my nightside table, which has a plate of lemon bars. "Try one of those, and then tell me about Penelope. How is she doing?"

Kelsey looks at the plate, covered in plastic wrap, then eases a bar out. She takes a bite, smiles. "Good bar," she says and then finishes chewing. "As to Penelope, she's remarkably resilient. All things considered, she's doing really well. The first month was the toughest — she had such separation anxiety that I took her everywhere with me. Every bathroom visit, every shower, but we got through it." Her mouth is gritted at the memory, but then she pats my hand and says, "We have Rob to thank for that. The family therapist he recommended was wonderful. I don't know that Penelope would've gotten on track as quickly without therapy. Frankly, I think our entire family would be a mess, if we hadn't had help."

I nod. "I'm glad it worked out so well for you guys," I say. "And thank you for coming by. I know it's hard when you're just here for a short visit."

She rolls her eyes. "We'll always come see you, especially when we're in town. Luke is going back at the end of the week, but Penelope and I will stay for two more weeks, and we're going to come visit you until you get so sick of seeing us, you'll wish we were gone."

"Never," I say.

"Oh, you haven't seen Penelope throw a tantrum,"

I laugh. "Well, I might as well get used to it, times two."

"I still can't believe you guys are having twins," she gushes.

"Believe it. There are definitely two in here. Two very rambunctious boys. Rob says he and Paul fought all the time, which worries me that my twins are fighting in utero."

Kelsey laughs. "I'm pretty sure they are not kickboxing in there."

I don't know. Maybe they are.

"So, how goes it on the name front?"

I laugh. "Rob's brothers are having fun with me, but I'm not sure exactly how."

Kelsey crinkles her nose, confused. "What is that supposed to mean?"

I point to the nightstand, where the plate of lemon bars sits. Next to it are three sheets of paper. Kelsey finishes the lemon bar she's eating and picks up the lists. She looks at the first one and reads it aloud.

"The Donnelly five," she says slowly.

"Yes, George says they're his suggestions for baby names. Read them."

She looks back down at the paper. "Michael, Marlon, Jackie, Randy, and," she pauses and looks at me unsteadily. "Tito?"

"Yes," I say. "It's weird, right?"

She shrugs. "A little, but they almost named Rob Ringo, right?"

I shake my head. "No, no one was ever really going to name him Ringo. Richard maybe, but not a stage name." I tap the lists in her hand. "Look at the next one; it's from Paul."

She moves the top sheet of paper to the bottom of the stack and looks at Paul's list. "Names to help the boys stay in sync," she reads. "What does that even mean?

I nod vigorously. "I have no idea. But at least the names are better," I say, recalling them: Justin, Joshua, Chris, Joey and Lance.

She smirks. "I agree, there's definitely something weird about these lists." She tosses Paul's and George's lists on the bed. "One more. Let's see." She looks at John's list and laughs. "'Names to ensure Osmosis?' Again, I haven't a clue what he's talking about." She looks the list up and down, before reading it aloud to me. "Donny, Alan, Wayne, Merrill, Jay and Jimmy."

Kelsey drops the last list atop the bed with me. "I'm not an expert in naming, but I'd avoid Donny Donnelly."

I can't help but laugh at that. Then I fart. I hate pregnancy digestion. "I'm sorry," I say.

"Don't worry about it. I've been there and done that." She gathers the lists neatly and folds them in half. "What does Rob say?"

I shake my head. "Hasn't seen them. He'll be back tomorrow."

"He went to a wedding?"

"Yeah, we were both supposed to go, but obviously I couldn't. It was the wedding of the first patient who had the spinal recalibration technique done on her. The technique that didn't work. Rob convinced her to try the revamped procedure after my success, and she's been up and walking. So, he was over the moon that she invited him to the wedding," I tell her. "He's also going to see Molly's brother while he's there."

Kelsey nods and eyes the lemon bars like she wants another. I motion for her to take one. "When's Rob due back?"

"Tomorrow night. Then, he'll be hanging out here with me until the twins are born. Maybe I'll ask Patricia what she makes of the lists when she stops by tomorrow."

Kelsey purses her lips. "So, you really do get along with your mother-in-law? You've forgiven her for trying to murder you?"

Not the warmest, fuzziest conversation, but worth having. "You do realize I've been on bed rest for the last month, and I have two more months on bed rest if all goes well? Patricia has come to visit me every day, and she has been pleasant and funny and friendly, and I just recognize that she's not the same person she was back then. So, we're moving forward. Besides, she made the lemon bar you're eating."

Kelsey puts down the bar.

I laugh. "She's not going to poison her grandchildren."

Kelsey lifts the bar, sniffs it, gives me a dubious look, and sets it back down. "If you say so."

"Speaking of family members who tried to kill us, how is the Greg/Emmie situation?"

Kelsey shakes her head, sighs. "Horrible," she admits, leaning forward. "Luke won't talk to Emmie at all. She's tried to make peace with him, but he says he wants nothing to do with her as long as she's married to Greg."

I reach out and pat Kelsey's hand. It's a horrible situation to be in, and why I'm glad Patricia and I have been able to bury the hatchet. Family strife is just a burden to everyone. "Have you said anything to him?"

She nods. "I've told him that he can't ask his sister to leave her husband. As awful as the things Greg did were, he did them for her. He stood by her through months of treatment and he's still with her. I don't want to see Greg, but I told Luke he's welcome to see Emmie without him. He's just unmovable on this. He sees her staying with Greg as her condoning his behavior. But, I don't know. Y'know if Luke did something awful to help me, I don't think that I would leave him."

I nod. I don't think Rob would ever do anything like that, but would I leave him if he did? That's a good question. One I'm glad I don't have to answer. "Give it some time. I didn't forgive Patricia overnight."

Kelsey picks up the lemon bar and takes another bite. "Well, she's a pretty good cook," she says.

I laugh. "Maybe, but apparently this is the only thing she actually knows how to cook."

"Do you think you could talk to Luke, tell him how things have changed between you and Patricia, give him a pep talk about maybe forgiving Emmie? I know he's upset, but holding this anger toward his sister isn't good for him."

"I'll be glad to," I say. "And you just remember it doesn't happen overnight. It takes time."

She nods. "Well, I'm glad we have time," she smiles. "Finally, we're not pressed to flee or escape. We've got all the time we need and I plan to enjoy it."

"You should," I say. "We all deserve a little peace right now."

# ALSO BY RJ CRAYTON

## LIFE FIRST

"I was completely intrigued by this book from the very first page. There were fairly few characters in-keeping with the story, but they were all extremely well thought out. I really think RJ Crayton should be expecting calls for film rights because this played out in my mind as I read it like a really great film…. It gripped you like King Kong and would not let go until you had finished the book."

-BestChickLit.com

## SECOND LIFE

"Twists and turns with a dash or two of betrayal."
-Amazon Reviewer

"I just cant give the twists away, but you will be sat on the edge of your seat."
-Amazon Reviewer

## FOUR MOTHERS

Sometimes, a mother's flaws are dangerous... Four stories. Four mothers. Four crises. One great read.

# ABOUT THE AUTHOR

RJ Crayton grew up in Illinois and now lives in the Maryland suburbs of Washington, DC. She is the author of the Life First series of novels, which includes Life First and Second Life. Prior to writing fiction, Crayton was a journalist, writing for newspapers, including the *Wichita Eagle* and *Kansas City Star*. Crayton also worked for several trade publications, including *Solid Waste Report*, *Education Technology News*, and *Campus Crime*. Her first novels were published in 2013. *Four Mothers*, a short story collection, was published in June 2014. Crayton is a monthly contributor to the Indies Unlimited (http://www.indiesunlimited.com/author/rjcrayton/) blog and a regular contributor to the Institute for Ethics and Emerging Technologies blog (http://ieet.org/index.php/IEET/bio/crayton/). When she's not writing, Crayton spends her time being a ninja mom (stealthy and ultra cool, like moms should be) to her son and daughter. You can find out more about her at http://rjcrayton.com.

CPSIA information can be obtained
at www.ICGtesting.com
Printed in the USA
LVOW07s2354040617
536938LV00011BA/65/P